august 2, 2011

A Crafty Killing

**Center Point
Large Print**

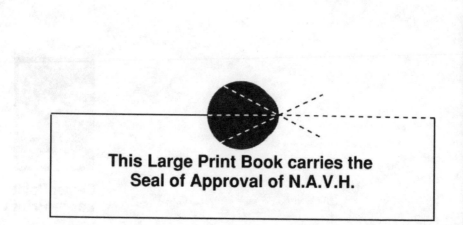

**This Large Print Book carries the
Seal of Approval of N.A.V.H.**

A Crafty Killing

LORRAINE BARTLETT

CENTER POINT LARGE PRINT
THORNDIKE, MAINE

This Center Point Large Print edition
is published in the year 2011 by arrangement with
Berkley Books, a member of Penguin Group (USA) Inc.

The text of this Large Print edition is unabridged.
In other aspects, this book may vary
from the original edition.
Printed in the United States of America
on permanent paper.
Set in 16-point Times New Roman type.

ISBN: 978-1-61173-095-1

Library of Congress Cataloging-in-Publication Data

Bartlett, L. L. (Lorraine L.)
A crafty killing / Lorraine Bartlett. — Center point large print ed.
p. cm.
ISBN 978-1-61173-095-1 (lib. binding : alk. paper)
1. Artisans—Fiction. 2. Artists—Fiction. 3. Large type books. I. Title.
PS3602.A83955.C73 2011
813'.6—dc22

2011011495

Acknowledgments

Tales of Victoria Square have been with me for a long time, and I'm so glad that I'm finally getting a chance to share them with readers.

I'd like to thank my critique partners, and all-around cheerleaders, Gwen Nelson and Liz Eng. I also got reader input from my Guppy Sisters in Crime Sandra Parshall, Nan Higginson, Marilyn Levinson, and Jan Fudala, as well as Kat Henry Doran, and members of the 13th Precinct Writers.

Thanks, too, to my editor, Tom Colgan; his former assistant, Niti Bagchi; and all the terrific people at Berkley Prime Crime; and to my wonderful agent, Jessica Faust.

I hope you'll visit my website and sign up for my periodic newsletter at www.LorraineBartlett.com.

One

Ezra Hilton lay sprawled at the bottom step of the staircase, facedown in a puddle of his own congealed blood. He'd probably broken his long, proud nose when he hit Artisans Alley's carpet-covered concrete floor, Katie Bonner decided. She wondered if McKinlay Mill's funeral director could make Ezra look presentable for a viewing.

Katie took a ragged breath and cursed her practicality. But that would be what Ezra would have wanted. At least, that's what she *thought* he would have wanted.

"Are you okay, ma'am?" asked the lanky, uniformed deputy, Schuler by the name tag on his breast pocket.

"No. But I guess that's to be expected. Mr. Hilton was my husband's business partner. My business partner now, I guess. My husband died in a car accident last winter," she explained unnecessarily. She didn't add that they'd been separated at the time. It was still too painful to revisit those memories.

After putting two fingers through the left leg of her panty hose that morning, Katie knew it was going to be one of those days. She'd had no idea it was going to be *this* bad. Not that the death of a seventy-five-year-old man should have come as a shock. But Ezra had been such a lively old coot. And dying so soon after Chad . . .

"Did Mr. Hilton have any enemies?" the deputy asked.

"Enemies?" Katie repeated. "Ezra? Of course not."

The deputy looked toward the cash desks at the front of the store. "The cash register's empty. The drawer was open when we got here. Do you know how much would've been in the till?"

Katie blinked, open-mouthed. "No. We could run the total, though—"

The deputy caught her by the arm before she could move more than a foot in that direction. "We'll wait for the tech team to dust for prints."

"Oh, of course." Then it dawned on her just what the deputy was saying. "You can't think that someone"—she had to swallow before voicing the impossible—"that someone killed him?"

Schuler looked back down at the dead man. "Looks like blunt trauma to the back of the head," he said without emotion. "The ME will have to determine the time of death."

Katie looked down at the still form on the floor and the rusty patch of dried blood staining the snowy hair on the back of Ezra's head. Tears stung her eyes and a lump rose in her throat. "Robbery?" she ventured.

"Most likely," the deputy agreed.

Katie had to take a shaky breath before she could speak again. "Thursdays are typically slow in this business." Not that she knew from personal experience. Her late husband had told her that on more than one occasion. "There couldn't have been more than a couple hundred dollars in the drawer."

"People have been murdered for a lot less," Schuler said. "The side door was unlocked. Could someone have had an appointment with Mr. Hilton after hours?"

"I don't know. I have a regular job. I'm not part of the day-to-day routine here at Artisans Alley. I was on my way to work when I saw the patrol cars in the lot and figured I should stop in to see what was up."

Schuler nodded. "Is there any chance Mr. Hilton kept an appointment calendar?"

"I could look," Katie said and took a step to her left, in the direction of Ezra's office.

Again Schuler held her back. "We'll wait until our chief investigator gets here."

Katie's gaze returned to the still figure on the floor. Ezra dying peacefully in his sleep wouldn't have been a shock, but murder? Katie searched the pockets of her suit jacket, found a balled-up tissue, and wiped her nose.

She wasn't the only one who needed a hanky. A woman older than she sat on a Victorian horsehair sofa in the dreary cluttered booth across the way, wiping away tears as she answered another uniformed deputy's questions.

"Did she find him?" Katie asked, with a nod in the stranger's direction.

Schuler nodded. "Do you know her?"

Katie shook her head.

"Her name is Mary Elliott. She says she's the co-owner of the tea shop across the Square."

Though her face was twisted with grief, the woman conveyed an aura of mature elegance that her pastel blue jogging suit couldn't disguise. The shoulder-length blond hair in a loose ponytail at her neck accentuated the firm lines of her neck and chin. She had to be at least twenty years older than Katie's thirty, but she carried it well. Two spilled cups of take-out coffee stained the rug near Artisans Alley's side door. The woman must have dropped them upon finding the body.

Embarrassed to witness the other woman's flood of emotion, Katie brushed a piece of fuzz from her drab gray wool skirt, the pleated one that always made her feel pudgy, and studied the toes of her scruffy sneakers. She'd change out of them once— if—she ever made it to work.

Shouldn't she be crying, too? Ezra was her business partner, for God's sake. But she couldn't break down. At least not yet. She'd shed far too many tears in the last year. Instead, Katie rummaged through her purse for a peppermint. She unwrapped it, popped it into her mouth, and immediately scrunched it, the sharp, sweet flavor

10

instantly delivering what was, to her, comfort. She tucked the wrapper into her pocket.

Outside, a car door slammed. A man appeared in the open doorway, carrying what looked like a big green tackle box. He had to be the medical examiner, Katie realized, who was closely followed by a plainclothes cop, his badge pinned to the lapel of his raincoat. Was that a lab team and a crime photographer behind them?

"Do you need me?" Katie asked Schuler, glancing down at Ezra's polished Florsheims. "I'll need to make some calls in the office. And I'll look for Ezra's calendar, too."

"Oh, no," the deputy warned. "You'll have to make your calls from another phone. This entire building is now considered a crime scene. We don't know if anything else was taken."

"Okay. I'll be in my car—the blue Ford Focus in the lot."

Again Schuler nodded, and left her to confer with the other police personnel.

Katie turned, hugging herself against the morning chill as she headed back to her little sedan. She really should call her boss, Josh, first, but decided against it; she wasn't up to an argument. Why couldn't he have gone to Syracuse on business today and not yesterday?

Katie settled herself behind the car's steering wheel, grabbed the small address book from her purse, and hunted for attorney Seth Landers's

11

name. As McKinlay Mill's only lawyer, Seth knew just about everyone in the village. He'd handled the legalities when Chad bought into Artisans Alley, and he'd advised Katie after Chad's death. Katie and Chad hadn't filed any paperwork on their separation. Maybe she'd been in denial, hoping they'd reconcile. It hadn't mattered in the long run.

Katie dialed the lawyer's number, grateful she'd taken her cell phone from the charger before start- ing out this morning, and got through to his secretary, who quickly transferred her to the lawyer.

"Seth, I've got some bad news. Ezra Hilton is dead."

"Dead? Oh, I'm sorry to hear that," he said calmly. "In his sleep?"

"No! A robbery at Artisans Alley. It looks like someone snuck up on him from behind, hit him over the head, and killed him."

"Good grief." She heard him take a breath. "When did this happen?"

"Probably last night. One of the other merchants in the Square found him."

"Katie, did you know Ezra named you executor of his estate?"

"Me? But I hardly knew him," she cried.

"You were his partner," Seth said.

"On paper only." Executor of Ezra's estate? She exhaled, raking her fingers through the hair curling around her collar, the enormity of that responsibility only just beginning to dawn on her. She reached into her purse for another peppermint, unwrapped it, and crunched. "Is there anyone I should notify? Any relatives?" she asked around the shards of candy.

"Just a nephew in Rochester. If you want, I can take care of that for you."

"Yes, thank you." The last thing Katie wanted to do was dump that kind of news on some poor, unsuspecting survivor. "Did Ezra leave any"—she closed her eyes and swallowed—"funeral instructions with you?"

"I'll have to pull his will from the files, but I think so. I'll call Mr. Collier at the funeral home to make sure."

"Thank you," she breathed. She looked through the car's windshield, taking in the rambling old wooden structure that was Artisans Alley. "What should I do about the Alley?"

"You're already a limited partner, so there's nothing to keep you from conducting business as usual. The estate still has to go through probate, but it's in your best interest to keep Artisans Alley open—if that's what you want."

Seth's tone on that last part of the sentence gave her pause, but she plowed on. "How long will probate take?"

"Anywhere from six months to a couple of years, depending on the complexity of the estate."

"Swell. Do I have to remind you I've already got a real job?"

"Now you have two," Seth said.

"What should I do next?"

"Can you sign the Alley's checks?"

"Yes. Ezra added my name to the bank accounts and I signed a signature card right after Chad died."

"Then you're in business. It wouldn't hurt to talk to Ezra's accountant, too."

"Thank you, Seth. I already feel better just talking to you."

"I'm glad to help in any way. Where can I reach you?"

"My cell phone, and maybe Ezra's number at Artisans Alley, if they let me back in. I won't know until later today." She gave him the numbers.

"I'll get back to you on what Ezra wanted in the way of a funeral. Knowing the old man, I'll bet he set that up in advance. He was very much a no-nonsense kind of guy."

"If you say so," Katie said. She'd barely known the man.

Seth said good-bye, and Katie folded the phone closed. Before she could put it away, she noticed a solidly built woman with short-cropped gray hair and oversized glasses charge across the parking lot, heading straight for her car. Katie cranked open her window, trying not to prejudge a woman who would willingly go out in public dressed in a garish purple polyester pantsuit left over from the nineteen seventies.

"I just heard Ezra Hilton died," the woman

barked. "Are you the new owner?"

"Uh—I guess so," Katie answered, startled by the newcomer's directness.

"Edie Silver," she said, extending a beefy hand. "I'm a crafter. I crochet and paint, and I make the most gorgeous silk flower arrangements you'll ever see, if I do say so myself. Will you be renting booth space to crafters? Mr. Hilton never would." Her voice vibrated with disapproval.

"I don't know."

"If crafters are coming in, *I* want to be at the top of the list. Take down my name, will you?"

Dazed, Katie pawed through her purse to find a small spiral notebook and a pen, and then dutifully copied down the information.

"When will you be making a decision?" the woman badgered.

"I don't know."

"I'll call Artisans Alley in a day or so for your decision." With a curt nod, Edie stalked back toward the fringe of the crowd that had gathered in front of the Square's tiny wine and cheese shop, The Perfect Grape.

Katie stared after her, appalled. Ezra's body had only been discovered within the hour and already the vultures were circling. She replaced her phone in her purse and nearly jumped as a slight, well-dressed woman—on the high side of fifty—suddenly appeared in front of her still-opened window.

"Am I disturbing you?" the woman asked and bent low, the remnants of a Brooklyn accent tingeing her voice. Her dyed-black pageboy emphasized her pale face.

"Uh . . . no," Katie said.

"I'm Gilda Ringwald. I own Gilda's Gourmet Baskets across the Square." She offered her hand.

Katie took it, surprised at the strength of the slight woman's handshake. "I'm Katie Bonner. Have we met before?"

"Briefly. At dear Chad's wake. Such a nice young man," she said and shook her head, her expression somber.

Those days after Chad's death were a blur, but Katie did remember writing a thank-you note for a lovely gift basket filled with luscious chocolates and fattening cookies that had arrived at the apartment.

"The whole Square has already heard about poor Ezra's passing. Naturally, we're all in shock. He was the Merchants Association's driving force, you know. I don't know how we'll manage without him. I expect you'll be in charge of Artisans Alley's affairs, won't you?"

"For now," Katie admitted.

"You're not going to close the Alley, are you?" Gilda asked, an edgy note coloring her tone.

"For today, at least. Long term . . . I don't know."

Gilda nodded over the roof of Katie's car. "There's already a crew from Channel Nine rolling

16

tape. I'll speak to them on behalf of the merchants." She sighed, clasping her hands. "Ezra would've jumped at the chance for this kind of publicity. For the Alley and the Square, I mean."

She was right about that. And Ezra's PR efforts had paid off. He'd turned a decrepit warehouse into an artists' cooperative. On the strength of his labors, the surrounding houses had been converted to boutiques and specialty shops like Gilda's Gourmet Baskets.

The result was Victoria Square—a budding tourist destination on the cusp of becoming truly successful. With decent marketing, its gaslights and the charming gingerbread facades on the buildings could bring in visitors on their way to Niagara Falls, some eighty miles west, as well as customers from nearby Rochester, New York.

"Artisans Alley's our anchor," Gilda continued, her voice firm. "The rest of us need it to pull in shoppers and keep us afloat."

That was a rather cold assessment of the situation. Had Gilda forgotten that a man had been killed?

"The Merchants Association will probably call an emergency meeting in the next day or so," Gilda continued. "I hope you'll come."

"I'll try." Katie caught sight of the dashboard clock, realizing she still hadn't called her boss to explain her absence.

As though taking the hint, Gilda straightened.

"I'll let you know about the meeting. In the meantime, I'm so sorry about Ezra. I just hope his death isn't a fatal blow to Victoria Square, too."

The woman turned on her heel and walked back to her store. With no one else coming her way, Katie realized she could no longer avoid the inevitable, again flipped open her phone, and punched in her work number. It rang once, twice.

"Kimper Insurance, Josh Kimper speaking."

"Josh, it's Katie—"

"Where the hell are you?" he bellowed, so loud she had to hold the phone away from her ear. "Do you realize there's no coffee and I've got a client meeting in five minutes?"

"Sorry, Josh, but my late husband's business partner was killed overnight. As minority owner, I'll have to take care of things at Artisans Alley here in McKinlay Mill for at least today."

"I don't appreciate a last-minute call like this, Katie," Josh barked.

Katie bit back her anger. "I'm sure Ezra didn't plan on being murdered."

"Murdered?"

"The police think it may have happened during a robbery attempt last night."

"That's too bad," he said, with no hint of sympathy. "But you can't let this affect *your* life."

Katie knew Josh meant he didn't want Ezra's murder to affect *his* life.

Josh Kimper's abrasive personality alone qualified him as the boss from hell. He'd given Katie a job as office manager when she'd been desperate for work with flexible hours while finishing her graduate degree. Four years later Josh liked to remind her of it on a daily—if not hourly—basis. Since Chad's death, he'd gotten used to her putting in fifty- and sometimes sixty-hour weeks. Katie had preferred immersing herself in office routine rather than facing her empty apartment—her empty life. And, she wasn't ashamed to admit, she needed the overtime money.

Paying a good salary was Josh's carrot to keep her at the agency. She made much less than Josh, of course, but then, he was the talent, as he so often liked to tell her. That left Katie with the drudgery.

"The coffee's in the cabinet. I brought in homemade chocolate chip cookies yesterday. They're in the jar on the counter. Put them on a plate, lay out napkins, and everything will be fine."

"You'd better be in tomorrow," Josh grated. "We can't let the filing go for more than a day."

You could always do it yourself, she thought, but held her tongue. "I'll tell you my plans as soon as I know them."

"And I'm not paying you for today either," he said.

"Then I'll take a day of vacation. I still have more than a week left."

"And you always wait until it's inconvenient to take it. You'd better be here tomorrow," Josh ordered again and hung up.

Eyes narrowed, Katie stuck out her tongue at the phone.

"Do you always end your conversations that way?" came an amused male voice from outside her still-opened window.

Chagrined, Katie stabbed the phone's power button and forced a smile for Deputy Schuler. "Only on days like today."

"This is Detective Ray Davenport, our lead investigator." Schuler stepped away, revealing the stocky, balding man Katie had seen earlier. She eyed the ratty raincoat. Was he trying to channel an old Columbo rerun?

Davenport nodded at her. "Ma'am."

Or maybe he was channeling Joe Friday.

Katie studied the detective's nondescript face, wondering if his no-nonsense demeanor was a defense mechanism he'd erected to shield him from the results of the violence he saw on a regular basis. Or could it be he was just grumpy? But then, grumpy was an apt description of her current emotional state.

"What can I do for you, Detective?" Katie asked, trying to be helpful.

The older man opened a worn notebook and took a pen from the inside pocket of his raincoat. "Did the deceased—uh, Mr. Hilton—have any family?"

"Deceased." The word made it sound so . . . permanent. Then again, it was.

"Apparently Ezra had a nephew. His lawyer is contacting him," Katie said.

"And that man's name is?" Davenport prompted.

"Sorry, I don't know." She gave him Seth's name and phone number, which he dutifully jotted down.

"Did Mr. Hilton always close the place by himself?"

Katie lifted her hands from her lap and shrugged. "I don't know."

Davenport frowned. "Who might've seen the deceased last, ma'am?"

"I—"

"Don't tell me—you don't know," Davenport supplied, slapping his notebook closed. "Would you have a list of all the vendors who rent space at Artisans Alley? We'll want to talk to everyone to see if they saw something or can tell if anything else was taken from the building."

"I'm sure there's a list somewhere in the office. I just don't know where to put my hands on it. Ezra was pretty much a one-man show—from handling the paperwork, to arranging publicity, to manning the register if need be. From the looks of it, he may have spread himself far too thin."

"And that," the detective said with a penetrating gaze, "could be what got him killed."

Two

The doors to the medical examiner's van slammed shut, intensifying Katie's hollow sense of loss. Knowing they'd autopsy Ezra, cutting him open, removing his organs—desecrating his body—made her shudder.

The vehicle's engine roared to life, and the blue Suburban pulled out of the lot, heading back to the city.

"Good-bye, Ezra," Katie whispered, and stared at the vacant space for a long time before turning back to Victoria Square's communal parking lot lined with rubberneckers, including customers and proprietors of all the boutiques. With the show now over, some of them were already skulking back into the warmth inside the shops.

Katie shivered in the brisk autumn breeze. Lake Ontario was only a mile or so down the road, funneling a Canadian cold front their way. God, she felt empty.

She retrieved another piece of candy from her skirt pocket, unwrapped it and popped it into her mouth, and then bit into it, grinding it with her molars. Artisans Alley's great hulk of a building looked even shabbier since Chad's death. The faded painted sign over the entrance was covered in insect-dotted spiderwebs. Without Chad to spearhead the holiday decorations, not so much as a cornstalk heralded the harvest season or Halloween only a week away.

Chad had been a vendor at Artisans Alley for three or four years before his death—though he considered the booth filled with his paintings and artwork to be more of a hobby than a true money-making venture. He enjoyed the camaraderie of his fellow artists, as well as the opportunity to expand his knowledge to market his work. Four months before his death, and without consulting Katie, he'd put up their combined savings for a ten percent interest in Artisans Alley.

"The roof was in bad shape, and the bank wouldn't give Ezra another loan," Chad had calmly explained, as though jeopardizing their financial security was nothing for them to worry about.

The Bonner marriage had foundered after that. For years they'd scrimped and saved, dreaming of owning and operating an upscale bed-and-breakfast —the English Ivy Inn—on or near Victoria Square, with Chad the amiable host and Katie serving as the power behind the scenes, managing the financial end as well as the day-to-day operations. The derelict Webster mansion on the east end of the Square was the perfect location. They'd plotted and planned for more than two years to buy it and had been on the verge of submitting a bid when dear, sweet, gullible Chad had fallen for Ezra's sales pitch, convincing him Artisans Alley would quickly return their investment tenfold.

So far, Katie hadn't seen a dime.

Not that Chad hadn't worked at improving Artisans Alley's bottom line. The addition of something as simple as arranging for the business to accept debit cards had made Artisans Alley more profitable within a month. But Chad had had to choose his battles carefully. Although a businessman for more than half a century, Ezra wasn't eager to adopt newfangled ways. And he'd decreed the business remain an artisans-only arcade, which kept the booth rental at only seventy-five percent of capacity, at least during a good month.

"Mrs. Bonner?"

Katie turned. An elderly lady, her carefully coifed, honey blond hair covered by a plastic weather bonnet—more, Katie suspected, in deference to the wind than any threat of rain—had broken away from a knot of other old women on the fringe of the parking lot. Her wrinkled face gave testament to her decades on the planet. Pretty blue-and-white beaded earrings hung from her earlobes, with a matching necklace just showing at the base of her neck. Though lithe and spry in body, the old lady's watery blue eyes were shadowed with grief. She held out her heavily veined hand. "I'm Rose Nash, one of Artisans Alley's artists."

Katie gingerly took the woman's hand, careful

not to exert any pressure for fear of crushing the delicate bones under the crepe-like skin.

"Everyone's saying Ezra was murdered," Rose said, her voice shaky with suppressed tears.

"I'm afraid it looks that way."

Rose let out an anguished sigh, her brows puckering. "I've been at Artisans Alley since it opened twelve years ago. I speak for a lot of the artists when I say this place means more to us than just a business or a hobby. It's our lives. Our social club. We're family. What will we ever do without Ezra?"

Katie didn't know how to respond. Chad had been friends with these people—had socialized with them—while she had been intent on getting her degree and working and reworking a viable business plan for the English Ivy Inn. She sensed another pitch to keep the place open was on its way and wasn't up to hearing it. "It's too soon for me to make any decisions. I'll have to wait to hear Ezra's will and find out who the heirs are. For now, I'd like to keep the place open." She didn't add, *until I can find a buyer.*

Rose's look of joy was to be short-lived.

"Only I can't manage it," Katie said.

"Why not?" Rose asked, sounding almost childlike.

"I have to support myself. My husband Chad's investment in Artisans Alley never paid off. That's why he had a full-time job teaching English at the McKinlay Mill High School."

"But there must be something we can do to keep it running," Rose cried.

"I suppose I'll have to hire a manager. There's still the problem of paying one. I haven't had a chance to go through the books. All I can tell you is—"

Rose's look of anguish nearly broke Katie's heart. "I'll try."

Rose reached out, squeezed Katie's shoulder. "God bless you, Mrs. Bonner."

"Call me Katie," she insisted, feeling like a rat.

Rose's lips trembled and she glanced at the ugly old hodgepodge of a building. "We were all so sad when Chad passed. He loved Artisans Alley as much as the rest of us."

Katie's throat tightened. *Don't weaken. Don't let her—or anyone else—persuade you not to sell the place. You'll end up living in your car if you do.*

Rose patted Katie's arm and turned away, heading back to her waiting friends.

Katie ducked under the crime-scene tape and reentered Artisans Alley. A pensive Deputy Schuler stood next to Detective Davenport. A six-by-six-foot chunk of carpet was missing at the bottom of the stairs where Ezra had fallen. Evidence, no doubt. What was left was a toe-snagging hazard for patrons who'd head for the twenty or so booths upstairs. She'd have to duct-tape the rough edges before they could open the store again.

"You can go in the office now, ma'am," Detective Davenport said. "I found a list of the artists and made a copy. Besides the cash, nothing else appears to have been taken or disturbed—but in a place like this, who can tell?"

Who indeed. Every booth seemed to contain hundreds of items.

"Of course, half your vendors will be calling us back, saying they've been robbed and demanding police reports to file with their insurance companies."

Katie frowned. "That's a pretty cynical statement, Detective."

"Ma'am, I've been on the job twenty-eight years. I've seen it all and then some."

Katie squelched the sharp retort on her tongue. Instead she asked, "Did you find any fingerprints?"

"A few. But they might turn out to be the victim's—or any of the other artists who might have used the register yesterday. Can you come up with a list of likely candidates?"

Katie shook her head. "I know in the past Vance Ingram was usually Ezra's backup. I'm surprised he's not already here. You could ask some of the other artists how to contact him. There still may be a few of them out in the parking lot."

"Thank you, ma'am."

Already Davenport's bored monotone and his overuse of the word "ma'am" began to annoy Katie.

"Call me if you think of anything that might

help us," he said and handed her his card. He glanced up at the timbered ceiling. "Damn fire trap," he muttered, shook his head, and took his leave.

Katie scowled, suddenly feeling protective of the sprawling old building—Chad's nightmare investment.

"Are you leaving, too?" she asked Deputy Schuler.

"I'll be around, ma'am," he said, and a ghost of a smile raised the corners of his mouth. "McKinlay Mill is part of my assigned patrol area."

Katie followed him into the wan sunlight. Sure enough, the group of elderly women was still camped out on the edges of the parking lot, and they seemed only too eager to answer any question Detective Davenport posed for them.

Katie watched as Schuler got into his patrol car and drove away; then her attention turned back to Detective Davenport, who consulted his list of artists during his talk with the ladies. He spent only a couple of minutes conversing with the women, and then he turned for his own unmarked car.

Rose Nash considered the people at Artisans Alley to be family. Why didn't the detective try to wrangle the family gossip out of those women? He said he'd been on the job for twenty-eight years. If he was anywhere near retirement, he could just be going through the motions—not caring if he ever found out who killed Ezra. Was his lack of interest a symptom of short-timer's syndrome or was he simply burned out—or worse, incompetent?

Katie couldn't help glaring at the detective as he pulled out of the parking lot. She and Ezra had never been pals, but even he deserved better than the disinterest this cop displayed.

As she turned toward Artisans Alley, a curtain of depression settled around her shoulders. In addition to her regular job, Artisans Alley and all it entailed would be her responsibility, too.

Swell.

Ezra's desk more resembled a junk heap than a place of business. Stacks of paper teetered precariously close to old cups of half-drunk coffee that grew science experiments and begged to be spilled. Katie itched to tidy the place, but first things first. She searched through the mess until she found a file marked "Accountant," hauled out the Yellow Pages from under stacks of rubber-banded Artisans Alley's brochures, opened it to the section marked "CPAs," and hunted for the accountant's name.

The call to James Morrison didn't go well. He outlined Artisans Alley's long list of creditors, and advised her to take a good look at the books. Unless the Alley turned around in the next few months, it would go under—taking Chad's investment with it—and probably all of Victoria Square as well. The chances of a buyer taking on that kind of debt were nil.

Katie thumbed through more of Ezra's files,

finding three loan payment books. It didn't take a financial genius to see that Ezra was behind on two of them.

"Oh, boy," she breathed, wishing she'd taken more of an interest in the place since Chad's death. A coffee-stained ledger proved to be a record of rent checks collected. Listed by booth number, each vendor's name had been carefully printed in what had to be Ezra's own hand. Quite a few of them were in arrears: Donner, Frances, Hingle, Mitchell, and more.

Good grief! Two or three of them were almost a year behind in their payments. How could Ezra have let the situation deteriorate like that? Why hadn't he hounded the vendors to pay up or make them leave Artisans Alley?

Her stomach twisting with anguish, Katie set the ledger aside and tackled the stack of bills, most of them at least a month overdue. The cash flow—or what there was of it—was definitely out of kilter.

Chad had told her that when Ezra first bought the building, the old apple warehouse had been divided to house up to four small businesses, as well as Artisans Alley. Ezra figured with that space leased, there'd always be income, since his artist vendors only paid on a month-to-month basis. All but one of those rental spaces was currently empty. It housed a photography studio. Apparently the previous lease holders had been so successful, they'd moved into larger quarters on Victoria Square.

Chad had wanted to hire Fred Cunningham of Cunningham Realty to list the vacancies, but Ezra wouldn't hear of it. Fred represented the owners of the old Webster mansion, and she and Chad had consulted with him on many occasions as they'd saved to buy the old colonial-style building. Unfortunately, miserly old Ezra felt he was perfectly capable of renting the space himself. He'd been wrong, and the little shops had sat vacant for months—some more than a year. If Katie couldn't fill them with retail establishments, she'd let them out as office space. And she would hire Fred to do it PDQ.

It was after two when Katie opened the middle drawer of Ezra's desk, looking for a pen that didn't skip, and found a brass key with a card tag attached. By now she recognized Ezra's handwriting. It read, "Chad's pad."

Her heart raced, and she clasped the key so hard it bit into her palm.

After a ferocious argument that sent Chad flying out their apartment door, he'd lived in a storeroom somewhere on the Alley's second floor, which had been totally illegal, and definitely not safe, given the age and condition of the building. How many times had Ezra encouraged Katie to come by to empty out that room? How many times had he invited her to become more involved with Artisans Alley?

She hadn't, of course. For a long time she

31

couldn't even think about the place without anger boiling through her. Artisans Alley—and Ezra—had ruined her marriage. The place had seduced Chad with its siren's song. It had caused him to empty their bank account, to abandon their dreams of running a bed-and-breakfast for an interest in this . . . this decaying money pit.

Katie unclenched her fist, staring at the key and the dents it had made in her hand, her anger flaring once again.

If it hadn't been for Ezra and his unnatural need to keep this sorry excuse of an enterprise going, Chad would still be alive.

Katie's throat tightened and tears threatened as she remembered her last sight of Chad laid out in his casket—dressed in his best suit, his waxy face lax, his hands folded over his abdomen, looking like no one Katie had ever loved; certainly not the man she'd lived and shared so much with. Six months later, the memory continued to haunt her dreams.

Pocketing the key, Katie got up from her chair. The vendors' lounge was just outside her office. "Lounge" was a definite misnomer, for it was not a place to hang around and pass the time idly. "Stark" was a better description. There was a table, where lunches could be eaten, an apartment-sized fridge, a microwave, and a coffeemaker. An out-of-date calendar hung on one of the drab brown walls, but there was no other decoration.

Katie crossed the room in a hurry and entered the main showroom to wander Artisans Alley's aisles, hoping to shake off the restlessness that prickled beneath her skin. Poor lighting made the area look dingy. Already she could see so many ways to improve the operation—and its bottom line. Had Chad seen the same things? Had Ezra been just too stubborn to take her husband's advice?

Dust-collecting objets d'art held little allure for Katie, who'd grown up in a house without them. It was Chad's interest in the arts—and their long-term goal to open an inn with perhaps a minigallery—that had brought them to McKinlay Mill in the first place. The mills had shut down more than a century ago, leaving nothing but fruit farms to take up the economic slack. Now, thanks to Victoria Square, the little town was on the verge of a financial reawakening. The new marina on the lakeshore might help draw in more visitors, too.

Katie twirled a lock of her hair around her middle finger, an idea glimmering in the back of her mind. Bringing Artisans Alley to life was the only way to resurrect her dreams of opening a sumptuous bed-and-breakfast inn. No one in his or her right mind would buy this place in its present financial state, but if she could bring it to the break-even point, someone with a love for the arts might be able to turn it into a smashing success.

For the first time since Chad had invested in the place, the possibilities of its success intrigued her.

33

She'd been running on autopilot for far too long. It was well past time to take an interest in the place. Because if she didn't, she could kiss Chad's seventy-thousand-dollar investment good-bye forever.

Katie found herself drawn to and then climbing the stairs to the balcony that overlooked the main showroom. Bypassing the overhang, she entered the first of the warren of rooms that made up Artisans Alley's loft area. It must've all been used for storage at one point, she mused, taking in the booths and shelves now filled with pottery, paintings, sculptures, and other handcrafted items. The booths petered out as she neared the back of the large open area. A thick layer of dust covered the taped lines on the old plank flooring, the markings delineating possible rental spaces. She estimated another twenty artists could easily occupy the space.

Making a circuit of the area, she noticed a locked door on the south end. Chad's pad?

The key from her pocket easily slid into the lock, which clicked as she turned it. For a moment she was afraid to enter. A Chad she no longer knew had lived behind the door. Not that they hadn't communicated. In fact, their conversations had improved from barely civil to quite friendly during the months they had lived apart before his death. There'd be no unfriendly ghost inside, she chided herself, and opened the door.

The darkness inside was complete, the feeble light from the loft doing little to illuminate the gloom. Katie groped along the edge of the door-jamb, found and flipped on the light switch. A bare bulb overhead flared to life, barely illuminating the tiny room.

Chad's coffee-table art books filled shelves lining the walls of the tiny room, which couldn't have measured more than eight by ten feet. In front of them were stacks of Chad's unsold, unframed paintings—priced and ready to sell—ones he said he didn't love. She'd kept seven or eight of his favorites, but had taken them off her walls after Chad's death. Maybe it was time to hang them again.

A cot, neatly made up, filled the nearest corner with a small pine nightstand and pottery lamp beside it. A sagging upholstered chair and floor lamp were the only other furniture. A small oriental-patterned scatter rug beside the bed was one of the few cheerful accents. An easel at the end of the bed held an unfinished canvas of lovely cosmos swaying in a breeze—one of Katie's favorite flowers. Chad's artist's palette was clean, as was the brush that sat on the top of the shelf.

Katie's throat constricted. Everything must have been as he'd left it more than six months before. She wrinkled her nose at the dry, stuffy air. Chad had left their homey, comfortable apartment for this horrible, barren little room?

A wide-striped Hudson Bay blanket, serving as a bedspread, lay wrinkled where someone had sat on it. Ezra? Had he come here to mourn Chad?

35

She stepped inside and noticed a book—she could tell it was a journal—lying on the cot's pillow, just daring her to open it. A box hidden in the back of her closet held the journals Chad had kept since his teen years. She'd respected his privacy and had never opened one of them—not even after his death.

Katie approached the bed. "I'm not afraid of anything it might say," she told herself, her words sounding hollow in that morbid little room.

She picked up the journal. It was nothing special. No tooled leather cover, just a cheap book of lined paper. Something Chad had probably bought at the McKinlay Mill Dollar Store. Katie flipped through the pages and recognized the cursive script that was indeed his handwriting.

Along with jotting down his thoughts and feelings, Chad had used the journal as a place to sketch ideas for future paintings. One of them was of a large pansy. He'd even filled in the petals and leaves with colored pencil. It was pretty. A note jotted just under it said, *I'll paint it for Katie. Maybe when I give it to her, she'll take me back.*

Katie frowned. She'd never seen the finished painting. It wasn't among those canvases stacked on the floor of this tiny room. Maybe he'd changed his mind about finishing it.

The breath caught in her throat as she read a sentence for the next day's entry. *I dreamed of Katie again last night.*

She slammed the pages shut, all the heartache

from their months of separation—and then the loss at his death—welling up within her again.

Then again, maybe she *wasn't* ready to confront Chad's innermost feelings at their separation. Still, she couldn't leave the journal there. Chad's body might be buried in the McKinlay Mill Cemetery, but the unassuming book contained at least a small piece of his soul.

Journal in hand, Katie closed and locked the door to the little room and headed back to Ezra's shabby, littered office. Setting the book on the desk, she slumped back into Ezra's grungy office chair, staring out the window to the parking lot and the rusty Dumpster, and to the gray, cloud-filled sky above it. All her dreams for the future had died with Chad.

She checked the pocket of her skirt, but found no more hard candies. Damn.

Katie looked down at the cover of the journal on the desk before her. No. If she was honest with herself, her hopes had died the day Chad had invested in Artisans Alley.

"Katie?"

Katie started at the sound, and then anger flared through her at the sight of Vance Ingram standing in the office doorway—the man Chad had considered to be second in command at Artisans Alley. Vance always reminded Katie of a skinny Santa Claus, thanks to his snowy hair, neatly trimmed white beard, and blue eyes half hidden behind gold wire-frame glasses. At that moment, she wasn't feeling quite so charitable.

"I came as soon as I heard. What in blazes happened?" Vance asked, his voice shaking.

"Where were you last night? I thought you always helped Ezra close."

Vance winced at her tone.

She hadn't meant to sound so accusatory.

"I was"—Vance hesitated—"called out of town."

The lack of conviction in his voice made it sound like the lie it probably was.

"It was only for one night," he continued. "How could I know—"

Katie waved a hand to stop his explanation. "It's up to the police to figure out who killed Ezra and why. He trusted few people. You were one of them."

Vance ignored the compliment, looking guilty. "Did you find him?"

She shook her head. "Mary Elliott, one of the Victoria Square merchants, did." Vance nodded. "Ezra had to be coming down the stairs or standing at the base of it when someone hit him from behind, and probably fractured his skull," Katie said. "The till was empty, but it looked to me like someone took the money to cover for killing him."

"Who'd want to do that?" Vance asked.

"That's what the police are asking. Did Ezra have any enemies? Any problems with the artists or maybe bill collectors?"

"He had no enemies that I know of. Ezra could charm your socks off—if he wanted to."

"And if he didn't?" Katie prompted.

Vance shrugged.

Katie glanced down at the stack of bills and payment books still spread across the desk before her. "Did you or any of the other artists make an investment in Artisans Alley?"

Vance shook his head. "Not unless you consider the rent we paid for our booths as an investment." He let out a mirthless laugh. "More like pouring money down a drain. As far as I know, Chad was the only one Ezra ever let invest in the place. To tell you the truth, I think he wanted Chad to take over for him someday. He was real fond of your husband. It nearly broke Ezra's heart when Chad died."

Mine, too. Katie thought about what Vance had said, or maybe it was the *way* he'd said it. Could he have been jealous of Chad's relationship with Ezra? She'd probably never know.

"I figured I was the only one with a financial stake here. That's why I've tried to take charge," Katie said. "I've been going through the files. What I've found isn't pretty. Artisans Alley is in deep financial trouble. Did Ezra confide that kind of information to you or any of the others?"

"No. In fact, I think it irked him when Chad would question him about it. I saw what Chad was trying to do and Ezra fought him at every turn," he said bitterly. "But without Chad, we would've closed long before this. Most of us have just been hanging on out of habit."

Jealously and admiration? Maybe she was reading Vance all wrong.

Katie set the ledger aside. "Walk with me," she said, getting up from her chair.

Vance followed her into the main display area. Shrouded in shadows, the place looked anything but inviting. "Take a look around," she said. "What do you see?"

He frowned and shrugged, his gaze taking in the uninteresting space. "Art."

He was so familiar with the place he probably didn't see the mishmash of incandescent and fluorescent lights; the path-worn, spotted tan carpet rippled where it had been stretched; the dark, bland plank walls and ceiling, and the virtual sea of ugly dark brown Masonite pegboard dividing the booths. Did he smell the dry wood—sense the aura of hopelessness?

"What's the dominant color?" Katie asked.

Vance's frown deepened. "Brown."

"And how does that make you feel?"

He let out a whoosh of air, the lines around his eyes creasing. "Depressed."

"Not conducive to a good shopping experience, is it? The only improvements made in decades appear to be the new checkout counters and the showcases in back."

"Ezra hired me to build them. They've only been in about a month."

Katie shook her head. "Two tiny improvements in a sea of neglect."

She started walking again, with Vance following in her wake. Pausing at Booth 12, she pointed at a dirt-caked spade, a rusty hoe, and a dull scythe, which leaned against the wall. "Here's an impressive sculpture made of old farm implements. Except they're filthy. And this carpet looks like it's never been vacuumed."

"Each vendor is responsible for keeping their own booth clean. Ezra supplied vacuum cleaners for their use. I guess not many of the artists take advantage of it."

Katie sauntered into another booth, which featured handwoven articles, including several beautiful wall hangings that would have shown better with decent lighting. A shelf held more items, including a small box full of colorful woven bookmarks, no doubt made on a hand loom from silky yarns. Waving her hand at the untidy heap of woven rag rugs that overflowed an old steamer trunk, Katie asked, "See anything you'd want to buy in here?"

Vance gave the booth a quick once-over. "Not especially."

"What if I—" Katie sorted the rugs from the placemats, then arranged them by color, draping them artistically over the trunk—something the vendor should have done on a regular basis. Did the vendors just abandon their booths, or were their sales so lackluster they couldn't be bothered to come in to tidy their booths on a regular basis? She finished her reorganization and stood back to admire her work. "What do you think?"

Vance shrugged. "It looks a bit better."

"Just think how much more merchandise the artists would sell if they put a little imagination into their displays."

"Didn't Chad tell me you had a background in marketing?" Vance asked thoughtfully.

She nodded. "I can't understand why none of the artists has painted their booths. It's so god-awful bleak in here."

"That was Ezra's idea. He didn't think one vendor should have an edge over another. He wouldn't allow anyone to paint or put up wallpaper. Believe me, I'm not the only one who fought with him over that on more than one occasion."

"As far as I'm concerned, every vendor can do what they want in the way of decorating their booths if they think it will increase their sales."

"I'll take you up on that," Vance said gratefully.

Katie scowled. "One of the merchants on the Square told me Artisans Alley is the big draw here. Well, it won't be if we don't turn it around—and fast."

"What are you suggesting?"

"For one thing, we have to rent the rest of the available booths. Now."

Vance's expression slackened. "Not to amateur crafters. Ezra would never allow—"

"Ezra's dead," Katie said. "And Artisans Alley will be, too, if we don't pump some life into it." Hands on hips, Vance advanced into Katie's personal space, suddenly looming over her. "You've never shown any interest in this place. What makes you think you can just waltz in here and change everything now?"

Katie stood firm. "I own ten percent of this business. I'm also the executor of Ezra's estate. That gives me the authority to do what I think is best for Artisans Alley. Including selling it outright." She let out a breath and softened her voice. "This place was Chad's dream, as well as Ezra's. I don't want to see it fail just because they're both gone. Will you help me save it?"

Vance turned away, his jaw twitching in repressed anger. Katie badly needed an ally, and if she'd just blown it—

Finally, Vance exhaled loudly and turned back to face her. "It'll be a hard sell. The artists don't want to share space with low-end crafters."

Katie didn't back down. "If they're the only ones interested in renting space here, then there's really no choice."

Three

"It's kinda dreary in here," Edie Silver said, glancing around Artisans Alley's uninviting lobby. The large, carpeted foyer had been painted white a long time before, but was now a timeworn yellow, marred by scuff marks and the remnants of aged masking tape still clinging to its walls, which were pocked by old nail holes.

"Can you make it look festive for Halloween?" Katie asked as her stomach grumbled. It was after six and she hadn't even taken time for lunch.

Edie's gaze narrowed. "What's your budget?"

Katie sighed, thinking about the few bills in her wallet. "Twenty-five dollars."

Edie rolled her eyes. "Honey, you don't want help—you want a miracle."

"Here's the deal—you make this area look attractive and prove to me that crafters can draw in customers, and I'll rent you space. Same terms as the rest of the artisans."

"Why the change of heart?" Edie asked, squinting up at her.

"I'll level with you. This place is going broke. It's full of artists who know a lot about their particular craft but haven't got a clue how to market their merchandise. Ezra's strict rules enforcing booth uniformity didn't inspire the artists to work on their displays either."

"A lot of them couldn't hack it in *real* galleries, ya know," Edie said snidely. "The commission of fifty or more percent is a killer. And of course, a lot of 'em are only here for the social aspect."

"So I gathered. The artists apparently aren't motivated to pay their rent now—and will feel even more belligerent if I have to raise it just to keep the place afloat."

Edie's frown twitched as she took another long look around. "I suppose I could get some orange and black crepe streamers at the dollar store. Maybe a couple of paper pumpkins. I might even have a line on some hay bales. . ." Her gaze traveled up and down the uneven walls, taking in the total space. "Yeah, I think I can do it."

"How soon?"

Edie smiled. "How late are you willing to stay here tonight?"

"As late as you need."

Katie awakened Saturday morning to find the gray clouds lower and darker than they'd been the day before. A light drizzle added to the gloom. Perfect retail weather, as Chad liked to say. She left a message for Josh on his voice mail. The insurance office was open a half day on Saturdays. She said she'd take the hours as vacation, and then headed straight for the local McDonald's, where she snagged a cup of coffee and a Sausage Egg McMuffin.

On her way out, Katie paused to read the banner headline from behind the glass front on the newspaper dispenser: *MCKINLAY MILL BUSINESSMAN MURDERED.*

Swell, she thought, feeding coins into the machine. She opened the door, grabbed a paper, nearly letting the spring door slam shut on her hand. Folding the paper, she tucked it under her arm before heading for her car.

Minutes later, she arrived at Artisans Alley, noticing a slight figure standing by the side door, wrapped in a beige raincoat over dark slacks, a black kerchief tied tightly under her chin, and huddled under a bright red umbrella. Katie gathered her breakfast, newspaper, keys, and purse, and headed for the building.

"Hello!" she called. The woman turned and Katie halted abruptly and found herself staring at the woman, whose left cheek was marked by the ugliest wart Katie had ever seen: big, round, and tall. She'd never known a wart could be tall before this.

"H-Hello," she tried again. "Can I help you? I'm Katie Bonner—one of the new owners of Artisans Alley."

The older woman smiled, the movement of her cheek seeming to increase the size of the growth. "I'm Ida Mitchell. I'm supposed to be working

46

today. I'm in charge of the tag room," she said proudly, and held out her hand to shake, but Katie juggled too many things to be able to take it.

"Sorry," she apologized. Ida Mitchell; the name sounded familiar. Hadn't she seen it in the ledger listing artists who hadn't paid their rent?

"Can I hold something for you?" Ida offered.

"Um . . . yes, thank you," Katie said, eager to get out of the rain. She handed over her breakfast bag and the already-damp newspaper, sorted through the keys, and unlocked the door, desperate not to have to look at Ida's face.

"What is it you sell?" Katie asked, fumbling for the light switch.

"Lace. I make it myself. It's very delicate work. The light's on the other side, dear," she directed.

Katie squinted into the darkness, and located the switch. "Oh. Thank you. Do you sell a lot of it?"

"Of what?" Ida asked.

"Lace."

"Oh, no. Not much call for it." Which would account for her not paying the rent on her booth.

With the light now on, Katie watched as Ida shook the drops from her umbrella before carefully closing it and fastening the Velcro tie around it. She placed its cord strap over her wrist. "After you," she said brightly, and followed Katie through the corridor that also served as a storeroom, and into Artisans Alley. Sadly, except for the lobby, the place hadn't undergone a miraculous transformation in the hours since Katie had locked up the night before. Where were the shoemaker's elves when she really needed them?

Ida handed back Katie's items and clasped her hands together, smiling brightly. "It's time for me to get to work."

"Just what is it you do?" Katie asked.

"As manager of the tag room, it's up to me to make sure that the artists get their little price tickets back. That way they can compare them to the computerized inventory they get with their checks each week."

Katie vaguely remembered Chad comparing his little square of paper with his price tags to a printed form of items sold. It wasn't unknown that mistakes were made in data entry; returning the tags to the artists was a chance for them to double-check their sales with the computer printout that accompanied their weekly checks.

"I take great care in taping those tickets down in an orderly fashion. I also cut up the sheets of paper and write down the week-ending date and the booth number. That takes a lot of time, you know."

"I didn't," Katie admitted.

Ida's head bobbed solemnly. "Yes, yes. It's quite important work."

"How long have you been a vendor?" Katie asked.

"For as long as we've been open," Ida answered, and beamed with pride.

Was she aware that Ezra had died? Or was she perhaps . . . special?

"Did you watch the news last night, or perhaps read this morning's paper?" Katie asked.

Ida shook her head. "Oh, no. Television is a tool of the devil. And I don't get the paper. It's full of bad news."

"Did you know that Ezra—"

"Mr. Hilton," Ida corrected her. "It's disrespectful to call someone our senior by their first name, you know."

Whatever.

"Mr. Hilton has died," Katie said as gently as possible.

Ida's right hand flew to cover her mouth. "Oh my goodness! Please tell me you're trying to fool me."

"I'm sorry, but he . . ." Could this woman handle the truth? "He passed on yesterday," she finished.

Ida's mouth trembled, her gigantic wart jiggling.

It was an awkward few moments before Katie could think of anything to say. "I'm sorry." *Talk about lame.*

"Is that why all the police cars were here yesterday and the Alley was closed?" Ida asked.

"Yes," Katie said.

"Whatever will we do without Mr. Hilton?" the older woman cried.

"We're going to carry on. Ezra, er, Mr. Hilton would've wanted that."

Ida sniffed. "Yes, he would." Despite her

49

conviction, her eyes still swam with tears. "Oh dear, oh dear."

Katie reached out, gave the woman's shoulder a hesitant pat.

Ida threw back her head, her body stiffening. "Despite this setback, I must not shirk my duty. Would you like me to turn on Artisans Alley's main lights, or do you want to do it yourself?"

"I think I can handle it," Katie said gently.

"Very well." Ida turned and marched off in the direction of the cash desks.

Okay. And how many more times that day was she going to have to break the news to artists, customers, or creditors?

Katie's stomach growled, reminding her of her cooling, uneaten breakfast, and she turned for Ezra's office. She pushed Ida from her thoughts, but not the problem of the deadbeat artists. She'd have to address that—and soon.

Shrugging out of her coat, she settled it on the back of Ezra's grubby office chair and sat down at the desk to contemplate the breakfast before her on top of her newspaper. Now that the vendor entrance was open, she expected more of her dealers would begin to show up and she hoped most of them would bypass the transformed entryway. She wasn't up to arguing about the inclusion of a crafter on the premises.

As she ate her breakfast sandwich, she decided it might be a good idea to greet the artists as they showed up for work. She tossed the grease-stained paper wrapper into the trash, grabbed her coffee and the newspaper, and went back to the main staircase. Perching on the bottom step, which faced the side entrance, she sipped her coffee, reading the paper's top story as she waited for the next vendor to arrive. The report made Ezra's death sound so . . . sensational. She'd heard it said there was no such thing as bad publicity, and hoped it was true for Artisans Alley's sake.

The rest of the paper held no interest for her so she folded it and set it aside. Her gaze strayed to the missing patch of carpet at the base of the stairs. Was that blood or dirt that stained the concrete? She'd have to do something about it. The simplest solution would be to add a strip of new carpet from the bottom step back to the wall. That would also take care of the messy coffee spill. She'd add calling a carpet installer to her list of things to do today.

The outside door opened and a tall figure was silhouetted in the dim light of the short corridor leading into the main showroom. He pushed a heavy-duty dolly ahead of him, and then closed the outer door.

Katie stood, reminding herself that retail was like show business, and the show must go on. "Hi!" she called cheerily.

"Are we open today?" the man asked.

"We sure are." She shoved her hand forward.

"I'm Katie Bonner, Chad Bonner's wife. I'm sort of in charge for now."

"Peter Ashby."

She shook his large, callused hand. Tall, blond, and ruggedly handsome, Ashby looked like he'd just walked off a movie set . . . or maybe an old Marlboro billboard. His plaid flannel shirt and padded vest didn't hide his muscled arms and torso. The word "hunk" lingered in Katie's mind.

He looked down at the floor and the missing carpet. "Is this where it happened?"

She nodded. "The sheriff's detective cut up the rug. It's just as well. We'd have never gotten the blood out of it."

He shook his head and frowned. "It's a damn shame about Ezra. He really kept this place together."

"Where's your booth?" Katie asked, glad to change the subject.

"Upstairs on the balcony." He pointed up to his right.

She looked up. A balcony ringed the cavernous room; its five-foot wooden railings overlooked the main showroom. "I guess it'll take me a while to put faces to names, and names to booth numbers."

"I'm number sixty-four. Any chance I can move downstairs soon?"

"I don't know that there are any openings. I guess it depends if we lose any vendors," she said, thinking about the artists who hadn't paid their rent in weeks or months. "What do you sell?"

"Resin statuary. Life-sized copies of Victorian cemetery art. Maybe you noticed them?"

"I'm afraid I haven't spent a lot of time upstairs," she said. "What do people do with these statues?"

"Decorate their gardens, mostly. Right now I have twelve different pieces. I'm expecting a shipment of new merchandise in the next week or so. I'll give you a ten percent discount on any piece you want," he offered.

"Sorry. I live in an apartment." After what she'd been through this past year, the last thing Katie wanted was some gruesome reminder of death staring at her while she watched TV at night.

"Does garden statuary sell at this time of year?"

Ashby raised an eyebrow, his mouth quirking down. "I've had good luck so far. This is my second fall at Artisans Alley. Christmas is coming—the best time of the year for retail."

Cemetery statues as Christmas gifts? Katie resisted the urge to shudder.

"Will you be here all day?" she asked, to change the subject.

Ashby nodded. "I'm scheduled to work today. Ezra usually left a job sheet on the main cash desk. I generally walk security, or carry out large pieces for customers. Sometimes do odd jobs. Do you need something done?"

"Yes. I want to make sure gawking customers don't congregate around this staircase. Could you keep an eye out for that and break up any bottlenecks?"

"Sure thing." He smiled, his white teeth resembling pristine white marble tombstones. "Well, I'd better get up to my booth to restock. Glad you're here, Katie. Maybe now we can upgrade the place—attract a more discerning clientele."

It was Katie's turn to raise an eyebrow as Ashby bent to pick up the large cardboard carton. She studied the rest of his body as he carried the heavy box up the stairs. He wasn't even breathing hard as he turned the corner and disappeared out of sight. He might be a snob but, yup, he was a hunk all right.

Before the end of the hour, another five artists had arrived to spruce up their booths before reporting for their work assignments. Rose Nash was among them. Upon arriving, the older woman, bedecked in matching beaded earrings, necklace, and bracelets, must have thanked Katie at least ten times for allowing Artisans Alley to reopen.

As Ashby had mentioned, Ezra had written up a detailed work schedule, which Katie found pinned to the bulletin board in his office. He had placed Rose and another woman at the cash desks, along with two more women to wrap the smaller, breakable items. Ashby and another man were assigned to walk security, and Vance had said he'd arrive before opening. Even so, Katie worried they might be shorthanded if hordes of the curious showed up.

Sure enough, the news of Ezra's death had been well reported in the local media. Ghouls and curiosity seekers arrived in droves. At precisely ten o'clock, Katie opened Artisans Alley's main, plate glass double doors to a crowd of twenty or more people, who rushed into the store as though they were competing in a marathon, their presence lending a macabre, carnival atmosphere.

And just as inevitably, the vendors who'd shown up to work demanded to know why a nonartisan was stationed at the front of Artisans Alley, selling what more than one deemed "crap," not "crafts."

"Halloween is only a week away. Why not capitalize on it?" Katie had said with a forced smile. Edie Silver had outdone herself. The spicy scent of pumpkin pie potpourri permeated the entryway, which looked like a Halloween fun house with fake tombstones, hay bales, cornstalks, and the inevitable paper skeletons. Maybe it was in poor taste, considering Ezra had just been murdered, but they were symbols of the season and lent a festive, not morbid, aura to the lobby. Edie's tabletop displays of cornucopias overflowing with gourds, resin scarecrows, pumpkin candles, and her amber-and-orange dried flower arrangements were splashes of color against the rest of Artisans Alley's dull background.

Most important, people were spending money —and not just for her items.

Many of the artisan vendors had also shown up,

and one by one they drew Katie aside, demanding to know what was going on. Vance always seemed to be hovering in the background, eavesdropping. The gossip ran rampant. Everything from the place would be closing tomorrow, to the rent would be doubled the next week. Everyone asked Katie when she would call a meeting to discuss Artisans Alley's future.

"How about tonight?" she suggested, and decided to hold it after closing. Since Artisans Alley was the most important part of Victoria Square, it made sense to invite the rest of the merchants, too.

Leaving Vance in charge, Katie headed across the Square. Her first stop: Gilda's Gourmet Baskets.

A brass bell over the door tinkled as Katie entered the boutique filled with browsing customers. She breathed in the scents of chocolate, wood, dried basketry, fresh-brewed coffee, and vanilla. Gilda Ringwald was waiting on a customer and flashed a be-with-you-when-I-can smile. That was okay; it gave Katie a chance to give the place a quick once-over.

Baskets of all shapes and sizes filled the shop— some filled beyond capacity, only the colorful cellophane wraps holding in all the goodies. Shelves lined the walls with a variety of delights: jellies, jams, teas, soaps, loofahs, cookie cutters, and gardening gloves. Any kind of hobby or interest was represented in some way, shape, or form. A basket filled with fresh breads sat on the old-fashioned wooden counter. Katie had no doubt the just-baked delights had been carried across the Square that very morning from Tanner's, McKinlay Mill's only bakery.

A doorway connected this shop with the one next door—The Perfect Grape wine store. Katie peeked through and saw more baskets containing wine, cheese, and an assortment of cookies and crackers—an eminently satisfying combination. Were the two shops linked financially as well?

Katie couldn't help smiling at the perfect blend of synchronicity the shops evoked. Why had she avoided the Square for so long? It was everything she and Chad had hoped for—everything they'd planned to be a part of.

"Mrs. Bonner," Gilda called, delighted.

"Call me Katie, please."

"Business is booming," Gilda whispered, then cleared her throat, as though realizing that observation may not have been in good taste. "I spoke with most of the merchants about an emergency meeting, but we haven't yet decided on a time to gather. Perhaps Monday."

"I came to invite you to a meeting I'm having with the Alley's artisans early this evening. Maybe we can kill two birds with one stone."

Gilda nodded. "I'd be interested in attending." She lowered her voice. "Have you heard anything from the police about Ezra's murder?"

"Nothing so far. I'm not sure if I should call

them either. They were going to do an autopsy today. I don't know when they'll release the body for burial. I guess I should talk to Mr. Collier at the funeral home."

Katie realized she sounded wishy-washy, but at that moment she felt she'd lost touch with the take-charge woman who'd been in control at Artisans Alley only minutes before. She changed the subject. "The meeting's at seven. Can you make it?"

"I'll make it a point to be there. I'm sure the other merchants will, too. Have you met them?" Katie shook her head. "Why don't you go introduce yourself," Gilda suggested. "They're all dying to meet you."

Dying? After what happened to Ezra, it was a poor choice of words.

"I'm on my way," Katie said, and started for the door. She paused, turning back to face Gilda. "You have a wonderful shop. I'm sorry it took Ezra's death to get me in here."

Gilda's smile was gentle. "Then don't be a stranger."

Outside, Katie stood for a moment under the door's colorful striped awning, looking out over Victoria Square. Her gaze fell on the decrepit mansion to the east. Paint flakes the size of silver dollars hung from its weathered clapboards. The English Ivy Inn—what she and Chad had planned on calling it, should they ever have saved enough to buy it—was never to be. Still, in her mind's eye she saw it restored to its former glory, with new landscaping in place, and cascades of ivy and yellow rambling roses climbing on more than one trellis.

Katie looked back at the ugly brown monstrosity that was the Artisans Alley and sighed.

Squaring her shoulders, she headed for the tea shop.

Like the morning, the afternoon was a blur of new faces and names, all strangers, all anxious, and all putting their faith in Katie to make things turn out right.

Katie sat at Ezra's—now her own—desk and marveled at the newly created order. What had seemed like an insurmountable mess turned out to be relatively organized once she figured out Ezra's haphazard filing system. Still, it would take weeks to go through all the accumulated paper in the file cabinets.

Vance had handled just about every crisis that arose during the day—from disgruntled customers to a tape jam in Register 1. Katie had all but decided to ask him to manage the place. She just had to figure out how to pay him.

Edie Silver told Katie that she'd already spread the word that crafters could now rent space. Already Katie had heard from five interested artists. If she could rent all the empty booths, it would mean an extra three thousand dollars a month in revenue.

She'd probably have to raise the rent anyway, but she'd give it a month to see how things worked out.

It was after four, though, and she still hadn't made the call she'd been dreading. To avoid it just a little longer, she picked up Chad's journal and flipped through a few of the pages.

January 2nd

AA is a good acronym for this place—Artists Anonymous—or maybe Artists-Destined-To-Remain Anonymous. It's full of odd ducks and social misfits. That Ida Mitchell lives and breathes to tape down price stickers, treating the task like it was the most important job in the world. Then again, I've never had another vendor's price tags on my weekly sheet. Poor Rose Nash must be really lonely. She drops everything to come in and work at the register whenever another vendor skips his or her scheduled shift—which happens far too often. Ezra ought to lay down some tough rules. Those who can't—or won't—work, should have to pay extra, or have a surcharge applied to their sales. That would get the deadbeat vendors to show up on their workdays. The excuses they make are worse than those of my ninth grade students who don't do their homework and howl when they flunk my quizzes.

Katie frowned, closing the book and setting it

aside. She'd hoped for words of encouragement from Chad, not a blunt assessment of the troubles she was likely to face. Still, she might have to bring up the subject of additional fees at the meeting that night.

Her gaze returned to the silent phone. Putting off the call wasn't going to make the news any better. She punched in the numbers on the black touch-tone phone, and listened as the phone rang.

"Collier's Funeral Home. How may we be of service in your time of need?"

"Mr. Collier, it's Katie Bonner."

"Oh, Mrs. Bonner. You're no doubt calling about Ezra. No need to worry. Mr. Landers has already made all the arrangements, per Ezra's instructions. Has he spoken with you about it?"

"Not yet. I probably should have called him."

"The coroner released the body earlier this afternoon. I have a preliminary copy of the death certificate if you'd like to see it—the official documentation will be recorded with the county on Monday morning."

"Yes, I'd like to see it, thank you. Was it blunt trauma as the deputy said?"

"Yes. But I don't think Ezra suffered," Collier said, his voice gentle.

Thank God for that, Katie thought.

"I thought Monday night for the viewing, and Tuesday morning for the burial. Would that be convenient for you?"

"I haven't spoken with Ezra's nephew, but it should be all right." Katie paused, wondering how to tactfully bring up the subject of cost. "Did Ezra make any financial arrangements?"

"Yes, it's all taken care of. Ezra was a practical man and made the arrangements more than a year ago."

Katie frowned at the dichotomy of Ezra with his natty suits and polished Florsheims taking care of his funeral expenses yet leaving his supposedly cherished Artisans Alley languishing. At least it was one less financial worry for her.

"Thank you, Mr. Collier."

The undertaker promised to call her with the final details and said good-bye. He hadn't mentioned speaking with the Sheriff's Office. But maybe that was standard procedure. Still, it didn't seem like Detective Davenport had done much investigating. As far as Katie knew, he'd only spoken with a couple of the merchants on the Square. She'd thought he might show up during the day to speak with the artists, but he hadn't done that either. Maybe it was his day off . . .

Don't get involved, Katie told herself. It wasn't her job to find out who'd killed Ezra. And yet what if Davenport didn't even try to find the murderer? It could be someone involved with Artisans Alley—or on the Square—right now. That thought brought her no comfort.

"I'm not going to think about it," she said aloud.

"Think about what?"

Startled, Katie nearly jumped. "Seth. Are you trying to give me a heart attack?"

"Never," Artisans Alley's lawyer said, and entered the office. Dressed in an oatmeal-colored sweater, matching slacks, and a droplet-speckled raincoat, the small-town attorney gave off an instant aura of trust. At forty, he was ten years older than Katie, but unlike many of his peers, he still sported a full head of sandy-colored hair, and a frame that suggested he worked out on a regular basis. How such a handsome, decent guy had evaded matrimony for so long was a mystery to her.

"I just spoke to Luther Collier at the funeral home. He said you'd made all the arrangements. Thanks."

Seth waved a hand to brush it off. "I'm happy to help. I dropped by to see how you were doing."

"So far, so good." She glanced at the dusty-faced clock on the wall. "And we've only got another forty-five minutes until closing. It's been a good day for sales."

He nodded and leaned against one of the khaki-colored file cabinets. "I spoke with Ezra's nephew, Gerald."

Something about his tone told Katie this might not be good news. "And?"

"He seemed a lot more interested in Ezra's will and what he was likely to get from it than what happened to poor Ezra."

Katie's stomach tightened. "Is it out of line for me to ask? Not for myself . . ." she quickly explained. "For the Alley. There're a lot of people's hopes riding on your answer."

Seth nodded. "Ezra split his assets evenly between the two of you."

"Ohmigod," Katie breathed. She'd hardly known the man. "Was it a recent will?"

"Dated a month ago."

"Good Lord. Do you think Ezra had a premonition of his own death?"

Seth shook his head, his lips quirking downward. "The old man expected to live forever."

Not if he prepaid for his own funeral, Katie thought.

"It did seem kind of odd at the time," Seth continued, looking thoughtful. "Ezra was in a terrible rush to get the new will written. Maybe he'd recently spoken with Gerald and wanted to make sure Artisans Alley would go on without him. I think he knew you'd try to keep it running. That *is* what he wanted."

Katie digested that piece of information. Then why hadn't Ezra invited her to take on more responsibility? He probably assumed she'd been in mourning for Chad.

That was true, of course, but it was her own financial need that took precedence. Chad had scoffed at the idea of life insurance. Not a good decision, especially as the local school board had cut back on teacher benefits. Like a lot of men under thirty, Chad felt invincible. Insurance could wait until later, he'd reasoned. And then he'd been killed. The funeral had set Katie back thousands. For months she'd worked overtime just to pay it off. And Ezra *had* asked her to come by. In fact, just days before his death he'd left a message on her answering machine. She should have made time to sit down and talk about the business. Her reply was always "next week," or "soon."

"Don't be surprised if Gerald Hilton shows up tomorrow," Seth said. "He asked me a lot of questions about Artisans Alley, things I couldn't answer. Like square footage, insurance, and such."

"What do you think he wants?"

"Between you and me, a quick liquidation of assets. That can't happen until after probate, and I told him so. You might want to prepare yourself for a fight. He doesn't seem the easygoing type."

"Swell." Katie leaned back in her chair, idly twisting her wedding band. "I'm having a meeting with the artists and merchants from the Square at seven to talk about the Alley's future. Can you join us?"

Seth shook his head. "I have a prior commitment. But I'll be at the funeral home on Monday night, and perhaps the service on Tuesday morning." He glanced at his watch. "I'd better get going."

She nodded and rose, wrapping her arm around his, and then walked him to the exit. "Thanks for dropping by. You're a good friend, Seth."

He reached for her hand, squeezed it, and then leaned forward to kiss her cheek. "See you Monday, Katie."

She blinked, her hand automatically going to where his lips had touched her skin. The kiss had been a surprise. A pleasant one. She found herself smiling after him.

Katie made her way past a cheerful Edie, who was waiting on a customer, and paused at the Alley's main entrance to wave as Seth's car pulled out of the parking lot. Out of the corner of her eye she saw the lights were now on in the Square's pizza shop. She hadn't had a chance to make contact with the owner and decided to dodge the raindrops to do so.

A row of heavy brass bells on a thick strip of age-darkened leather hung on the plate glass door, jingling loudly as Katie entered. Inside, the enticing aromas of pizza and spicy chicken wings battled for prominence, and the heady fragrances nearly lifted Katie off her feet.

"Can I help you?" asked a tall, beefy guy of about thirty. A Rochester Red Wings baseball cap sat atop his head, covering dark wavy hair, which stuck out over his ears. He wore a blue Angelo's Pizzeria T-shirt, faded jeans, and sneakers. A white dishcloth at his waist made a makeshift apron. He pounded a round of flour-powdered dough, forming it into a flat circle.

"Are you Angelo?" Katie asked.

"Andy Rust. The place was called Angelo's when I bought it last year. Can I help you?"

She reached out to shake hands, realized his were occupied, and pulled her hand back. "Katie Bonner. I was Ezra Hilton's business partner."

"Sorry to hear about him dying." His words held no warmth.

"Thank you. I've tried to meet all the other members of the Merchants Association to—"

"Then count me out," Andy said, bitterness coloring his tone. "I'm not a member."

"Oh. I just thought—"

Andy looked up, his eyes cold. "Some of the merchants don't think a pizza parlor fits the hoity-toity Victoria Square image."

"Oh, well . . . I'm sorry to hear that. Doesn't everybody love pizza?"

Brows furrowed, Andy stared at her for a moment, then shrugged and laughed. "Not around here. What can I do for you?" he said, his voice softening.

"I'm having a meeting at seven for the artists and other merchants on the Square to discuss Artisans Alley's future. Would you like to join us?"

Again he stared at her. "Saturday's my busiest night of the week. I really can't spare the time."

"Oh, well, maybe you could combine business with pleasure. I'd like to order a couple of sheet pizzas. It might help break the ice with the artists."

"As you said, everybody loves pizza." As he

took her order, she couldn't help noticing the way his brows furrowed as he concentrated. It was kind of . . . cute. "What time do you want them delivered?" Andy asked.

"Just before seven. Thanks."

This time he wiped his right hand on his make-shift apron and reached to shake hers. "Thank you, Katie," he said and held on, his deep brown eyes staring into her own. "I've been open almost eighteen months and you're the first merchant to order something from me."

Katie laughed nervously, still aware of his warm, dusty hand in hers. "It probably won't be my last. I'm a pizzaholic."

His answering smile charmed her. "Then I hope there's no cure."

Four

Katie smiled, gritted her teeth, and endured yet another bone-crushing handshake from one of the artists. Stationed at Artisans Alley's lobby entrance, she wanted to greet every artist as they arrived for the meeting. In her left arm she held a clipboard, and dutifully checked off each name on the copy of the phone list she'd found in one of Ezra's desk drawers.

"Glad you could make it," she said to a grim-faced man who followed the stream inside, heading for the main staircase, where Rose Nash directed them to empty loft space above.

Once again dressed in her raincoat and kerchief, and still clutching her umbrella, Ida-with-the-giant-wart Mitchell shuffled along with the pack. "Good evening, Katie," she said, her grin wide and her eyes looking slightly crazed. Katie tried to keep her gaze from the flaw on the woman's cheek, but it was so glaringly obvious.

She forced a smile. "Hello, Ida. Thank you for coming. I see you're feeling better this evening."

Ida nodded sweetly. "Mr. Hilton's in a better place now. I'm rejoicing for his good fortune."

Had anyone explained to Ida that Ezra had been murdered?

Katie shook her head and watched as the clueless woman continued on her way. When she turned back, Katie recognized the Red Wings cap on a head above the crowd. She shook hands and greeted everyone else as she waited for the man to shuffle forward.

"Where do you want these?" Andy Rust asked, hefting the pizza boxes.

"Upstairs, to the left, thanks."

Andy nodded and followed the others inside.

Vance arrived, bringing up the rear of the crowd, with a teenaged boy in tow. "Hey, Katie. This is my son, Vance Junior." The kid actually winced at the introduction. "He's going to watch the door and send up any latecomers."

Katie clasped the gangly young man's damp palm. "Nice to meet you, Vance Junior."

"Call me VJ," the boy insisted.

"I really appreciate this, VJ." She looked at Vance Senior. "I need to get my notes from the office. I'll meet you upstairs, okay?"

"All right."

Katie hadn't considered the logistics of stuffing sixty-plus artists and nine or ten merchants into Artisans Alley, and wished she had. Of course, the only suitable open space was upstairs in the loft-like, unoccupied area Ezra had reserved for new artists. Vance had also shown her more storage space nearby that could be converted to vendor booths. Thanks to the interest Edie Silver's friends had shown by their calls requesting vendor space, Katie already anticipated the increased revenue.

Seating was also a problem. They had virtually none. Vance had scrounged six or seven folding chairs and a couple of tables to put out the pizza. While he'd set them up, Katie had taken a trip to the grocery store for disposable cups, napkins, and soda, and to restock her dwindling supply of hard candy. When she'd first decided to hold the meeting, she hadn't anticipated feeding a crowd, but free food often put people in a more receptive mood to hear bad news—and that's the only kind she had to deliver.

More than half the pizza had already been scarfed up by the time Katie reached the meeting area. People had gathered in knots, with conversations buzzing in the warm, dusty old loft.

Katie sought out a familiar face and made a beeline for Edie Silver. "Thanks for coming."

"Are you kidding? I wouldn't miss it. Looks like I'll need to restock. Most of my merchandise is already gone," she said, her expression smug.

"That tells me crafters *can* sell here."

"I always knew it." Edie raised a hand to wave to someone.

Katie looked around. "Do you know any of these people?"

"Heck, I know most of 'em. We do a lot of the same shows."

"Shows?"

"Art festivals, canal days, and holiday craft sales. There's a slew of big shows every year in the Rochester area. I only do the local ones, but some of these folks go all over the state and even out of state to sell their stuff."

Katie blinked. "If you guys mingle in other venues, why was Mr. Hilton so prejudiced against . . ." She hesitated before finishing, "Low-end crafters?"

Edie shrugged, not in the least offended. "A purist, I guess. A lot of highbrow artists think craft means crap. But people on a budget can afford to spend twenty bucks on a pretty eucalyptus swag when they can't afford a primitive-style painting to hang over the fireplace in their tract house. When can we talk about my booth location?" she asked, changing the subject. "The lobby's great, but I want a more secure space."

"How about first thing tomorrow morning?"

Edie nodded and smiled. "Guess I'd better grab some pizza before it's all gone."

She'd taken only a step away when another, much younger, woman—petite and blond, and closer to Katie's age—took her place. Smartly dressed in a denim jacket, black turtleneck, tight jeans, and black leather boots, the newcomer was the epitome of business casual. She looked vaguely familiar. Hadn't Katie seen her in the local supermarket or drugstore?

The woman stuck out her hand. "Katie Bonner? I'm Tracy Elliott."

For a moment the name meant nothing. Then, "Are you related to the woman who runs the tea shop?" Katie asked.

"She's my mother. Sorry I was out when you came by earlier. My computer monitor blew and I had to drive into Rochester to get a new one." She rolled her eyes. "It'll be years before a decent computer outlet comes to this hick town."

Katie didn't see what that had to do with selling tea and pastries, but she didn't get the opportunity to ask.

"A lot of our business is on the Internet. Check us out," Tracy said, handing Katie a business card. "I can't bake worth a damn, but I wanted to be part of the shop. When I suggested we sell some of Mom's blended teas online, it seemed like I'd found my niche. Now we make more money on that than the shop itself."

"Then, why—"

"Are we a part of Victoria Square? It's Mom's hobby. And . . . well, she had other reasons for being a part of the Square." Tracy didn't elaborate. "Ezra was a great guy, but he kept both feet firmly planted in the twentieth century. I offered to build him a website. It would be a good marketing tool for Artisans Alley. He wouldn't take advice from a woman—let alone someone young enough to be a granddaughter. Mom says you're part owner. If you want a website, I'd be glad to set the whole thing up for you for a competitive price."

"That's awfully nice of you. Thanks."

"Why don't we talk about it tomorrow? Mom makes the world's best scones. Drop by the shop before opening and try them out."

"I'd like that. And please help yourself to some pizza before it's all gone."

Tracy's gaze traveled over to where Andy Rust lingered at the fringe of the crowd. "Thanks, but no thanks. Talk to you tomorrow," she said, and filtered back into the throng.

Katie looked over at Andy again. Hands thrust into his jacket pockets, he leaned against one of the massive hand-cut support beams, having obviously decided to hang around for the meeting. What could the merchants possibly have against him? He seemed a decent, friendly enough guy. And surely a pizza parlor wasn't *that* detrimental to the livelihood of the rest of the Square. She'd have to find out what was really going on. But that could wait until later.

Katie consulted her watch, saw that it was already after seven. Public speaking was not her forte, and the plastic smile she'd been wearing for the last half hour was already beginning to droop while the butterflies in her stomach multiplied. Katie resisted the impulse to crunch another lemon drop she'd squirreled away in her pants pocket, and instead sorted through her notes. Why oh why hadn't she joined the debating team back in high school, or perhaps the local Toastmasters chapter? To distract herself, she counted heads. When she got to fifty-five, she decided it was time to start.

"Can I have your attention? Please gather around so I don't have to shout."

Vance was suddenly at her side, setting down a black box covered in knobs and dials. "It's my son's karaoke machine. It can double as a sound system." He unraveled the cord and plugged it into a wall socket, then handed her a microphone.

Katie cleared her throat and tapped the mike. "Testing." A squawk of feedback echoed through the loft.

The buzz of voices died as Vance adjusted a dial then nodded for her to continue.

"Thank you all for coming on such short notice. We're here to talk about Artisans Alley's future. But first, let's have a moment of reflection in memory of the Alley's founder, Ezra Hilton."

Everyone bowed his or her head. Silence fell over the stuffy, low-ceilinged room. Katie saw a tissue or two dab at damp eyes. She counted to ten before beginning again.

"Thank you. Now, before we start—"

"Have the police got any idea who killed Ezra?" Rose Nash asked, her voice thin and anxious.

"If they do, they haven't shared that information with me. Of course, I'll let you know if I find out anything. And I urge you all to cooperate with the Sheriff's Office if they should decide to interview you."

"Are you going to increase security?" a man up front asked. "What if someone else breaks in to rob the place? I've got lots of valuable items in my booth and I don't make enough to afford insurance."

Was it worth voicing that Ezra had probably known his killer, making the issue of security virtually moot? Probably not.

"I'll consider it," Katie promised, then cleared her throat. "I've spoken with Ezra's lawyer, as well as his accountant. We can continue to stay open during probate, but we've got some serious cash flow problems."

"You're not going to raise the rent, are you?" came a belligerent voice from the back.

"There's a good possibility I'll have to do just that. Or I may have to charge a service fee. Believe me, that's not what I want. Unfortunately, to stay afloat, I'm going to have to run the place like a business—not a hobby. That doesn't mean we can't have fun and socialize, but it's imperative that we rent out all the vacant booths as soon as possible."

"We don't want crappy crafters here," another unidentified male voice declared.

"The area where we're standing can accommodate up to twenty artists," Katie said. "I've already spoken to six crafters who are eager to start paying rent immediately. Unless you have any alternatives, I'm going to rent out that space."

A wave of grumbling rolled through the loft.

"What do you think, Vance?" Peter Ashby asked.

"Better to have crafters come in than to have to shut down," he said.

Katie silently blessed him for backing her up.

"Then let them make up the shortfall," Ashby said. "Let's see a show of hands. Who votes for the crafters to pay more in rent?"

"Aye," went the collective voice.

Katie waved them quiet. "This isn't a democracy, Mr. Ashby. For now, at least, everyone will pay the same rent per square foot."

Again, a rumble of disapproval rolled through the crowd.

"There's also the problem of late rents. In checking Ezra's books, I've found that some twenty percent of you are between two and six weeks late. Several people haven't paid their booth rental in months. There'll be an amnesty period of two weeks, then I'm afraid those still in arrears will have to vacate their booths."

Silence and shocked expressions greeted that grim statement. Ida continued to smile blandly.

"I realize that a lot of you barely make your rent, let alone a profit, and raising the rent would be a financial hardship. The solution to all our problems is bringing more artists into Artisans Alley. Advertising costs money, something we're in short supply of. As you saw in the entryway today, Edie Silver found plenty of customers ready to buy her merchandise."

"Yeah, and she took away our customers," someone said.

Edie glared at the jerk.

"I checked Ezra's records for last Saturday. Today's take was forty percent higher," Katie said. "I can't say that was entirely due to Edie's merchandise, but she nearly sold out, and that didn't hurt Artisans Alley's bottom line."

"The Merchants Association has an advertising budget and the Christmas push is about to start," Gilda Ringwald volunteered. "That always brings in customers." Her voice faded. "Ezra always took care of that."

"What's wrong with word-of-mouth advertising? It's free," came another voice.

"That's important, too. But we have to have something special to draw the crowds in," Katie said. "I propose we set up a committee to explore ways of enticing new customers to come visit. Any volunteers?"

Several hands rose above the sea of heads. Katie recognized Rose Nash and Edie Silver as belonging to two of them. "Rose, could you take down the names of those interested? Thank you. What we also need to think about are long-term strategies for keeping Artisans Alley going—to bring in customers, and to get them to spend money."

"All this is irrelevant," came a voice from the back of the crowd. Katie hadn't seen the distinguished, middle-aged gentleman enter. Clad in a three-piece suit, with slicked-back black hair and a debonair manner, he elbowed his way through the assemblage.

"And you are?" she asked.

Without asking, the man jerked the microphone from her hand, then turned toward the crowd. "My name is Gerald Hilton. Ezra Hilton was my uncle. I want you all to know that once probate is finished, there isn't going to be an Artisans Alley."

"So much for allaying the fears of our artists," Katie began, once the crowd had cleared out and she and Gerald Hilton were alone in what she already thought of as her office. She'd wanted Vance to sit in on the discussion, but Hilton was adamant that it be just the two of them.

"It doesn't do any good to encourage them. Or you, for that matter. I've made up my mind. We're selling Artisans Alley."

"I agree."

Hilton blinked, obviously not expecting that answer.

"In order to get a good price, we need to offer a going concern," Katie continued. "The business as it stands is in imminent danger of failure."

"That's immaterial. We're not selling it as a going concern."

79

"Then what's the point—"

Hilton shook his head in a condescending manner. "My dear young woman, have you ever heard of the Radisson Hotel chain?"

"Of course."

"They've been interested in buying this property for the past two years. My uncle refused to sell, despite the chain's very generous offer."

Chad had never mentioned that. But then, had Ezra ever told him?

"Why would a big hotel want to locate here in McKinlay Mill?"

"They own a share in the new marina. The area is on the verge of exploding with development opportunities and it would be well worth it for you to carefully consider their offer."

"I've lived in the village for the past four years and the rumors of development have been around for a lot longer than that. I haven't seen the offer and only have your word on it."

"I assure you, what I've said is true."

"And I assure you, I'm not interested."

"Are you out of your mind?" he blurted.

"No. My plan has always been to be a part of Victoria Square." Hilton didn't need to know just exactly what those plans entailed, and with that belligerent attitude, he didn't deserve to know either. "It's in the best interests of Victoria Square for Artisans Alley to remain the anchor, and to do that, it needs to be solvent."

"Just who do you think you are making plans for this establishment? I've done my homework, you see, and—"

"I don't think you have," Katie said, crossing her arms over her chest.

"I beg your pardon?"

"We're not selling to any hotel chain. And obviously you haven't done your homework. At least, not in the area of partnership agreements."

"Ah," he said, ready to dismiss her again. "I've spoken with my uncle's attorney. He said the assets were evenly split between the two of us. Although God knows why my uncle chose you."

"Because I already happen to be a partner in the business."

Hilton's eyes widened in surprise. Obviously Seth hadn't told him everything.

"I already own ten percent of Artisans Alley. Legally, I'm the only one who can make any decisions about the business. When probate is completed, I'll own fifty-five percent of Artisans Alley. It's unfortunate for you, Mr. Hilton, but the person with the biggest portion of the pie gets to call the shots."

Hilton said nothing, but his eyes bulged, his temper smoldering.

He paced the short distance to the door and back. "It would seem we've come to an impasse. There has to be a compromise."

Katie didn't bat an eye. "I don't think so."

"You're being unreasonable."

"I'm sure you heard what I told the artists. I don't intend to run Artisans Alley as your uncle did. I don't consider it a hobby. You may be right. McKinlay Mill could be on the verge of an economic explosion. And if it is, Artisans Alley can be a large part of the draw. The future of Victoria Square depends in part on its survival—so do the livelihoods of a lot of other people in the village."

"I'm not interested in other people," Hilton declared.

"Why am I not surprised?"

Hilton's eyes narrowed. "You'll change your mind, Ms. Bonner. I guarantee it."

Katie straightened to her full height. "Not in this lifetime."

"You said it," Hilton grated. "I didn't."

Five

"He threatened you?" a wide-eyed Vance asked after Hilton had stormed out of Artisans Alley, although Katie suspected he'd been behind the door with his ear pressed to the keyhole during the whole heated discussion.

"It sounded like that to me," she said, leaning back in her chair. "But then, he was angry, and I can't say I blame him. I'm sure he was just blowing off steam."

Vance shook his head. "I might agree with that, Katie, if Ezra hadn't been murdered."

"You can't think his own nephew would—"

"If the land this old building sits on is worth that much, who's to say he wouldn't?"

Katie frowned, and then went back to sorting through the papers on Ezra's desk—her desk. "Other than Hilton, how do you think the meeting went?"

"There was talk of inviting the robber to come back and rub *you* out."

Katie looked up, her mouth dropping open, and then saw the amusement in Vance's eyes.

"Ezra should have been more honest with everyone about his financial problems," Vance continued. "Our artists are good people. That's why . . ." He reached into the breast pocket of his flannel shirt, withdrew a wad of folded papers, and handed them to her. "There're at least ten checks there. I'm sure you'll have the rest of them before closing tomorrow."

Katie felt her eyes fill with sudden tears. "Oh, Vance, thank you."

"I didn't coerce anyone. They paid up voluntarily. Nobody wants to leave. And they want Artisans Alley to stay open, too."

Katie felt her throat closing. Was it gratitude or something else she felt for this old place and the friends Chad had left behind?

Clearly embarrassed by her waterworks, Vance headed for the door. "There's a light out in the lobby. I'd better replace the bulb before I leave."

"Vance, wait. There's something I've been meaning to ask you since yesterday."

He turned to face her, his face impassive.

"I want you to manage Artisans Alley. I'm not sure what I can pay right now, but you obviously know more about running this place than anyone else. We need someone to take on the day-to-day responsibilities. Someone who cares about the place. Someone who—"

Vance shook his head, his voice somber. "No."

Katie blinked, surprised by his quiet refusal. "It doesn't have to be permanent, just until we find someone—"

"I'm sorry, Katie, but I can't." Vance turned and opened the office door.

"I can't do it, Vance. I have a regular job that pays well and gives real benefits. I can't afford to leave it. My boss is already fuming because I've blown off a day and a half, I—"

"I'm sorry," he said without even looking back, "but I can't do it either." Then he was gone.

Katie sank back in her chair, panic churning inside her. Just when she thought there was a chance—however small—that things could work out, something else went wrong. Why would Vance, a retiree who many already considered to be Artisans Alley's second-in-command, refuse?

Would Chad's journal hold a clue?

Katie located the book, and flipped it open at random, running her fingers over the pages, searching for Vance's name. She found it, near the back of book, and read the entry.

February 26th

Vance and I have a bit of a love-hate relationship going. I love him—and he hates me. Or at least it seems that way. I think he's jealous of my friendship with Ezra. But then, he has gone to bat for me several times when I've challenged Ezra on how AA is run. I've been trying to convince Ezra we should do what antique co-ops do: rent shelf space. If artists do well with a shelf, they might just rent space with us. I asked Vance if he'd build them, and he liked the idea—and the idea of getting paid to do it, too.

The rest of the account had to do with where the new shelving should be put. Chad thought it should be near the registers—likely the last stop customers made before paying for their purchases. Instead, Ezra had opted for them to be hidden in the back of the first floor.

Katie sighed. Chad's words hadn't given her any insight into Vance. Since it was written eight months before Ezra's death, it also hadn't given Katie any insight as to where Vance might've been the night Ezra was killed.

Once Chad had left her, Katie spent many a lonely evening baking her great-aunt's favorite recipes. She enjoyed the process of carefully measuring the ingredients, and beating the batters by hand with an old wooden spoon. The problem was, she couldn't possibly eat the bounty of cookies, cakes, and quick breads. Her boss, Josh, had been the happy, although not necessarily grateful, recipient of all those sweets, so it was with real pleasure that Katie baked a batch of her Aunt Lizzie's shortbread for the vendors at Artisans Alley.

The building felt cold and damp on Sunday morning, as though it had reverted to the apple warehouse it had once been. Katie didn't know enough about the old building's mechanics to even attempt to coax more heat out of the mishmash of blowers and machinery. And she wasn't sure she could afford the extra gas . . . or did it run on oil or electricity? Maybe she shouldn't bother, hoping that lights and the customers' body heat would warm the place. She sighed. She still had a lot to learn about Artisans Alley.

She set the plate of shortbread on the table in the center of the vendors' lounge, and made a fresh pot of coffee so that all would be ready by the time the day's workers arrived. She unlocked the side door—what she now thought of as the employee entrance—and headed for the cash desks up front. A glance at Ezra's work schedule on the cash desk confirmed that six of the Alley's artists had signed up to work that day. Ezra had devised a good system to staff Artisans Alley. Each vendor worked four days a month—that way Ezra didn't have to pay wages and worry about payroll taxes—but six didn't seem nearly enough for a building of this size. She'd have to rethink that strategy, and quickly, too, as she'd need to worry about staffing the place for November and the holidays to come.

As the clock ticked toward the 10 a.m. opening, Katie was still the only one on the premises. She could run a cash register if she had to, but doing that, plus walking security, in addition to attending to matters in the office, was more than one person could reasonably do. If no one showed up by ten fifteen, she might have to close.

She couldn't afford to do that either. You didn't make money with the doors locked tight.

"Anybody here?" called a familiar voice from the vicinity of the side, employee entrance.

Katie looked up. "Rose, is that you?"

"Katie?"

At least Rose had decided not to address Katie so formally. "Mrs. Bonner" reminded her of Chad's late mother, who hadn't been the nicest, friendliest woman. Like the worst fictional mothers-in-law, Mrs. Bonner had believed no woman was good enough for her son—especially Katie. And Mrs. Bonner—she'd never even asked Katie to call her by her first name, let alone "Mom"—had made it clear minutes after Chad's funeral service that she wanted nothing more to do with Katie.

The night that followed had been the loneliest night of Katie's life.

Rose appeared around the corner and strode up to the counter, untying her kerchief as she approached. "Good morning, Katie. Isn't it a lovely day?" she asked cheerfully. "I'll hang up my coat and be right with you."

Heartened by Rose's greeting, Katie parked herself by the cash desk, firing up the computer and making sure that there was change in the cash drawer to start the business day. She needed to get another roll of quarters for Register 1, she reminded herself. And she still hadn't called the security company to learn the combination of the safe. That would have to wait until Monday. Yet another item on her ever-growing to-do list.

Rose trundled back up to the register, decked out in a brown skirt suit with amber beaded jewelry adorning her ears, neck, and wrist. Katie also noticed the steamy romance novel Rose clutched in her hand.

Rose blushed. "Romance novels are my sin. Since my Howard died, they're my only vice."

Katie smiled. "Maybe I should try them." She winced as her voice cracked on the last word.

Rose's lips trembled as she patted Katie's hand. "A pretty girl like you doesn't need to worry. You'll find another someone. You have a long life ahead of you."

A long, lonely life, Katie thought, then shook her head to banish such thoughts from her mind.

Setting her book down, Rose rubbed her hands. Artisans Alley wasn't exactly toasty warm first thing in the morning. "Boy, it's cold in here today."

"And I know nothing about powering up the heating system," Katie admitted.

"Vance will take care of it when he gets in," Rose assured her.

"Shouldn't he be here by now?"

Rose sighed. "His wife, Janey, has multiple sclerosis. Lately it seems her bad days outnumber the good, or so I've heard."

Katie tried to squelch her irritation at Vance, reminding herself she wasn't the only person on the planet with problems.

"I'm surprised Ida hasn't shown up. At least I didn't see her coat hanging in the tag room," Rose said.

Ida-with-the-giant-wart. Much as she tried not to think of the woman that way, Katie just couldn't help herself. "Does she come in every day?"

Rose nodded. "Most days." She leaned in and spoke conspiratorially. "Ezra let her slide when it came to paying her rent."

"Yes, I know."

"I can tell you, that's caused hard feelings among more than a few of the artists."

Especially you? Katie wondered, but somehow refrained from saying it aloud. "I can understand that. But Ezra's gone now. If Artisans Alley is to stay afloat, everyone has to pull his or her financial weight. Including Ida."

"That won't go over well. The woman has more than one screw loose. I try not to talk to her because she talks in circles. It's maddening."

Katie shook her head, trying to suppress a grin. "Duly noted." She glanced at her watch. "Showtime." With her key ring in hand, Katie headed for Artisans Alley's main entrance.

Several people stood outside the door, waiting to enter, including a woman Katie recognized from the previous morning. Repeat customers were always good for business.

Katie unlocked the door and welcomed her customers before returning to the cash desks. "Do you think you can handle things here, Rose? I have some work I need to get done in the office."

"If I have a problem, I'll call you on the PA. Besides, Cheryl and Gail will be here in a few minutes—church services end at ten thirty. They're always late, but they *will* be here."

Katie nodded, took a step toward the office, then hesitated. "Thank you, Rose. For being here," she said, suddenly flustered. "You've already worked more than your scheduled hours, and from what I understand, you've been doing it for a long time now." She didn't have to elaborate just *where* she'd gotten that piece of information.

"I told you, Artisans Alley is like my second home. The people here are like family to me. Now you're a part of our family, and we'll take care of you, too."

A smile tugged at Katie's lips. "Thanks, Rose."

Feeling just a bit more secure, Katie headed back to the office, opened the door, and turned on the light to find the room knee-deep in paper. Every file cabinet and desk drawer had been dumped. A gale gusted through the broken window over the desk.

"Oh no," she groaned, her stomach flip-flopping as adrenaline coursed through her. *First Ezra, now this!*

Katie swallowed. "I will not cry," she commanded herself, and took a deep breath. "I will not cry," she repeated. Instead, she bit her lip, turned on her heel, and made her way back to the front of the store and the wall phone near the cash registers.

Rose stood behind the counter, her nose already buried in her novel. It was too early for any sales to be rung up. She looked up. "Is something wrong?"

Katie nodded and, hands shaking, picked up the phone, punching in 911.

"I'd like to report a break-in."

"Is anything missing?"

Sunday was apparently Detective Davenport's day off, so he'd taken his time to arrive at Artisans Alley. In contrast, Deputy Schuler had arrived only minutes after Katie reported the crime. The younger officer wasn't happy when she'd refused to close Artisans Alley, so he stood guard over Ezra's office, detouring any curious customers who ventured too close.

"Since I didn't know what was in the files to begin with, and I couldn't touch the mess until you got here—how would I know if anything's missing?" she asked tartly.

Detective Davenport's glare could have blistered paint. Katie refused to be intimidated.

He watched the tech team dust the room for fingerprints. "Once they finish, you can go through everything and attempt an inventory."

Swell.

"Have you gotten any further with Ezra's murder investigation?" Katie asked.

Davenport gave her a long, level stare. "I'm making progress. I'll let you know if anything develops in the way of fingerprints," he said, nodding at the tech still at work.

"Thank you," Katie said politely—albeit through clenched teeth.

Davenport gave her a curt nod and headed for the exit.

"Wait a minute!" Katie said, hurrying to keep up with him. "Aren't you going to speak to the vendors who are here? They might know something that happened the day—night—Ezra was murdered."

Davenport didn't slow his pace. "I've got a timetable for doing that, and it's not on my list of things to do today," he said over his shoulder.

"How about the robbery angle? Did you find any fingerprints on the cash drawer?" Katie asked.

"Only the victim's."

Katie walked double time to keep up. "How about the murder weapon? Any ideas on what the killer hit Ezra with?"

Davenport exhaled, irritation causing the wrinkles on his brow to deepen. "No, ma'am, and I wouldn't be at liberty to discuss it with you if I did."

"Just what is the county paying you for, Detective?" Katie said, losing her patience.

Davenport stopped, pivoting to face her—his expression a scowl. "Today they're not paying me anything. If you'll excuse me," he said and continued for the exit.

Deputy Schuler caught up with Katie. "I'll be leaving, too, ma'am. You might want to call your security firm to get the windows wired. Right now only the doors are covered. It's a big hole in your security."

"I've already called them. They'll come by sometime tomorrow. In the meantime, I've got to get the glass replaced." She walked him to the exit.

"Detective Davenport will never win any personality contests," Schuler said, "but he is good at his job. And he's had a hard time lately—at home."

Katie refrained from commenting. With such an abrasive personality, Katie could well understand it.

"I know you want Mr. Hilton's murderer found, but you'd be better off letting us handle it," Schuler added.

"Are you saying I shouldn't ask questions?" Katie asked.

The deputy frowned. "A man has already been murdered. And when someone has killed once, it's easier the second time. I'd sure hate to think your curiosity might cause *you* to be the killer's next victim."

Six

No mob of customers crowded Artisans Alley's aisles as they had the day before. Still, Katie got the impression that those who had crossed the county to shop there weren't exactly regulars either.

With the deputies now gone, things had definitely settled down and no doubt the sold-out Buffalo Bills game had influenced a number of potential customer/rubberneckers to park their bodies in front of their TVs rather than park their cars in Victoria Square's lot.

Vance hadn't shown up, so it was up to Katie to fumble with printer glitches and all the other mundane problems that arose that morning.

Long after the midday rush, Rose assured Katie everything was under control. With that in mind, Katie figured she could risk taking an extended break.

She snuck out of Artisans Alley's back entrance and threaded her way through the cars in Victoria Square's parking lot, heading for Tea and Tasties. When the heavenly scent of baking met her halfway, she breathed deeply and quickened her pace.

The brunch crowd was long gone and the shop's front door was locked. The darkened storefront looked anything but welcoming, but a car parked at the side of the building told her that someone was still inside. Katie went around to the back of the store and knocked on the door marked DELIVERIES.

Wiping her damp palms on the back of her jeans, Katie rocked on her heels, waiting for someone to answer. Over the years she'd lost con-tact with old friends. Thanks to their full-time jobs, Katie's schoolwork, and Chad's booth at Artisans Alley, the couple had scant time to build or maintain outside friendships. Since Chad's death, Katie had occupied herself working long hours at Kimper Insurance with little time for anything else—with the exception of her baking hobby, that is. Now, when she really needed it, her support system was definitely lacking. Had Tracy's invitation the evening before only been polite conversation? The thought depressed her.

Finally the door rattled open. Mary Elliott greeted her, wiping her hands on her apron. "Hello, Katie. Tracy said you might stop by, but we were expecting you much sooner."

"I was detained," Katie said simply, grateful for the cheerful welcome.

Mary frowned. "Yes, we saw the police cars. Please, come in."

Katie stepped into the cocoon of warm air, her eyes wide with envy as she took in the banks of ovens on the far wall. The kitchen's center island workstation contained sacks of opened flour and sugar, bowls of separated eggs, and tubs of spices. Despite the chaos of the work area, the rest of the room was spotless. A rack of trays stood nearby, filled with fresh-baked cookies. Envy burned within her. Oh, if she could only have such a wonderful kitchen to bake in.

"I think I've died and gone to heaven," Katie said, and took in yet another deep lungful of the heavenly aromas.

Mary pursed her lips, swallowing. Katie had forgotten the poor woman had found Ezra's body just two days before. Swallowing down guilt, and not wanting to bring more attention to her stupid remark, she asked for Tracy.

Mary stepped over to the wall and pressed a button. A harsh bell sounded in some other part of the converted house. Moments later Tracy appeared, dressed in tight jeans, a bulky blue sweater, and black suede high-heeled boots, looking comfortable, yet smart. "Glad you could make it, Katie. Have you had lunch?" she asked.

"As a matter of fact, no. And after everything that happened this morning, I could sure use a pick-me-up." Did that sound like too blatant a plea for a freebie? And truthfully, Katie felt that a shot of whiskey was more likely to hit the spot, but she didn't voice the idea.

"You're in the right place for tea and sympathy," Tracy said, her voice welcoming. "Come on into the shop."

97

"Put the kettle on, Tracy. The walnut scones will be out of the oven in a few minutes," Mary said, and went back to her work.

Mary had been occupied with customers the day before, so Katie had only told her about the vendors' meeting before hurrying on to Nona Fiske's quilt shop. Now she had a real opportunity to study the shop, and was absolutely delighted. Several small tables, with seating for two or four, lined the west wall. Linen-covered, each table held a bud vase with a pink or red carnation and a spray of baby's breath. The opposite wall housed a large refrigerated case, filled with all sorts of tempting sweets, a counter, and a lovely antique cash register. Dainty rose-patterned wallpaper decorated the walls, with a teacup border edging the ceiling. An old oak schoolhouse clock told Katie it was already after three. Shelf upon shelf of floral teapots and matching cups or mugs, tea cozies, and toast racks were available for sale, as were the packages of imported blended teas Tracy had mentioned the day before.

"The scuttlebutt is Artisans Alley had a break-in overnight," Tracy said, and moved behind the counter.

"That's true. My office was ransacked. There's no telling if the burglar found what he was looking for."

"This is getting downright scary. That's why I insisted on being here this afternoon. I don't want

Mom working here alone anymore." Tracy sighed. "Do you have a tea preference?"

Katie shook her head. "Anything's fine."

Tracy grabbed a teapot from one of the shelves. "How about Earl Grey? It's my favorite."

Katie nodded, taking in the soothing atmosphere, something she'd hoped to convey if or when she opened the English Ivy Inn. "Your shop is lovely. It makes me want to pull out my checkbook and buy everything in sight."

Tracy smiled. "That's just the ambiance we'd hoped for."

"Of course, the reality is—" Katie started.

"You don't have to tell me," Tracy said. "Discretionary spending has been on the wane for a long while now. That's why Mom still takes on the occasional catering order. She's working on one now. We had a rough first year, but we're already pulling in a modest profit. I'm praying that continues."

Was that yet another veiled reminder that Victoria Square's merchants were dependent on Artisans Alley for their survival?

Katie took a seat and stared at the linen tabletop. "By any chance do you have time to listen to a sob story?"

Tracy's smile was warm. "All the time you need."

While Tracy made the tea, Katie poured out her troubles, starting with the break-in, and back-tracking to her heated discussion with Gerald

Hilton the evening before. She even told Tracy about her job at Kimper Insurance, and how unhappy she was with the way Josh treated her.

Tracy served the steaming brew in delicate, primrose-patterned bone china cups. "Sorry about your day job, and it sounds like Gerald hasn't got a leg to stand on. Serves him right for being so mean to the artists."

Mary joined them, bringing in a tray laden with still-warm scones piled on a three-tiered plate, sweet butter, raspberry jam, and clotted cream to the table. She served, placing a paper-doily-covered plate before each of them.

"I don't know what I'm going to do about a manager for Artisans Alley," Katie said. "I don't know anyone else who's qualified to take over, or even who I can trust. I guess I'll have to call an employment agency." She took a bite of the warm, crumbly confection, savored it, and swallowed. Good as it was, it couldn't hold a candle to the scones her beloved Aunt Lizzie had made.

"Why don't *you* take charge yourself?" Mary asked, adding a dollop of clotted cream to her scone.

"Me? There's no way. I have a real job."

"A job you don't really like," Tracy added. "And it sounds like you're vastly overqualified for it, as well. You ought to make use of that marketing degree of yours."

"I tried getting jobs in the field, but all the big Rochester firms keep downsizing and firing—

100

not hiring—workers. Besides, I have no practical experience in marketing. At least at Kimper Insurance I have health care and other benefits."

"Like what?" Mary asked.

"Vacation, for one."

"Which your boss gives you a hard time about using," Tracy reminded her.

"Working for Josh Kimper isn't the best job in the world," Katie admitted, "but it's stability. I can't possibly give it up for Artisans Alley. Especially when I don't even know if I can keep the place afloat until Christmas—let alone beyond."

Mary put a hand on Katie's shoulder. "You don't have to make up your mind today, dear. Think about it tomorrow when Artisans Alley is closed." She glanced at the clock. "Oops. I've got some mocha chocolate chip cookies in the oven. They're due to come out right about now." As if on cue, a bell rang in the kitchen. Mary rose from her seat and hurried off.

"Did you see Ezra's death notice in the paper this morning?" Katie asked, referring to the announcement notice Seth had placed in the *Democrat and Chronicle.*

Tracy nodded. "In case you didn't know, Mother and Ezra were . . . friends."

"Good friends?" Katie asked.

"*Close* friends," Tracy clarified, and Katie remembered Mary's sobs upon finding Ezra—her lover?—dead.

"If she'd like some private time with Ezra before the burial, I'd be happy to arrange it."

Tracy's gaze darted to the kitchen, then back to Katie. "I'll let you know. Thank you."

"Artisans Alley closes in about an hour. I'd better get back." Katie stood and started for the door, but then she turned. "Thanks for the tea—and the sympathy."

"I'll see you at the funeral home tomorrow night," Tracy said.

Katie headed for the door, and then stopped abruptly, her throat suddenly dry. The memory of Ezra's still body stretched out on Artisans Alley's floor filled her mind. "Oh my God," she breathed. "Ezra's really dead." She turned her tear-filled eyes toward Tracy.

Without hesitation, Tracy stepped forward and embraced her, patting her back sympathetically.

"I don't know why it hit me like this," Katie said, wiping at her eyes. "But suddenly I just feel so alone."

"You can handle this. It's not the end of your world. It's a new beginning," Tracy suggested.

"It's a beginning all right, but of what?"

Tracy didn't answer, just patted Katie's back some more.

"I'm sorry," Katie apologized and pulled away. "I didn't mean to dump on you like this."

Tracy smiled with a look of distant pain in her own eyes. "It's okay. What're friends for?"

Plywood covered Ezra's—now Katie's—broken office window, darkening the room and making Katie feel claustrophobic. She sat at her desk once more, sifting through yet more file folders from the mound on the floor. Once more she came across the key to "Chad's pad." Like it or not, one of these days she was going to have to deal with disposing of the items in there. Maybe in a couple of weeks. It might take her that long to work up the courage to read the rest of the journal, too.

Yeah, maybe in a couple of weeks.

Katie reached for another stack of folders and uncovered a framed picture, its broken glass long gone. A young man with curly blond hair and a blithe smile looked back at her.

"Who are you?" she asked, and naturally received no answer. The frame was dime-store etched metal—nothing spectacular—the picture a high school graduation photo.

Shrugging, she set the picture on the desk next to Chad's and wondered what she should do about her regular job the next day. Artisans Alley was closed on Mondays, so that gave her an extra twenty-four hours to make up her mind about the business's future. She'd have to tell Josh she had other responsibilities and would need more time off—to attend Ezra's funeral on Tuesday, and to hire a manager. She'd have to bust her buns trying to catch up with Kimper Insurance's Friday and

Saturday work. That still left the rest of the week to worry about.

Should she open Artisans Alley on Wednesday, or shut down and keep the place open only on the weekends for the time being? Maybe that was the best—her only—option. The artists were paying rent for a six-day week; to cut them back to two . . . they'd expect a rent reduction, and she couldn't afford that either. Would they leave in droves if she announced a cutback in hours? But what was her alternative? Maybe she could work part-time at both jobs—at least for a couple of weeks . . .

Katie realized she'd been sorting papers into piles, but she hadn't really looked at any of them. She set the hanging file folder aside and went through the closest pile once again.

One sheet in particular drew her attention: a simple loan agreement for five thousand dollars, typed on standard eight-and-a-half-by-eleven-inch white paper. Though properly dated and signed, the signature on the agreement was illegible. Ezra probably hadn't thought it important enough to type in the borrower's name. He knew who he was giving the money to. Katie studied the squiggly line—the handwriting was totally illegible. Did the signer think he or she was a movie star, or maybe a doctor? One thing was clear. The loan was due to be paid in full on October twenty-third.

The day Ezra died.

Katie read through the simple document once

more. Ezra had taken it seriously enough to write it all down, but he was damnably vague about who owed him the money. The loan was dated four months before Chad's death, and definitely did not contain the borrower's name beneath the signature. Would Chad have known about it? Had the money come from the Alley's funds, or was it a personal loan? Could the killer have ransacked the office looking for this one piece of paper?

Katie pulled out the rent checks Vance had given her the evening before, comparing the signatures. No, whoever signed the loan was not one of these artists. Who was to say it was an artist who'd asked Ezra for the loan? Did Ezra's bank send statements showing miniature versions of each Alley check or were they available as JPG pictures online? She'd have to check. Comparing them to the signature on the loan might be the best way to eliminate any artists as suspects. She'd have to make a trip to Ezra's house, since she hadn't seen any evidence of bank statements in the vast sea of dumped Alley files.

Katie glanced at the blue-ink signature on the loan. It bothered her that Ezra died the day he was to collect. Had the person confronted Ezra, asking for more time, been denied, and then murdered him for a lousy five thousand dollars? As Deputy Schuler had said, people were killed for a lot less. Either way, whoever borrowed the money owed it to the estate. And five thousand dollars would help keep the creditors from Artisans Alley's door.

No matter what, she ought to at least let Detective Davenport know about the loan. It could be a motive for murder.

She dialed the number on the card Davenport had given her on the day Ezra's body had been found, and listened to it ring four times before voice mail picked up. "You have reached the office of Detective Ray Davenport. Leave your name and number at the tone and I'll get back to you."

Swell, Katie thought. He was probably watching the football game on TV. Okay, so she didn't like the man. Still, she did as instructed, figuring Davenport would no doubt get back to her on Monday morning. She told him she had something important to tell him concerning Ezra, left her name and number, and hung up the phone. As Katie sat back in her chair, a flash of movement caused her to look up.

Vance stood in the doorway. "I owe you an apology," he said, and took a step forward.

Katie leaned forward and laid a file folder over the loan agreement. No need to advertise it. "What for?"

"I didn't give you an explanation of why I can't manage Artisans Alley. It was . . ." He trailed off, and then said, "Rude of me."

She waited for him to continue.

Vance didn't meet her gaze. "See, my wife. She's sick. She's got MS. I need to take care of her.

And, well, I can't promise I'd be available to be at Artisans Alley every day."

A logical explanation she didn't for a moment believe. Her great-aunt Lizzie always said a man who wouldn't look you in the eye had something to hide. Vance was definitely hiding something.

"Thanks for telling me," Katie said, knowing her voice sounded cold. It wasn't Vance's fault she was in this mess. She ought to blame Ezra as much as anyone, but she knew he'd much prefer to be sitting here worrying about unpaid loans and the mass of bills than embalmed at the funeral home.

"Do you know if any of the other vendors has business experience and might be able to step in?"

Vance shook his head. "Most of us are retired and do this as a hobby. We all depended on Ezra to handle the paperwork, the advertising—everything. Chad set up the computer so that we would get weekly printouts. Ezra liked to hand-write the checks, although the computer can do it. They go out on Tuesdays, you know."

Not this week, Katie thought. "It's going to take me a while to figure out how to do all that."

"I can help," he offered. "I just can't do it on a regular basis."

"Could you be available this week?"

"I've . . ." He hesitated. "I've got things to do tomorrow. And Ezra's funeral is Tuesday. You weren't planning on opening that day, were you?"

"I haven't decided. Probably not. With no one to

manage the place, I may not reopen until Saturday."

Vance's eyes widened angrily. "You'll piss off a lot of the artists if you do that."

"Maybe it'll motivate someone to find us a manager," she said, making sure to keep her voice level.

Vance seemed to squirm within his clothes. "I've got to get going. I've written out a list of instructions," he said and handed her a folded piece of paper. "Can you close by yourself?"

The last person who'd closed by himself was dead, Katie reminded herself. She glanced at her watch: four twenty-nine.

"Sure," she said, with more conviction than she felt.

"I'm sorry, Katie," Vance said again.

"Don't worry about it. You must put your family first."

Vance swallowed and looked like he wanted to say something—then thought better of it—and turned to leave her office.

Katie sighed, uncovered the loan agreement, and stared at the Courier typeface. Ezra had probably written up the agreement on the old portable typewriter that sat in the corner. Was that so there was no record in the computer, or had the computer only been there for Chad and Vance's use?

Katie bit her lip. She should put the document somewhere safe. But first she'd make two photocopies on the tabletop copier behind her.

Placing the original on the platen, she did just that. Folding one of the copies, she put it in her purse, then made a new file folder tab and put the other copy and original away in the cabinet.

Next, she read through the paper Vance had given her. Neatly printed block letters guided her through every step needed to close the place. Step one, warn the customers that Artisans Alley closed in twenty minutes, and then after they were all gone, lock the doors and do a walk-through to make sure the place was secure. Empty the cash registers and lock the day's receipts in the safe. Only she didn't have the combination to the safe. Did Vance? Maybe she could lock them in the file cabinet. It wasn't the best solution, but she didn't want to take that kind of money home and make herself a target for a mugging either.

Katie looked up at the ugly plywood covering the hole where her window had been and sighed. "Oh, Chad, why did you have to die and leave me in this mess? You, too, Ezra."

She read through Vance's list a couple more times, memorizing it, before heading for the cash desk. She picked up the phone and pressed the public address button. "Artisans Alley will be closing in twenty minutes. Please bring your purchases to the front desk. Closing in twenty minutes."

Rose Nash, manning Cash Desk 1, with a string of five customers in line, gave her a thumbs-up and a smile. She had no wrapper, so Katie stepped in to help. Katie recognized one of the women as having been standing behind the door at opening. Could she have been shopping at Artisans Alley for nearly seven hours?

"Oh, isn't this cute," Rose proclaimed, examining a small, handmade greeting card in a clear protective sleeve. She removed the gummy price tag from the plastic. "Someone's birthday coming up?"

"My sister's," the woman said proudly.

"Tell her 'Happy Birthday' from Artisans Alley," Rose said. "That'll be three dollars plus tax."

The woman handed over a fistful of dollars and change. Katie eased the card into a small brown paper bag before handing it to the customer.

"Will we see you tomorrow?" Rose asked.

"Maybe," the blond-wigged older woman said with a shrug. "Have a nice evening."

"You, too!"

The customer walked away.

Rose turned to Katie. "She's our best customer. Comes in every day. Now if we could just get her to buy something over five dollars, we'd all get rich."

Katie smiled, but it quickly turned to a frown. Artisans Alley's income came from renting vendor space to the artists, but if their sales were so lackluster, it was no wonder they found it hard to pay their rents.

Within minutes Artisans Alley emptied out, and Katie followed the last customer to the door and locked up for the night.

The tag room was just to the left of the main double doors. Clad in her raincoat and scarf, Ida exited the little room and turned off the light. "Hi, Katie. All but the last batch of tags have been sorted and taped down," she reported. When Katie had last ducked into what she had begun to think of as "Ida territory," she'd seen the older woman bent over the table, carefully lining up the price tags that had been removed from merchandise.

"See you on Tuesday," Ida chirped and headed for the side—vendor—exit.

"We won't be open on Tuesday," Katie called. "Tuesday is Ezra's funeral."

Ida stopped short. "Oh, dear. But I'm used to coming in here on Tuesdays. What will I do if I can't come here?"

Was her routine that engrained? "Stay home?" Katie suggested.

"Why would I do that?"

"Because Artisans Alley will be locked up. We won't be open."

Ida seemed to need time to think about that. "Oh."

"Perhaps you'll consider attending Ezra's funeral service on Tuesday morning."

Ida frowned. "Maybe." She started off toward the vendor exit once more, her steps slower.

Katie waited until the woman was out of earshot before she turned to Rose. "Does Ida have some kind of emotional or mental problem?"

"I'd say so. She calls that big ugly wart on her

cheek a beauty mark, which is certainly not what I'd call it."

Nor would Katie.

Rose giggled. "I told you she had more than one screw loose." She changed the subject. "I'll do the walk-through with you if you'd like," Rose volunteered, and she stayed until Katie had completed every task on Vance's list before she retrieved her coat from the tag room.

"You did great today, Katie," Rose said, her good cheer giving Katie a much-needed boost of confidence.

"Thanks, Rose."

"Are you leaving now? We could walk out together."

Katie shook her head. "I have a few more things to do in the office, then I'll be off."

"Do you want me to wait with you?" Rose asked, sounding anxious.

"Oh, no. You've been on your feet all day at that register. I'll be fine here alone."

Rose pulled out a silk kerchief from her coat pocket and tied it around her tight blond curls. "Then I'll see you tomorrow night at the funeral home," she said, her voice cracking. She swallowed hard, and Katie gently patted her shoulder. Then Rose cleared her throat and straightened. "I'll say good night, then."

Katie walked her to the door and locked it behind Rose before heading back for her office. Artisans

Alley felt cavernous and empty without another living soul within it, and she found the silence unnerved her. Katie took the paper sack full of cash, checks, and credit card receipts from the two registers and locked them in the back of one of the file cabinets, crossing her fingers that the burglar wouldn't make a return visit.

She tidied up the desk and remembered the lack of dinner opportunities in her refrigerator at home. About the only things in her cupboard were bags of flour and sugar, a couple of cans of cat food, and a bag of kitty kibble for her cat, Mason. Her wallet was empty, thanks to the pizza and soda she'd paid for the previous night, and she didn't feel up to a trip to the grocery store and the ATM machine. Maybe kitty kibble would make a good snack, after all. In the meantime, she plucked a butterscotch sweet from her pocket, unwrapped it, popped it into her mouth, and crunched it—letting the chunks of sweetness begin to dissolve on her tongue.

Pocketing her keys, she shrugged into her jacket, collected her purse, and headed for the side exit, turning out lights as she went. Finally, only the light from the exit sign over the door to the showroom pierced the gloom. The darkness pressed in around her, sending a shiver of unease down her neck.

Ezra had died only feet from where she now stood. Murdered. Probably by somebody he'd known.

Katie turned her back on the shadows and set the burglar alarm as Vance had taught her to do the night before, and then she locked the door behind her. As she groped her way down the short dark corridor toward the outside door, she pulled her car keys from her pocket and promptly dropped them.

"Swell," she grated, stooping down to paw the drafty floor.

Had Ezra's murderer made his—or her—escape down this same corridor? Mary Elliott had found the door open the next morning, assuming Ezra had opened it for the vendors, but it had apparently never been locked the night before.

Snagging her keys, Katie straightened, fumbled for the handle, and turned it, throwing open the door and welcoming the cold evening air as she fled the enclosed space. The door banged shut.

A furtive glance around the near-empty parking lot told Katie several mercury vapor lights had burned out, leaving the sea of asphalt around the building bathed in shadows. Was the Merchants Association responsible for the lot's upkeep? How were Artisans Alley's customers going to feel safe when she didn't?

She turned her back to the Square, glancing at the tall bushes in need of pruning that flanked the doorway. Another job she'd see was done within the week.

Wedging her purse under her arm, Katie inserted the brass key in the lock, turned it, and jumped as something jabbed her in the ribs.

"Stick 'em up!"

Seven

Katie whirled, arms flailing, her heart pounding as she beat at the intruder with her purse.

"Hey, hey!" Andy Rust protested, covering his head, shying back from the blows.

Katie jumped back, crashing into the closed door. "What the heck do you think you're doing?"

Silhouetted in the dim light, Andy thrust his hands in his pockets, managing to look like a guilty schoolboy. "The lot was nearly empty. I was worried about you closing all alone. It was just a little joke. Sorry if I scared you."

She hoped the heat of her glare would singe his hair. "Next time, don't do me any favors."

"I said I was sorry. Look, come on over to my shop and let me make amends. A nice jolt of cola ought to pick you right up."

Katie sized him up. He did look contrite. "Include a slice of pizza and you've got a deal."

"How about a nice fresh calzone?"

"I could go for that," she admitted, grateful her dinner dilemma was now history.

Within minutes Katie had shed her jacket and sat atop a stool inside the pizzeria, sipping a Coke and watching Andy behind the counter, tossing pizza dough into the air with flair. A string of teenaged boys came and went, taking pizzas in padded hot covers out to their cars for delivery. Andy had one assistant assigned to the ovens while he fabricated each of the pizzas. The guys worked like a well-oiled machine, one taking the phone orders when the other was too busy to do so.

"You two move like a choreographed dance," Katie marveled, nearly burning her mouth on the steaming-hot and tasty cheese-and-pepperoni calzone.

Andy's smile warmed her. It had been a long time since that had happened. She swallowed back a twinge of guilt, thinking about Chad. She shook the hurt away. "Is it always this busy?"

"Football season's my most lucrative time of the year, but it'll slow down after eight. We only take orders until ten o'clock on Sundays—unless there's a late game."

"Then you go home?"

"Then we clean up. I'll be back at noon tomorrow to get the dough ready."

"Sounds like a busy life," she said.

"That's what it takes to be successful. You've got to pour your heart and soul into your business if you want it to thrive."

Katie laughed. "How does your significant other feel about that?"

"I wouldn't know. She left me," he deadpanned.

"Oh. I'm—I'm so sorry," Katie stammered, embarrassed.

Andy waved off her concern. "It's okay. I like to

work. It keeps me from dwelling on the past—and out of the poor house."

Andy's words reminded her of her most pressing problem: hiring a manager. Could Artisans Alley be rescued from the brink of bankruptcy, let alone thrive, without someone who cared about it taking charge?

"I've got a lot to learn about running a business," Katie said. "Like how and when to take the money to the bank. I'd feel vulnerable going to the night deposit drop."

"Vary the times and days you do your banking. Otherwise you're a prime robbery target," Andy advised. "And don't keep more than your operating expenses in cash on the premises. Don't give creeps a reason to rob you."

"Do you think Ezra operated that way?"

"If he was any good at his job, he did."

That was debatable. Still, the register had only recorded some four hundred dollars in sales for the whole day of his death, and that was money long gone. The safe was still locked—and no one but Ezra had had the combination. Katie would have to call a locksmith. Could Ezra have cleaned out the register before he was murdered, giving the thief a reason for hitting the old man?

Andy passed another pizza to his assistant.

"Are you going to the funeral home tomorrow night?" Katie asked.

Andy shook his head. "Although it might not be

on network TV anymore, Monday Night Football's still great for pizza sales. I might try to make the Tuesday morning service, but I don't know. What have you heard from the cops?"

"I spoke to Detective Davenport this morning." She told Andy about the break-in. "I tried to call him later today, but all I got was his voice mail. Unless he's working behind the scenes, he doesn't seem to be putting much effort into solving the crime."

"Crimes," Andy corrected, "if the motive was robbery."

"Sounds like you know about police work. Were you ever a cop?"

Andy choked on a laugh as he started on another pizza. "Hardly. Let's just say I've had my share of brushes with the law."

Katie chewed slower on her calzone. Was Andy a criminal? To run a successful business in a small town like McKinlay Mill, he'd have to be a reformed one.

"You look like I just stole your Popsicle. Was it something I said?" Andy asked with a laugh.

"Uh, no," she lied.

Andy's gaze held hers. "Look, I'll level with you. When I was in high school, I got picked up for joyriding. Three times. It got so I could hot-wire a car in my sleep," he said, ladling tomato sauce onto a round of dough, then swirling it to cover the entire surface.

"Grand theft auto?" Katie asked.

"I spent some time locked up before I figured out I'd get my own car faster if I got a job and worked for it."

"Jail?" Katie asked, the word coming out a squeak.

"Same as. Juvenile detention," Andy clarified.

Katie watched as he grabbed a handful of shredded cheese, liberally sprinkling it over the sauce. Next, he dipped his plastic-gloved hands into containers filled with sliced bell peppers, mushrooms, onions, and broccoli, until the pizza was heaped with veggies.

"Gee, that looks good," Katie said, and took the last bite of the calzone. She licked her fingers, resisting the temptation to wipe them on her jeans-clad leg, and reached for a napkin from the counter dispenser.

Andy lifted the uncooked pizza with a wooden paddle and handed it to his assistant, a flushed-faced boy whose name tag read KEITH.

"I was lucky. My high school guidance counselor took an interest in me. She got me an after-school job in a pizza parlor," Andy said.

"In McKinlay Mill?"

"No, Rochester. I bought myself a car within six months. I worked there all through college. A couple of grants paid for the rest of my education. It took me five years, but I earned a degree in accounting."

"That sounds lucrative. What on earth are you doing running a pizza place?"

"It's a lot more interesting than staring at numbers all day. Besides, I got sick of the commute pretty quick—as well as working for someone else. I like being my own boss, and I like it out here in the sticks. I have a deal with the local high school. They send me their troublemakers, and I try to straighten them out before they screw up their lives like I did. Right, Keith?" he said. The boy's already heat-flushed cheeks blushed a shade darker.

Katie wondered what laws the blond boy had broken. Had he been arrested for vandalism? Robbery? Could one of Andy's truants have robbed—and killed—Ezra? An old man would be easy prey. What if—

"No, Katie, it wasn't one of my boys," Andy said, as though reading her mind. "They're all good kids. I promise you . . ."

But his words couldn't wipe away the suspicion that filled her.

"I'd better be going," she said, slipped off the stool, and struggled back into the sleeves of her jacket.

"I'll walk you to your car," Andy said, peeling off his gloves and reaching for his coat from a hook on the wall. "I'll be right back, Keith."

Andy followed Katie out the door and into the parking lot.

"I'm parked out back," she said, her breath vaporizing in a cloud.

They walked in silence, dodging puddles that

dotted the asphalt. The rain had stopped, but clouds still loomed overhead. Andy's revelation about his past, and those he employed, weighed heavily on Katie's mind. She shivered in the damp cold and decided in future she'd park under one of the lot's mercury vapor lamps.

Katie unlocked her car, and then turned to face Andy. "Thanks for the calzone, and for walking me out here. I have to admit, after what happened to Ezra, I'm a little nervous."

"McKinlay Mill is a safe place. Ezra's death was an isolated incident," Andy said. "It won't happen again."

Katie nodded, opened the door, climbed into her car, and started the engine. She waved at Andy as she pulled out of the lot, wishing she felt as confident as he did.

Katie balanced a plate of fresh-baked scones, her office keys jangling as she let herself into Kimper Insurance at six fifteen the next morning. Arriving early would give her almost a two-hour head start to catch up on the work that had accumulated during her absence on Friday and Saturday. She hoped the scones would be received as a peace offering.

As expected, Josh hadn't even attempted to keep up with any of the daily tasks that kept the office going. File folders and other papers littered Katie's desk, which had been clear when she'd left the place on Thursday afternoon.

She set the plastic-wrapped scones on the corner of her desk, hung up her jacket, and jumped into work. Her voice mailbox was also full. Katie transcribed the messages, coding them by importance. She'd return the calls later.

She was finishing the last of the filing when she heard the office door rattle at seven fifty. Katie steeled herself.

"It's about time you showed up," Josh said by way of a greeting.

"There's fresh coffee in the pot," she said, not bothering to raise her gaze to otherwise acknowledge his presence.

Josh tramped through the outer office to the small conference room that also served as a makeshift kitchen. Katie felt her blood pressure rising and wondered how long he would wait before picking a fight.

"I'm trying to run a business here," Josh hollered from the other room. "That means every day, not just when you feel like showing up."

Katie let the file drawer roll shut with a bang. Ten seconds, she thought—a new record—and considered Josh's next rebuke. Would it start, "I pay you too much," or "My clients deserve the best . . ."? Not *their* clients, despite the fact she'd helped him build the business these last six years. Since day one, Josh had never given her credit for the part she played in the company's success.

"I pay you too much . . ." Josh began, and Katie

tuned out the rest of the all-too-familiar speech. Eventually he'd run out of steam, slam his office door, and sit down at his desk to trim his fingernails . . . or some other time-wasting activity. She busied herself until that happened, then fielded the first of the morning's phone calls. Afterward she returned the calls she needed to make, but Ezra's wake, later that evening, never strayed from her mind.

Josh would pitch a fit when she told him she intended to take tomorrow off for the funeral. She wondered if she should host a gathering afterward for Ezra's friends and colleagues. Could Tracy and Mary Elliott cater such an affair, or was it thoughtless to ask Mary to do all that work when she hadn't yet recovered from her own heartache at Ezra's loss? Tasty as they were, Andy Rust's pizza, calzones, and chicken wings were hardly dignified enough for such an occasion. Katie wished she knew someone else in the restaurant business. With all his contacts, Josh probably did, but she wasn't about to ask for his advice.

Katie remembered her conversation with Tracy and Mary the day before. Why, exactly, *did* she want to stay at this job anyway? For health insurance? Vacation? Despite the present economy, she knew she could get another office manager's job in a heartbeat. Why had she put up with Josh's bullying tactics for so long? After all, she'd managed to accumulate more than a couple of months' rent. That would hold her until she located another, more satisfying job—maybe even one that paid more.

No. Quitting was out of the question. Making decisions without a clear-cut plan was just plain dumb. And Mary had been right. She didn't need to decide what she wanted or needed to do today. Like Scarlett O'Hara, she'd think about it tomorrow.

Josh emerged from his office at nine-oh-three, ready for Round 2. Monday meant the blue suit with the lighter blue shirt. Would it be the paisley tie or footballs? Basketballs in basketball season, hardballs in baseball season, with golf sprinkled in now and then. Katie looked up as Josh stopped before her desk. Bingo! Paisleys. Hands on hips, Josh planted his feet a foot or so apart, trying to look formidable. That, too, was a joke. Only a midget would be intimidated by this little Napoleon.

"I have to take another day of vacation tomorrow," Katie said, deciding to take the offensive.

Josh grabbed a scone and shook it at Katie, just inches from her nose. "Uh-uh. You've already had two days off."

"A day and a half," Katie corrected him.

"I need you here tomorrow afternoon while I firm up the Henderson deal."

"I have a funeral to attend," she said, not backing down.

"Then come into work afterward."

"Sorry, I need the whole day," she said, keeping her voice level.

Josh shook his head again. "You seem to have

forgotten just who runs this business."

Katie wanted to wipe that smug look right off his face, but somehow managed to keep her cool. "I have a moral and business obligation to be at Ezra Hilton's funeral tomorrow morning. Then, as Ezra's executor, I have other business matters to wrap up. We can talk rationally about getting coverage from a temp agency, or you can bellow and moan and threaten to fire me. Either way, I won't be in tomorrow."

Josh's face flushed and his eyes narrowed, but for once he held his temper in check. Still, his voice was low and as menacing as he could muster. "Where do you get off telling me how to run my business?"

"I've learned from experience not to even try. You don't listen," Katie said, knowing she was fueling the pending argument.

Josh's eyes widened in indignation. "What the *hell* has gotten into you?"

Katie stood, towering five inches over him. "Maybe I'm tired of the way you treat me, Josh. Of the way you belittle me in front of clients. How you think you can bully me simply because I'm on your payroll. And you know what, I won't stand for it any longer."

"You run that hoity-toity artisan joint for a day or two and think you know all there is to operating a business."

"No, I don't. But I know that common courtesy is

the key to good customer and employee relations, and I'm tired of not receiving it in this office."

Josh backed up a step, his lips parting as he began to breathe through his mouth—a sure sign he was about to explode.

In a split second Katie made her decision. She brushed past him, heading for the copier across the small office. Bending down to pick up an empty paper carton, she carried it over to her desk, then picked up her framed picture of Chad and set it inside the box.

Josh's eyes widened. "What do you think you're doing?"

Katie picked up the potted philodendron from her desk and placed it next to the picture. "Saving you the trouble of firing me. I quit," she said, and set her half-empty glass candy jar alongside the plant.

"You can't quit!" he cried, horrified.

Katie looked down at him. "Watch me."

"Wha? You, you—" Josh stammered.

Katie collected the few remaining personal items she'd accumulated in the office during the past six years, grateful she'd always traveled light. Last of all, she placed the plate of scones in the box.

"You have to give me two weeks' notice," Josh said, near hysteria.

She glanced at her desktop calendar. "Consider my resignation retroactive as of the twelfth. You can send my remaining vacation pay and last payroll check to my home address. It's in the Rolodex."

"You can't go! I need you—" he blurted out, as though suddenly realizing just what her contributions to running the office had been.

"That's not the impression I got," she said, extracting the office keys from her ring. "I'm sure you'll do fine on your own. Besides, I've heard you say many times that a monkey could do my job. Perhaps you can hire one from the zoo." She grabbed her jacket from the peg behind her desk, slipped it on, and collected her purse from the desk drawer. As a last act of defiance, Katie snatched the uneaten scone from Josh's hand, dropped it into the box, picked it up, and marched out of the office.

"Come back!" Josh hollered, but Katie ignored him and headed straight for her car.

She set the carton in the Focus's trunk, got in the car, and started the engine. It was only then that her hands began to tremble. Putting the car in gear, she drove to the exit and waited for a break in the traffic. Glancing in her rearview mirror, she saw Josh still standing in the parking lot. She could have sworn there were tears in his eyes.

Instead of heading home, Katie went straight to Artisans Alley. She took the carton from her trunk and transferred it to her new work environment, plunking Chad's picture, the philodendron, and her candy jar onto the back corner of Ezra's desk— her desk. She thought she'd feel terrified, giving up her financial security, but as she looked around the shabby office, exhilaration filled her. She knew the panic would come later.

First things first. She called Tracy, but it was too late to arrange for an after-funeral gathering. Tracy recommended Blueberry Catering in nearby Parma, who were only too glad to take on the assignment—for a surcharge, owing to the lateness of the order. They promised they'd arrive with an assortment of finger foods, cookies, and punch for one hundred, and set up in Artisans Alley's lobby. Thank goodness Edie Silver had already moved her wares to her new booth on the second floor the day before.

The repair guys showed up, took down the plywood, and replaced the window in Katie's office. She liked the sound of that: *her* office. After they left, she ignored the mess from the weekend break-in and spent the rest of the afternoon figuring out the computer program that would sort the inventory data and spit out vendor checks. After a few stops and starts, the computer complied. She was grateful Chad had left such precise documentation. Then she signed each and every one, and decided to buy a signature stamp before the next week. Writer's cramp was no fun at all.

The afternoon waned. Katie locked up Artisans Alley, stopped at the bank to make her first deposit, and was about to head home when on impulse she turned right instead of left at the village's main crossroad. Artisans Alley's survival might rely on the new marina. It was time to check it out.

The drive to the lakeshore took less than five minutes. Preoccupied with her job at Kimper Insurance these past eight months, Katie hadn't seen the extent of the development, and was surprised to find it farther along than she'd imagined. She parked her car in the little municipal lot and headed out on foot.

It was sad to see the seasonal businesses shuttered for the long, dreary, Western New York winter. The Hot Pointe burger and ice cream stand looked forlorn in the encroaching twilight. Sylvan's Souvenirs, which sold trinkets, banners, and wind socks, was also closed for the season. Outside its door stood a big ice freezer—a commodity not in demand in late fall—ready to fill the coolers for the fishermen's catches come summer.

The old Gray Gull Tavern on the water's edge had been newly shingled, looking a lot more upscale, and its name had been changed to The Pelican's Roost. Katie and Chad had eaten there often before they decided to save every extra penny in order to open the English Ivy Inn. She'd eaten a lot of boxed macaroni and cheese since those days. As in the tavern's previous incarnation, cheerful neon beer signs glowed in the front bay windows, and a blue-and-white-striped awning flapped over the deck out back, hinting at lunches and dinners alfresco in warmer temperatures. Had the changes been made in anticipation of increased foot traffic? But what about the name? No pelican had ever roosted in this part of the country—or ever would.

Pulling up her collar against the wind, Katie strolled farther down the street. A sign in front of Captain Jack's boat rental promised twenty additional slips come the new year, along with an expanded bait and tackle shop. She traveled on.

At the end of Thompson's Landing, the skeleton of what would be the new marina was already taking shape. The builder's announcement stated there would be room for more than one hundred boats, a bathhouse, and restaurant facilities—opening Memorial Day weekend. A cheerful banner said, SEE YOU THEN!

"I don't think they'll make it," she muttered to herself.

"Of course they will."

Katie whirled to find McKinlay Mill's most successful real estate agent, Fred Cunningham, striding toward her, his steel-colored crew cut standing up to the stiff breeze.

Fred paused beside her, pushed his glasses up the bridge of his nose, and crossed his arms over his chest, his tawny camelhair coat making him look like a chubby teddy bear. He fixed his gaze on the steel beams silhouetted against the gray sky. "She'll be a beauty." The pride in his voice was unmistakable. "And there's talk of building a water park closer to the village. Can you imagine that?"

"No," Katie admitted, feeling overwhelmed. "I can't."

"It's just what McKinlay Mill needs to put us on the map."

"Do you really think so?" Katie asked.

"Definitely. I was on my way to an appointment with a potential investor at The Pelican's Roost when I saw you standing here. You can't believe the interest that's been shown in McKinlay Mill in the last few months. Things are about to explode here on the lakeshore."

"You could be right," Katie admitted. "I was shocked at how Ezra Hilton's murder brought new customers to Victoria Square."

"That was unfortunate, but the killing was an aberration. Check the stats, my dear; McKinlay Mill is one of the safest communities in the state. And once boating season starts, nobody will even remember it happened."

"That's a sad commentary on Ezra's worth as a person," Katie said.

"Business is business," Fred said with a shrug.

Katie sighed. "I suppose you're right. And I'm glad I ran into you, Fred. I've been meaning to call you about listing the retail space in Artisans Alley."

Fred's eyes widened. "I like the sound of that. And as a matter of fact, I've got a client looking to open a dance studio. Can I bring her by later this week so she can look at the space?"

"You sure can."

"And I have another client looking for office space."

"The more the merrier," Katie said, a shot of hope coursing through her.

Fred sobered. "Ezra was a great guy, but not always the best businessman. I could've had that space rented out a long time ago, but he wouldn't give me a chance."

"I have every confidence in you."

"I'll give you a call tomorrow, and we'll talk more about it."

"Yes, please do. Will you be at Ezra's wake tonight?"

Fred shook his head. "Sorry, can't make it. I have two meetings this evening, and I'm showing warehouse space to another client at eight. The market around here is sure heating up." He looked at his watch. "Oh, gosh, I'm going to be late." He gave her a quick salute. "See you later, Katie."

Katie watched as Fred hurried down the sidewalk for the bar before she turned back to face the muddy expanse of land the marina would soon occupy. She thought about what Fred had said. If progress, in the form of new development, brought more people to McKinlay Mill, she had a better shot at pulling Artisans Alley out of debt, selling it, and fulfilling her own entrepreneurial dreams.

Development was supposed to be a good thing.

And if that was true, then why did it feel so wrong?

●●●

Katie made it home before the horizon completely swallowed the sun. As she feared, her fridge was still empty, and her cat Mason's stash of kitty kibble was no more inviting than it had been the night before. She made a fuss over, and then fed, the black-and-white cat, found a box of stale crackers, slapped some peanut butter on them, downed them with a tall glass of milk, and completed her dining experience for the night. After changing into the same black suit she'd worn to Chad's wake, she headed for Collier's Funeral Home.

The parking lot was empty when she arrived, but the front door stood open. Luther Collier met her, taking both her hands in his. "Mrs. Bonner, I'm so sorry we have to meet again under such painful circumstances."

The elderly, white-haired gentleman had been McKinlay Mill's undertaker for as long as anyone could remember, inheriting the business from his own father decades ago.

"Thank you, Mr. Collier."

"Ezra is in the Rose Room. He's our only client tonight. I'm sure there'll be a large turnout. He was respected by most of the community."

Only most of them?

Collier led her into the large room, which glowed with soft pink incandescent light—the better to give the dead a rosy complexion. Rows of folding chairs took up half the open area, leaving space for a receiving line and enough room to mingle. Comfortable couches lined the walls of the room, with end tables on either side bearing glowing lamps and boxes of tissues. At least ten sprays of flowers brightened the gloom that even the cream-colored walls and mauve draperies could not dispel. Katie hadn't thought to send flowers.

Katie's stomach tightened as Mr. Collier gripped her elbow and propelled her forward toward the coffin. Scrutinizing the dead always made her uncomfortable, reminding her of her own mortality. She'd decided on a closed casket for Chad, who'd died of head injuries from the crash. Luther had done his best, but she'd seen none of the man she'd married in the battered, lifeless husk that remained.

Ezra lay in the open coffin, his once-proud nose pointing toward the ceiling, his glasses clasped in his waxy, sallow-skinned hands. Seth Landers had made all of Ezra's arrangements. Had he gone to Ezra's house to pick out a suit?

"I don't even remember when I last saw Ezra alive," Katie murmured. She and Ezra had conducted most of their business over the phone. She'd brought the last of Chad's stored merchandise to round out his booth several weeks before, but she'd been in too much of a hurry to stay and chat with Ezra. Now she wished she had.

Collier's round, pink face loomed. He seemed to be waiting for praise for a job well-done.

"Ezra looks very . . ." Katie stumbled over a descriptor. "Natural."

No, he didn't. He looked dead. Someone had stolen what remaining precious days the old man might have enjoyed. Katie's fists clenched at her sides, her eyes filling with tears.

Collier patted her arm, misinterpreting her emotional state. "I'll give you a few moments alone with him," he said, and withdrew.

Katie stared at the casket's brass handles. "It's okay, Ezra, I'm going to manage Artisans Alley myself. I'll give it my best shot and keep it going for as long as I can." She raised her gaze to take in Ezra's still form, as inert as the earth he'd soon be committed to.

Katie sighed and turned away, checking out the flowers and reading the cards that accompanied them. The Artisans Alley vendors had purchased a large spray of gladioli—had Rose arranged that?—as had the Victoria Square merchants. Seth had sent a bouquet, and she was surprised to find one with her own name on the card. Seth must have ordered that, too. Trust him to take care of everything.

Mary Elliott had sent a dozen red roses. "For thine eyes did shine, and made me happy," the card read. The card on a bouquet of pink carnations and baby's breath, from Nona Fiske, declared, *Undying devotion.* Katie couldn't place a face with the name, although it seemed familiar. The rest of the cards were from strangers. Nothing from Ezra's nephew, Gerald, she noticed.

"Mrs. Bonner?"

Katie turned at the unfamiliar voice. Not totally unfamiliar, it turned out: Detective Davenport.

"I was beginning to think you'd given up investigating Ezra's death," she said, unable to hide her irritation.

"Merely being efficient. The victim's wake is the perfect time for me to speak with most of his friends and family."

And totally tacky, Katie thought, bristling at the detective's tone. "Before he was ever a victim, Ezra was a person."

"I realize that, but I'm sorry to say this isn't my only case."

"Have you done *anything* to find the murderer?"

Davenport exhaled, as though bored. "As I told you, that's why I'm here."

Katie crossed her arms over her chest. "Oh, and I suppose you think the murderer is just going to show up and stroll over to the coffin tonight?"

Davenport didn't even blink. "Quite possibly, yes."

Eight

Why did wakes so often resemble cocktail parties, Katie wondered. The only things missing were adult beverages and delicious finger foods. And of course, the participation of the guest of honor.

Laughter cut the air again. Katie glanced toward a knot of men standing near Ezra's casket, the tallest among them being that hunk Peter Ashby. Had he or one of the others just told a joke? Clad in beige Dockers and a brown bomber jacket, Ashby looked like something out of a movie, and had the eye of more than one woman in the room. Had he left his Indiana Jones fedora and bullwhip at home?

Katie had stationed herself at the doorway, hoping to meet, greet, and memorize the names and faces of everyone who'd come to pay their respects to Ezra, but soon realized the task was futile. It seemed that just about everybody in McKinlay Mill had shown up. Had they actually known Ezra, or had morbid curiosity drawn them to take a look at McKinlay Mill's first murder victim in decades?

Dry-eyed and pale, a demure Mary Elliott sat on one of the low couches against the wall, clutching a damp tissue and staring at nothing, while her stylishly dressed daughter, Tracy, stood nearby, looking bored. A prudish-looking woman with pursed lips and dressed in widow's weeds kept glaring at Mary from across the room, her gaze filled with hostility.

Gilda Ringwald, the basket shop owner, passed by and Katie snagged her. "Thanks so much for coming, Gilda."

"It was the least I could do for poor Ezra." Gilda glanced across the room at the body and shook her head sadly. "Such a shame."

A momentary, awkward silence fell between them, which Katie broke. "Has the Merchants Association set the time and place for their next meeting?"

"Thursday evening at Del's Diner. Six fifteen sharp. Can you make it?"

"I'll be there," Katie said. She nodded toward the grim-faced woman. "I'm having a hard time pinning names to faces. Could you remind me of that lady's name?"

"Nona Fiske. She runs the Square's quilt shop."

Katie remembered the card on the flowers: *Undying devotion.* "I understand she and Ezra were good friends," she bluffed.

Gilda leaned closer. "*Very* good friends. But that was before Mary Elliott opened her tea shop," she said, her voice filled with reproach.

"Were Ezra and Nona lovers?"

"I wouldn't go that far, but they were close enough that Nona thought about closing her shop and relocating once Mary moved in on Ezra. Seeing that woman walk across the Square to Artisans Alley every day with a plate full of goodies was like a stake in poor Nona's heart."

So, the way to a man's heart really *was* through his stomach.

It was hard enough imagining Ezra even having a sex life at his age—let alone with Nona Fiske. Perfect nunnery material there, with her prim collars, midi-length skirts, and sensible shoes. But then, maybe that was why Ezra had been attracted to the vivacious Mary Elliott, the complete antithesis of the Square's quilter. Mary looked at least ten years younger than her fifty-odd years, with a body a forty-year-old would covet.

Was it possible Ezra's death had been merely the result of a lover's spat? That didn't seem likely. Surely it made more sense to eliminate the competition rather than the object of one's affection. But Ezra had obviously known his killer—had let that person into Artisans Alley and trusted him or her enough to turn his back on them.

Katie changed the subject. "I'm hosting a reception at Artisans Alley after the service tomorrow. I hope you can make it."

"That would be lovely, thank you," Gilda said.

"Feel free to tell the others, too. Although I'll also have Mr. Collier announce it at the service tomorrow."

Gilda nodded, and then her gaze drifted. "Oh,

there's Ben Stillwell. Excuse me, but I must go speak with him." She hurried across the room, leaving Katie alone once more.

As she studied the faces around her, Katie realized she recognized only a few of the artists from Artisans Alley. She'd already spoken with Rose Nash, and was beginning to feel isolated among the crowd of strangers. Then Seth Landers walked through the main entrance. Although before this week she'd known the attorney only casually, she thought they could be more than friends. Especially since that kiss the other day . . . Okay, it was only on the cheek—but that still counted.

"How are you, Katie?" Seth asked, pausing before her and taking her hands in his own. His fingers were warm and dry, his touch sending a flutter of excitement through her.

"Pretty good, under the circumstances. I'm glad you could make it."

Seth glanced toward the casket, his mouth settling into a frown. "I hate these things. The person you'd really like to speak to is beyond reach."

Amen, Katie silently agreed.

"At least Ezra got a good turnout," Seth said, glancing around the room, taking in those who'd assembled to pay their respects.

"Including the police," Katie said.

Seth raised an eyebrow.

"That man in the trench coat," she said, nodding toward Davenport.

Seth turned, stared at the man in the rumpled raincoat, and frowned. "Who does he think he is, Columbo?"

Katie smiled. "My thoughts exactly. The one person I haven't seen is Gerald Hilton. I met him on Saturday. He didn't know I was already part-owner at Artisans Alley."

Seth's eyes twinkled. "You don't say."

"Why didn't you tell him?"

"Let's just say the younger Mr. Hilton was more than a bit arrogant, telling me how he wanted events to unfold. I listened without comment and he went away, very pleased with himself. Did he give you any trouble?" Seth asked, concern tingeing his voice.

"Not unless you count his threat of mayhem."

At Seth's startled expression, Katie explained, making light of the incident, but the attorney's expression remained somber.

"I'm sorry, Katie. I didn't mean to put you in that position."

She patted his hand. "I'm a big girl, Seth. And if I have any trouble with Mr. Gerald Hilton, I have a wonderful attorney who can put him in his place."

Seth squeezed her hand again. "I appreciate your vote of confidence."

Their eyes met and held. Seth's intense gaze seemed to penetrate her soul. Katie was the first to look away. "I may have done something extremely stupid this morning. I quit my job," she admitted.

Seth blinked. "That does sound a bit drastic."

"Artisans Alley needs a full-time manager and I was overdue for a change. I have a little money saved—I'll either sink or swim." Why did she sound a whole lot more confident than she felt?

"If you need advice, just ask," Seth said.

Katie smiled. "I will." She thought about his offer for a moment. "In fact, maybe you can advise me on something right now." She lowered her voice. "The guy who owns the pizza parlor next to Artisans Alley has a lot of high school boys working for him. Local troublemakers. He's supposed to be a positive role model for them. Should the police know about this, and if so, who should volunteer the information?"

Seth let out a sigh. "Ideally, he should have told the police. Is he here?"

Katie shook her head. "If I talk to Detective Davenport, and those kids had nothing to do with Ezra's death, I could be making an enemy of my neighbor."

"That is a dilemma," Seth agreed. "Do you really think one of those boys could have killed Ezra?"

Katie frowned. "I don't think so. I mean, Ezra had to have let his killer into Artisans Alley. Andy said none of the merchants ever ordered anything from him. So, unless Ezra was acquainted with one of the boys for another reason—like he knew their parents—he probably wouldn't have opened the door."

"What if someone waited for Ezra to leave, surprised the old man, and forced their way in?"

"It could've happened that way, I suppose," Katie said, her worry intensifying.

"Would you like me to talk to Detective Davenport?" Seth asked.

"No, it's my responsibility." Katie located Davenport across the room. "And I'd better do it now, before I lose my nerve."

Seth gave her an encouraging smile and she started off.

Davenport was conversing with Peter Ashby and a couple of the other artists. Katie waited for the detective to finish before interrupting. "Could I speak with you for a moment?"

Davenport stood there, staring at her—waiting.

"Privately," she amended.

He frowned, then nodded toward the foyer.

Katie felt all eyes on them as they left the room.

"Yes, ma'am," Davenport said once they were out of earshot.

She relayed what Andy had told her, and was surprised to see the detective's eyes light up.

"Interesting. I'll pay Mr. Rust a visit this evening."

"Do you have to mention where you got this information?"

He shook his head. "No, ma'am."

"And do you have to keep calling me 'ma'am'?" Katie asked, annoyed.

"Sorry, Mrs. Bonner."

That was nearly as bad.

"I phoned yesterday and left you a message. You didn't get back to me."

"I'm a very busy man," Davenport said in a monotone.

"I wanted to tell you that someone owed Ezra five thousand dollars. It was due to be paid the day Ezra died. I found the agreement yesterday, but I can't make out the signature."

Davenport's expression—and his voice—hardened. "You should have told me this sooner."

"When? You didn't return my call," she reiterated.

Davenport didn't back down. "That agreement is evidence. You'll have to turn it over to the Sheriff's Office. Where is it now?"

"In a file drawer at Artisans Alley. You can have it tonight if you want."

"Does anyone else know about this?" he demanded.

"No."

"Then you'd better keep it that way." Davenport's tone was serious, with just the hint of a threat in it.

"Maybe we could get signatures from all the artists and compare them," Katie suggested.

"The department will handle that," he said, his no-nonsense voice annoying Katie once more.

"Very well, Detective." Their gazes locked. The arrogant man unnerved her, but also reminded her of someone else. "Have you spoken with Ezra's nephew, Gerald Hilton?"

"Not yet."

"What *have* you been up to?" At Davenport's steely glare, she continued. "Mr. Hilton is eager to settle the estate. Before he found out about me, he thought he was in for a lot of money at Ezra's death. That could be a motive for murder, too."

"I'm quite capable of deciding what constitutes motive, Mrs. Bonner. I suggest you concern yourself with running Artisans Alley and leave the investigating to me."

"If you can spare the time." Katie turned on her heel, stalked forward, but then abruptly halted, unsure what to do next. Seth was surrounded by several artists—perhaps clients—and she decided not to intrude. She glanced at the clock: eight thirty—half an hour to go until calling hours ended.

She caught sight of Tracy, who waved and crossed the room to join her. "I'm so sorry we couldn't help you with the reception tomorrow."

"That's okay. I understand," Katie said, her nerves still jangled. She took a breath to steady herself. "The caterer you suggested assured me they could handle the job."

"They're great. Mom trained with them for two years before we opened our shop."

Katie glanced back at Mary. "How is your mother?"

"Pretty torn up." Tracy's voice had hardened, her lips growing thin. "She's taking Ezra's passing almost as hard as Daddy's death."

Katie wasn't sure what to say.

"In some ways, I think Ezra reminded Mom a lot of Dad," Tracy continued. "He was much older than her, too. Almost as old as Grandpa Wilson, but they fit, you know? They were happy, until Dad was sick for so long."

"Were Ezra and your father much alike?"

Tracy stifled a laugh. "No way. My dad was a retired dentist. He had a *real* life, his friends, and us, of course. It seems like Ezra only had Artisans Alley and the Merchants Association. Maybe that was all he really wanted." She looked back at her mother. "Mom would like to take you up on your offer of a private good-bye with Ezra. We could come here early tomorrow, if that's okay."

"I'll speak with Mr. Collier and let him know you'll be coming," Katie promised.

"Thanks," Tracy said.

Detective Davenport reentered the room, notebook in hand, and spoke with another one of the mourners.

"Boy, that guy wouldn't win any personality contests," Tracy muttered. "He's got a real attitude problem."

"You noticed that, too, huh?" Katie asked.

"What's he trying to accomplish with all these pointed questions? It was a robbery, plain and simple. Ezra was in the wrong place at the wrong time."

If only it were that simple, Katie thought. But

too many people seemed to have had reasons for getting rid of Ezra. From his greedy nephew, to his spurned lover, to someone unwilling to repay a relatively small loan. And how many other people might have had motives to kill the old man?

"Trollop!"

The shouted word cut across the quiet viewing room. Katie's head whipped around. A red-faced Nona Fiske stood before an open-mouthed Mary Elliott.

"What the . . ." Tracy began, and hurried off to intercede, with Katie following close behind.

"It's your fault Ezra's dead!" Nona screamed. "If you hadn't come to Victoria Square, Ezra would still be alive today."

Mary looked around at the crowd, whose attention was now riveted on the two women. "This isn't the place to discuss—"

"Don't you speak to me in that tone!" Nona bellowed.

"Ladies, ladies," Katie soothed, and rested a hand on Nona's elbow, intending to steer her away, but the older woman shook her off.

"Keep your hands off me."

"Could you please lower your voice?" Katie said, noticing Tracy pull her mother away from the ruckus.

"Look at her," Nona spat. "She came to Ezra's viewing with her bosoms hanging out—the brazen strumpet!"

Katie glanced back at Mary, who wore a modest scoop-necked shirt under a dark suit jacket. Hardly the wardrobe of a jezebel.

"Mrs. Fiske," Katie began in a tone her aunt Lizzie rarely used, but when she did—people listened.

"That's Miss Fiske," Nona corrected.

"Miss Fiske," Katie tried again. "I know you're very upset about Ezra's passing—we all are. But please—"

"And who are you to be taking over his business, making his funeral arrangements. It should've been done by his friends, people who loved and cared about him, not some opportunist—"

"That'll be enough, Miss Fiske." Though Seth towered over the quilt shop owner, his expression was kind, even sympathetic, and Katie was never so glad for someone to come to her rescue.

"Ezra had already planned his own funeral, and Mrs. Bonner is one of his legal heirs. I'm sure if you had known that, you wouldn't have said—"

Nona Fiske's face scrunched up and she burst into tears, her wrenching sobs causing those rubbernecking to turn away in embarrassment. "It's all her fault," she cried, pointing at Mary. "Things were fine on the Square until that harlot came along. I tried to tell that policeman about her, but he wouldn't listen. He said she had an alibi, but I know better."

Katie risked a glance at Davenport, who was

furiously scribbling in his notepad. So the detective *had* actually interviewed a few of the merchants. And about time, too.

Seth handed Nona a clean handkerchief, which she took, blowing her nose and wiping at her already red and puffy eyes. "I'll take you home," Seth offered, and Nona put up no resistance as he led her to the exit.

Katie let out a breath as she surveyed Ezra's remaining friends and colleagues, remembering Davenport's pronouncement that one of them had probably killed him.

She didn't want to speculate on just who that could be.

Nine

The next morning, Katie arrived at Artisans Alley before Ezra's memorial service to take down some of Edie Silver's Halloween decorations. Paper skeletons and pumpkins were absolutely the wrong theme for an after-funeral gathering.

The Blueberry Catering truck arrived right on schedule, and Katie left them to finish their setup, making it to the funeral home a full fifteen minutes before the service was to begin. The parking lot wasn't as full as she would have thought, considering the turnout the night before, and Katie entered the building with a heavy heart.

Gilda Ringwald and Mary and Tracy Elliott were the only Victoria Square merchants in evidence. Nona Fiske was conspicuous by her absence. Had she been too embarrassed after her outburst to show her face? After the previous evening's spectacle, Mary had been happy not to run into Nona again, and thanked Katie profusely for allowing her a private good-bye with Ezra. Neither Andy Rust nor Seth Landers had made it, but there were enough Artisans Alley artists to fill several rows of folding chairs that faced the open coffin. Also noticeably absent was Ezra's only surviving relative—Gerald Hilton.

Luther Collier's funeral service was general enough not to cause offense, and the personal remembrances of Ezra from people such as Vance Ingram and Rose Nash made it a fitting memorial to McKinlay Mill's leading citizen. Still, the lack of mourners bothered Katie. Most people probably had to work, Katie surmised, and then worried she'd be stuck with finger foods for one hundred.

By the time Katie made it back to Artisans Alley, the caterers had transformed the lobby with tables filled with food and urns with coffee and hot water for tea. She stationed herself at the main entrance just in time for the crowds to arrive.

"Good afternoon. Thank you for coming," she greeted total strangers, people who had not attended either the wake the night before or the service that morning. "Won't you sign the guest book?"

A number of Artisans Alley's artists and several merchants from the Square showed up to pay their last respects to Ezra. But still Gerald Hilton wasn't among them. Maybe she'd scared him off on Saturday.

Seth dutifully arrived, giving Katie yet another perfunctory kiss on the cheek. Well, a kiss was a kiss, even if brotherly.

"Glad you could make it," Katie said. "Sorry we missed you this morning."

"I'm sorry I can't stay. I had court this morning

and I've got appointments I wasn't able to reschedule this afternoon."

"I'm just grateful you diffused that nasty situation last night."

"Glad I could help. But I have something for you. I didn't think it appropriate to give it to you earlier." Seth dipped a hand into his suit jacket and came out with a set of keys. "They're to Ezra's house. If you've got time, you might want to check it out. You'll be responsible for disposing of the estate and paying off any debts."

Katie let out a breath. "Okay. I'm not reopening Artisans Alley until tomorrow anyway. I'll go as soon as all the guests leave."

Seth took in the oddly shaped lobby. "This is a great space."

"Yes," Katie agreed. "Chad said they often used it for special sales events."

"The lighting is much better than in the individual artists' booths. You ought to make it a gallery."

Katie looked around the empty walls. "Maybe I will. I just have to figure out how to charge the artists who'd use it—and referee the fights that are sure to break out among them."

Seth smiled. "You'll figure it out." He looked at his watch. "I really must be going."

"I'll walk you to the door," Katie said.

The rest of the guests seemed in no hurry to leave—at least, not until the food was all gone. Katie made the rounds and listened in on the latest local gossip—the main topic being the new marina. It was all everyone could seem to talk about. That, and Ezra's murder, of course.

The caterers cleaned up the mess, even vacuuming the carpets, then stood patiently waiting while Katie wrote a check with what seemed like far too many zeros. She winced as she signed her name, and hoped business would be booming on the weekend to make up for the expenditure.

After locking the doors and setting the security system, Katie started off for Ezra's home.

The old farmhouse on County Road 8 was in desperate need of some tender loving care, Katie observed, looking over the rusted gutters and peeling paint. The grass needed cutting, and one of the shutters had fallen off the house and lay haphazardly on the ground. Taking in the three-story structure, Katie noted there were no drapes on the upstairs windows. Cardboard cartons blocked them—probably a fire hazard.

Katie's heart sank. Clearing out and selling the place was likely to be a time-consuming project, and, in its present shape, not a lucrative one. If Gerald was so anxious to get his share of the estate, maybe he'd be willing to help with the cleanup.

Taking the keys from her purse, Katie inspected them, wondering which one opened the front door. None of them, it appeared. She went along to the back entrance and the door opened on her second try. A striped mass of tawny fur launched itself at her, howling and winding around her legs in a frantic figure eight.

"Oh, you poor kitty," she murmured. "How long has it been since you've eaten?" Sniffing the air, she realized it had been a while since the litter box had been changed, too.

The cat cried piteously as Katie searched the kitchen cupboards for its food. Why hadn't someone told her Ezra owned a cat? Surely Mary Elliott or Nona Fiske knew.

Katie found a can of cat food and emptied it into a bowl she grabbed from the drain board. The tabby danced around her ankles, threatening to trip her as she walked the few steps to the plastic placemat and empty water and food bowls on the floor by the fridge.

"That ought to hold you for a while," she said. While the cat wolfed its meal, Katie refilled the water bowl, then searched out the litter box, which she found by the washer and dryer. Five minutes later, she'd changed it, and went back to the kitchen to find her furry new friend furiously washing its front paws.

"What's your name?" Katie asked, petting the cat's silky head. But the cat's only answer was a resounding purr.

"I don't know what to do about you. I've already got a kitty," she said, thinking of Mason and knowing he wouldn't want to give up his status as king of the jungle.

She decided the cat's fate would have to wait a few days. She'd come twice a day to feed it until she either found it a home or, barring that, found time to take it to the vet to be checked for feline leukemia before bringing it to her apartment. No way would she compromise Mason's health. But she couldn't neglect this little one either. Probably a female, she decided, because of its size, but she wasn't inclined to check its anatomy to find out.

Taking a look around the large kitchen, she noticed how neat it was. The laundry room had been clean and tidy, too. Then why were boxes stacked in front of the upstairs windows?

She did a quick walk around the first floor, finding a cubbyhole home office, a bedroom, a bathroom, and a living room. The walls were in need of fresh paint, and the rugs were threadbare, but the inside of the house looked to be in pretty good shape. Had Detective Davenport been through to search for clues?

Heading up the creaking staircase, she found the doors of the three bedrooms closed. Upon opening them, she found each room filled, floor to ceiling, with boxes of receipts. They couldn't all be from Artisans Alley, Katie thought. Sure enough, the boxes were labeled, dating back to the late nineteen sixties, the accumulated records for Ezra's former business ventures—an appliance store that was open through the seventies, and a hardware store that had closed a year or so before he'd opened Artisans Alley.

Ezra's office may have been untidy, but on each of his archived boxes he'd recorded, in his precise handwriting, the nature and date of the receipts. Katie selected the one that held receipts for the previous three months and took it downstairs.

She set it on the recliner seat and tugged at the strip of strapping tape that kept it closed. It came off in a sticky curl that she shook from her hand.

Something hit her from behind, nearly knocking her from her feet. A tangle of furry legs and a tail tried to steady itself on her shoulder.

"Good Lord!" Katie gasped, her hands flying back to stabilize the cat, who, despite its precarious position, did not sink its claws into her skin. Intent on the tape, the cat jumped down to the chair.

"Oh no you don't," Katie said, grabbing the tape and rolling it into a ball, stuffing it into her jacket pocket. The cat hopped onto the armrest, looking for its now-missing prize, and then jumped onto the back of the chair.

Katie glanced up at the empty topmost shelf on the floor-to-ceiling bookcase. The cat must have leaped down from there. Had Ezra trained it to land on his shoulder?

She turned her attention back to the box, picking up a fat envelope from Ezra's bank, thumbing through the pages, which listed only the check numbers and amounts. Too bad banks no longer returned the cashed checks themselves; otherwise she would've had an opportunity to examine the signatures on the back. She still hadn't had an opportunity to go online to look—but what a time sink that would be.

Replacing the envelopes, she folded in the carton flaps. The cat was no longer on the chair. Katie looked up to see it sitting high atop the bookshelf.

"You think you're pretty smart, don't you?"

The cat closed its eyes, opened its mouth to speak, but no sound came out. It looked smug.

Grabbing the box, Katie headed for the kitchen. She heard a dull thunk from the living room, and before she'd grabbed her purse and keys from the counter, the cat was winding around her ankles, as though begging her to stay.

"Sorry—I gotta go, little kitty. But I'll be back to feed you tomorrow." Somehow she managed to juggle the box, her purse, and her key, and close the door behind her without the cat escaping.

Placing the box in her car trunk, Katie walked around to the driver's side, noticing for the first time the barn out back. It looked to be in about the same condition as the house. A late-model SUV sat parked next to its main door. Ezra drove a rusty old Chevy station wagon, which was still parked behind Artisans Alley. Yet Katie was sure she'd seen the SUV sitting in the Victoria Square parking lot during the past few days.

Closing her car door, Katie headed for the barn. She stood on tiptoe, and rubbed a hand over one of the dust-caked windows to peek inside. The interior was too dark to see anything clearly. She wandered over to the door. A shiny new lock hung from the hasp.

A heavy hand grasped her shoulder, yanking her around.

"What do you think you're doing here?"

Heart pounding, Katie tried to catch her breath.

"What am *I* doing here?" she repeated, staring into the depths of Peter Ashby's chocolate brown eyes. "I could ask you the same thing."

"I have a right to be here. I rent the barn from Ezra."

Katie pulled down on the hem of her jacket, straightening it, trying to regain her composure. "Since I'm in charge of his affairs, I guess you're now renting it from me. You wouldn't happen to have a written contract, would you?"

Ashby frowned. "Ezra and I had a verbal agreement. He charged me fifty dollars a month."

"Why so cheap?" she asked.

"The roof leaks."

Knowing the state of the house, she didn't doubt that. Still . . .

"What are you using the barn for?"

"Storing my merchandise."

Katie thought about the shiny new lock. "Anything else?"

"That's none of your business."

"You're wrong." She waited, but Ashby didn't

reply. "I'm afraid we'll have to renegotiate at the end of the month. That is, if you wish to stay," she said, knowing that only gave Ashby days to make up his mind.

"Hey, what is this? You're letting low-end crafters in Artisans Alley, and you're about to jack up the rent, too. You're a chiseler, lady."

Katie felt her cheeks flush. "I'm a business-woman. And if I want to stay in business, I have to charge fair market value for my properties. Including this one." She jabbed a thumb at the building behind her. "I'll be in my office at Artisans Alley all day tomorrow if you'd care to discuss it. Otherwise, I'll give you two weeks to vacate."

Ashby pivoted, heading for his SUV. "Bitch."

Katie watched as he got in, started the engine, and left a spray of mud when he spun the tires on the damp earth.

She had acted rather rashly, she reflected, but despite Ashby's good looks, his bluntness irritated her. Ashby had been the one to advocate charging the crafters more at Saturday's meeting. And if he could lie about what he paid Ezra for the barn rental, what else was he capable of doing?

The sun was already sinking into the horizon when Katie headed back to town. Besides Nona Fiske and Ezra's nephew, she'd noticed another person absent from the funeral and reception afterward.

The lights were aglow at Angelo's Pizzeria. She

159

pushed open the door to the wonderful smells of rising dough, pepperoni, tomato sauce, and melted mozzarella.

Andy Rust paused in his dough throwing, glowering at her—as happy to see Katie as Peter Ashby had been.

"Are we still friends?" Katie asked, keeping her tone light.

Andy didn't answer, tearing his gaze from her face and riveting his attention on the pizza he was making.

Katie stepped closer to the counter. "I could sure use a friend about now."

"I had a visit from Detective Davenport last night." Apparently friendship was the last thing on Andy's mind.

"Oh?"

"You sent him."

"I didn't. But I felt I had to tell him about you and your pet project."

"And I told you my boys weren't responsible for Ezra Hilton's death," Andy grated.

Katie saw Keith behind Andy, trying to look inconspicuous but listening nonetheless.

"I believe you. But the police wanted to know about any possible witnesses. Maybe one of your boys saw something—maybe . . ." But the excuses sounded phony even to Katie.

"I'm sorry, Andy. I don't believe any of the boys were involved. I've never known anyone who was murdered, and I want to make sure whoever killed Ezra is caught and punished. Can you at least understand that?"

Andy shrugged. "I guess so. I keep forgetting Hilton was your friend."

"Not a close friend, but he had been my husband Chad's friend and mentor." She offered Andy her hand. "We've both made errors in judgment. Can we try again?"

Andy frowned, puzzled.

"Stick 'em up," she reminded him.

Andy actually blushed. Still, he peeled off his plastic gloves, wiping his dusty hands on his apron. "I guess so."

They shook.

Katie let out a breath in a whoosh. "Do you ever take a break from work?"

"Not once I get here."

"How about lunch tomorrow? Are you free?"

"I could be," he said, the barest hint of a smile quirking his lips.

"One o'clock? We could go to the tea shop."

Andy shook his head. "I doubt I'd be welcome. What about the diner next to the grocery store?"

Katie nodded. "We can walk over together. I'll meet you here."

"Okay."

Katie hesitated, not wanting to leave. Despite the day filled with people, she felt starved for meaningful conversation and human companionship.

"I—I guess I'd better get going," she said at last.

"See you tomorrow," Andy said.

Katie gave him a quick smile and headed for the door.

She sorted through the keys on her ring as she walked to her car. She could fill a couple of hours looking at the box of papers she'd collected from Ezra's house. Maybe she'd make a few calls to see if she could find a home for Ezra's cat, too.

And maybe later, when the emptiness became too much to bear, she'd cry herself to sleep.

Ten

The sky was deep blue when Katie left Artisans Alley the following afternoon. A stiff breeze off the lake had chased the clouds away, and she hoped the clear skies were an omen of good things to come.

Andy Rust was already waiting outside his shop when Katie arrived at his doorstop at one-oh-three the next afternoon. "Sorry I'm late."

"No problem." He nodded, turned, and Katie dropped into step alongside him, heading up the sidewalk toward Main Street. "You look nice today. New hairdo?" Andy asked.

Katie smoothed a hand over the windblown hair at her collar. "Hardly."

"Then maybe it's the pink in your cheeks. It suits you."

Katie felt a flush rise from her neck.

"Everything cleaned up from the break-in?" Andy asked.

"I wish. I never seem to get time to work on it."

"Anything of value taken?"

"It's hard to say. But the files being dumped has given me an excuse to toss out a lot of old paperwork—stuff that's at least half a decade out of date. I'm afraid Ezra was a bit of a pack rat."

"Not surprising, considering he was in a business that stressed collecting things."

Katie smiled, grateful the tension between them was gone.

They turned the corner, heading for Del's Diner.

"Have you lived in McKinlay Mill long?" Katie asked.

"Most of my life. My parents are snowbirds—retired to Florida about five years ago. They've got a cottage on the lake where they still spend summers. I bought their house here in the village. You're not a townie. And you've got a Rochester accent."

"*You* could've been a detective. But I grew up in the suburbs, not the city. I went to Greece Olympia High School."

Andy smiled. "Ah, McKinlay Mill's arch basketball rival."

"They still are, I think. Funny how important that stuff seemed at the time."

"Not to me. Though if I'd been involved in sports, I probably wouldn't have gotten into trouble with the law."

"You look a healthy specimen now. Do you work out?" she asked.

"Weights, at the gym here in town. How about you?"

"I'm vying for the state couch potato title. I'm just lucky I inherited good genes."

The amusement in Andy's smile helped her

relax. It was fun to talk to a good-looking man, getting to know him. And it made good business sense to cultivate a relationship with Artisans Alley's nearest neighbor.

Del's Diner wasn't a charmer from the nineteen fifties as its name might have promised. The nineteen seventies strip mall lacked the aura of that bygone era. Wedged between the grocery store and the local gym, Del's was rather dark and the decor dated, but the food was good, and the coffee strong.

McKinlay Mill's luncheon rush was already over, and they found an empty booth with no trouble. Andy tossed his jacket on the seat next to him, but Katie shrugged out of hers, keeping it draped around her shoulders.

A portly bleached blonde of about fifty, in a white polyester uniform dress, black apron, and thick-soled shoes—Sandy, by her name tag—came around with the coffeepot. "Hey, Andy. The usual?"

"Sure. But I think Katie will want a menu."

"I'll just have a grilled cheese sandwich," she said.

Sandy nodded, poured coffee for them both, then bustled off for the kitchen.

"You must be a regular here," Katie said.

"I hate to cook," Andy admitted.

Katie laughed. "But that's how you make your living."

"Which is why I can't stand to do it for myself. I practically live here at Del's. How about you?"

"I can't say as I've been here more than half a dozen times."

It was Andy's turn to laugh. "I mean, do you like to cook?"

"Nope, hate it. Chad, my late husband, was the chef at our house. I think he started cooking as a defensive tactic. I have no interest in it. But I do bake—a lot."

Andy eyed her. "You must not eat much of what you make—at least you don't look it."

"I told you. I have good genes."

Andy doctored his coffee with sugar and creamer, his expression sobering. "Why did you invite me here today? I mean, it couldn't be just my charm and good looks." He handed Katie the bowl of sugar packets.

"There's that, too, but I guess I'm a little concerned. Why hasn't the Merchants Association asked you to join? Whether they like it or not, you're a part of Victoria Square."

"They *don't* like it," he said, "and I have no idea why."

Katie sipped her coffee, not sure she believed him. "Is it because of your past?"

He shook his head. "That was fifteen years ago. And unlike me, none of my boys has ever been in trouble with the law."

"You didn't answer my question."

"I've been blackballed. And I've got a pretty good idea who's behind it, too."

"Who?"

He shook his head.

"Would you *like* to join the Association?" Katie asked.

Andy toyed with his spoon. "I see the benefit of getting along with my neighbors. Unfortunately, the guy who used to own my shop *didn't* feel that way. He wouldn't contribute to the Square's upkeep—lighting, snow removal, resurfacing the parking lot, that kind of thing. My business is mostly delivery, so I don't need much parking. And to tell you the truth, when I took over, I didn't have the capital to afford it. Now I'm out of the red and could use another write-off. When I mentioned it to Mr. Hilton a couple of months ago, he said he'd take it up with the Association. So far no one's contacted me."

"I'm going to my first meeting tomorrow night. I'd be glad to bring it up."

"I'd appreciate it. Thanks."

Sandy arrived with two plates balanced on one arm, the coffeepot clutched in her other hand. She set the plates before Katie and Andy. Both contained a grilled cheese sandwich, pickle slices, and potato chips. She topped off their cups, then slapped down the check and a couple of hard candy mints. "Let me know if you need anything else," she said and departed.

"Hey, we think alike," Katie said, picking up half of her sandwich.

Andy smiled. "You know what they say about great minds."

Katie took a bite, chewed, and swallowed. "It's much better than I can make." She rearranged the chips on her plate, letting Andy guide the conversation, listening with real interest as he told her more about his business and his plans for the future.

Finally he paused, polishing off the last of his pickle slices. Katie took the opportunity to make her pitch. "Besides an evil nephew, Ezra left behind a darling little cat. You wouldn't happen to be in the market for a pet, would you?"

"I'm never home. It wouldn't be fair to the cat. Besides, I'm more a dog person. But tell me more about this 'evil nephew.'"

"Oh, that's just my perception of the man. He's probably no more despicable than Hitler or Mussolini, but I don't want to talk about him. Do you know any of the people at Artisans Alley? I mean, the merchants may never have patronized your place, but surely some of the artists have."

Andy nodded, swallowing the last bite of his sandwich. "I'm only on a first-name basis with a couple of them. Vance Ingram, Rose Nash, and Ben Stillwell. I'd probably recognize a bunch of other names from orders, but I can't say I really know any of them."

"I don't know any of them, so anything you can tell me would help," Katie said, and unwrapped one of the mints. While Andy took a few moments to think about it, Katie bit down on the candy.

Andy frowned. "Yo—don't you worry about your teeth?"

"I brush a lot," Katie said around a mouth full of candy splinters.

"Yeah, but you could crack a bicuspid or something."

She waved a hand in dismissal. "The artists," she reminded him.

"They seem like nice, decent people. But they'll place an order and only make small talk if they show up too early to collect it—usually after their shifts end at Artisans Alley."

Katie nodded, trying to hide her disappointment. She was going to have to find a confidant within Artisans Alley. Chad would have known everyone, although so far his journal hadn't included much in the way of personal assessments of the vendors. She'd have to make the time to sit down and actually read it.

But as she thought about it more, Katie realized the best person for the job had literally been right under her nose all along.

"Goodness, yes," Rose Nash said with a gleam in her eye, and motioned Katie closer. "I can tell you *everything* about *everybody* in this place."

169

"I'm not generally a nosy person," Katie said. "It's just that I need to get up to speed—and fast—with how Artisans Alley operates. And that means getting the lowdown on as many artist vendors as possible."

"I've been here since the beginning, so I guess I know just about everybody. We have a few new artists, but I think I at least recognize all the faces."

"Great. What can you tell me about Vance Ingram?"

Rose leaned against the counter, and then looked around to see if anyone was within earshot. Several customers browsed in a booth down the aisle, but none close enough to listen in. "Janey Ingram's MS has put a real strain on their marriage. Not so much now, but in the early days it was hard for Vance to take care of her and work a full-time job. Since he retired, it's been easier."

"Is he older than her?"

Rose nodded. "By about ten years. She went into remission a couple of years ago and that helped, but Vance hinted that lately she hasn't been well."

"He must be devoted to her."

"You'd think that, wouldn't you?" Rose said, her eyes wide—her expression enigmatic.

"You mean he's not?"

Rose looked around again, and then lowered her voice. "There was talk . . . but it's just gossip."

Katie's eyes widened.

A customer stepped up to the counter, laying

down her purchases. Katie watched as Rose carefully entered each item into the computer. Rose wasn't the fastest typist, and it took nearly five minutes before she finished making change and took the receipt from the printer.

"Thank you for shopping at Artisans Alley," Rose said, waved a cheerful good-bye to the customer, then turned back to Katie, ready to spill all. "Of course, it's just a rumor that Vance cheats on his wife," she said without missing a beat. "And I haven't heard anything more about it in years. Maybe he had a midlife crisis."

"How about Peter Ashby?" Katie asked.

"Oh, he's a creep," Rose said, not telling Katie anything she didn't already know.

"He's been renting the barn behind Ezra's barn."

Rose frowned. "Have you seen his product?" Displeasure colored her voice.

"He said he sold copies of Victorian cemetery statuary."

"It's downright creepy—just like him. And the prices he gets for the stuff." Rose shook her head. "Suckers will buy anything."

"I'll have to check out his booth," Katie said.

"It's funny, but Edie Silver was telling me that she's never seen a catalog for the kind of stuff Ashby sells. I mean, there doesn't seem to be a national distributor."

"Where is he getting his merchandise from?" Katie asked.

Rose's gaze traveled up to the balcony, where Ashby's booth was located. "That's a good question."

Katie looked up, too. "Maybe I'll go have a look now."

Rose nodded in encouragement.

Katie headed for the stairs. The first booth at the top right featured handmade paper articles—greeting cards, stationery, as well as seals and wax, specialty pens, and hand-bound journals. Nothing too spectacular, but it all exuded a certain "homey" charm nonetheless.

Ashby's booth was next door. He seemed to have more marketing savvy than the majority of artists. Stenciled, ivy-covered pillars decorated one wall. Fake plants in terra-cotta pots made a container garden around the merchandise for sale. Floodlights showcased a full-sized Victorian beauty with flowing, windblown robes that stood in the booth's corner. Katie had expected tombstone art, but three-dimensional cherubs and angels were the dominating theme, with only one example of each piece. All wore a facsimile patina of age. Paint or some other faux finish, Katie surmised. And they were warm to the touch—resin, as he'd told her, not marble or some other kind of stone.

Ashby had said he had a dozen designs, and that's just what his booth contained. An old-fashioned, purple velvet–covered photograph album sat on an antique oak plant stand, which was labeled

NOT FOR SALE. Katie flipped through the pages of pictures. Each statue was shown in a garden setting, or in the middle of an elaborate water fountain.

Katie's gaze kept returning to the haunting statue in the billowing robes. Its eyes were vacant, but the placement of the arms leaning into the wind made one think that at any moment she might take flight. What kind of monument had the original stood on? Was it a representation of a long-dead woman or maybe just an artist's interpretation of a woman at the turn of the last century, longing for some kind of fulfillment? How many had Ashby already sold? Katie tugged at the string tag hanging from the statue's finger and whistled at the sky-high price. She hadn't thought Artisans Alley could draw in customers willing to spend that kind of money on simulated antique statuary. But business must be good. Ashby said he was expecting a new shipment of merchandise within the week. That must be the reason for the shiny new lock on Ezra's barn door.

Had Ashby given Ezra a copy of the key for that lock? Did a landlord have the right to access his property—even if it was rented out? She didn't know, but no doubt Seth would. She'd have to call him and ask.

Something about Ashby's attitude the evening before still bothered her. He'd been angry to find her on Ezra's property. Why? What was he trying to hide?

Katie, you're getting paranoid.

As long as she was upstairs, Katie decided to wander around the rest of the balcony. Each vendor seemed to have a specialty. Booth 99 belonged to a potter, and its shelves were lined with bowls, plates, mugs, and even oil lamps. The stained glass booth was numbered 32 and belonged to Liz Meier, who was currently walking security. An artificial Christmas tree was decorated with a myriad of sun catchers, but the tree had no lights, and with nothing to reflect, the ornaments looked dull and unattractive. There didn't seem to be any electrical outlets in the booth.

Katie moved on, amazed at how much she knew about the various arts. Chad's lectures must have sunk in. Chad's booth was next, with his colorful floral paintings. His booth was one of the best. He'd added tract lighting to showcase his work, and Katie remembered he'd paid to have an electrician put in a new line. Too bad Liz hadn't done the same. The whole balcony needed better lighting. Another thing for the to-do list. She stared at the signature on a cheerful painting of daisies swaying in a breeze and felt a pang of regret—the tears came less and less as time went on—and she turned away.

None of the other booths interested her, and Katie decided her time would be better spent in conversation with Rose. If Detective Davenport wasn't going to strain himself to find Ezra's killer, her efforts to gather information for him certainly couldn't hurt.

A chill ran through her and she held the banister as she descended the stairs and again considered that she'd probably already met Ezra's killer. What kind of person murdered, and then resumed their life as though they'd never committed such a heinous act?

Peter Ashby? a niggling voice in her mind teased.

Distracted, Katie paused at the bottom of the stairs to admire a display of quartz rocks in a variety of shades that decorated Booth 8. This artist—a maker of beaded jewelry—had a good sense of how to best display merchandise. A hole in the display marked a successful sale. Next to the empty space was a lovely chunk of pink quartz. A little typed placard noted it helped promote restful sleep, and a beaded necklace and matching earrings of the same quartz beautifully polished hung above the rock.

Katie leaned closer and frowned. A brown stain marred one of the sharp edges of the stone, and stuck to it was a single white hair.

Eleven

"And no one's touched it?" Detective Davenport asked, standing before the display of colorful rocks, his eyes narrowed in suspicion.

Katie shook her head. "I've sort of been standing guard."

Davenport withdrew a pair of latex gloves from his raincoat pocket, and put them on with a flourish. He picked up the pink quartz and carefully inspected the stain before placing it in a paper evidence bag.

He turned to Katie, his expression dark—almost frightening. "Did you tell anyone about your find?"

Again Katie shook her head. "There were customers around. I didn't want to alarm anyone or bring attention to it."

"Who's the booth owner?"

"I don't know. But Rose Nash, our cashier, knows nearly all the artists. She can tell us. If not, I have the list in the office."

"We'll talk to her first," Davenport said, and turned away, heading toward Artisans Alley's entrance and the cash registers.

"Detective?" Katie called after him.

Davenport stopped, and swung his heavy head around to look at her.

"I'm sure you've been checking everyone's alibi. After that little altercation at the funeral home, I was wondering if Mary Elliott—"

He sighed. "Of course I checked alibis. At the time of Ezra Hilton's death, Mrs. Elliott was with her daughter—not that it's any of your business."

Katie ground her teeth, clenching her fists to keep from hitting him.

Davenport resumed his track toward the registers.

As expected, Rose hovered over the cash desk, her nose buried in her latest romance novel.

"Rose," Katie said.

Rose held up a hand to stall them. "One more paragraph." Her eyes darted back and forth as she scanned the page, then she threw back her head and smiled. "Wow! The hero and heroine just made love for the first time. Hot and steamy."

The lines around Davenport's mouth grew more pronounced.

"Um, Rose, you remember Detective Davenport, don't you?"

Rose straightened, wariness creeping into her gaze. With great care, she stuck a small piece of paper between the pages of her novel to mark her place. "Yes."

"Ma'am, would you know who vendor eight is?"

"Why, yes. It's me. Is something wrong?"

Katie's heart picked up speed. How would Rose handle the news that it was her property that had probably killed her dear friend?

Davenport carefully removed the pink quartz from the evidence bag. "Does this belong to you?"

"Yes, and it's a bargain at fifteen dollars." She went to take it from him, but Davenport snatched the rock back.

"Ma'am, where were you last Thursday evening?"

"Detective Davenport!" Katie cried. "You can't suspect Rose."

Rose's brow puckered in confusion.

"It's a standard question," Davenport said.

"I was at home all evening," Rose said, sounding bewildered.

"Alone?" Davenport accused.

"Yes. I've been alone for five years. Since my husband, Howard, died. What are you saying?" Rose turned frightened eyes toward Katie, as though suddenly realizing the reason behind Davenport's questions. "Is he going to arrest me? I'd never hurt anyone—especially not Ezra. He was my friend, he was—"

"We haven't established this object as the murder weapon," Davenport said. "However, if we do, we'll need to differentiate your prints— if there are any—from whoever else may have touched it. Can you follow me to headquarters? It'll only take a few minutes to fingerprint you."

Rose's breathing quickened, her frightened gaze darting back to Katie.

"Can it wait until we close?" Katie asked, her gaze darting back to Rose. She couldn't stand to see the panicked look in the old woman's eyes. "Then I can come with her."

Davenport hesitated, then, "I guess that'll be acceptable."

"Will you meet us there?" Katie asked.

"Just check in with the desk. I'll tell them to expect you."

Of course. Wednesday was probably his bowling night. No need to cancel his personal plans to wait for news on the possible murder weapon on his hottest case.

"That'll be fine," Katie said, though she hoped from her tone that Davenport knew she meant just the opposite.

Davenport nodded to the women, replaced the pink quartz in the bag, then headed for the exit.

Rose pulled a lace-edged handkerchief from her skirt pocket, dabbing at her suddenly damp eyes. "Katie, I swear, I didn't kill Ezra."

Katie drew the elderly woman into a tentative embrace. "I know. We'll work this out," she promised, patting Rose's bony back. She couldn't imagine Rose being able to lift the rock over her head, let alone smashing it—with enough force to kill—against Ezra's skull.

"As the detective said, it's more to tell who's handled the quartz. But if it'll make you feel better, I'll call Seth Landers for legal advice."

Rose's sniffles lessened and she pulled away. "Thank you, Katie."

A woman customer stood some ten feet away, hesitant to intrude.

"Can I help you?" Katie asked, trying to sound cheerful.

She rang up the sale herself, a delicate porcelain doll with a wardrobe of exquisitely handmade clothing. Rose fumbled as she wrapped the purchase, her hands trembling so badly she nearly dropped the doll.

"It's okay, I'll take care of it," Katie said. "Why don't you go sit in the tag room and visit with Ida for a few minutes. I can handle things out here, and I'll pull Liz off the floor to help."

"But then no one will be walking security," Rose said. "No, I'd feel better if I was doing something useful. If Liz will handle the register, I'll walk around. It's only for an hour until we close. That'll give you a chance to call Mr. Landers."

Five minutes later, Katie was back in her office dialing the phone.

"I'm sorry, but Mr. Landers is in court today. Can I take a message?" his secretary offered.

Katie relayed her find and their subsequent plans to go to the station, asking that the lawyer call her that evening.

She hung up the phone and took in the messy office. She hadn't had a chance to do more than a cursory pickup since the break-in. She'd have to come back later that evening to finish the job. And she needed to talk to Vance about collecting work schedules from the artists for the upcoming weeks.

Katie frowned, glancing down at Ezra's master schedule tucked into the side of the desk blotter. Vance's name had been jotted down for today. He'd never shown up or even called. Irked, Katie consulted the dog-eared Rolodex cards listing the artists' home telephone numbers. She found Vance's card and dialed. It rang six times before being answered.

"Hello?" A woman's voice.

"Mrs. Ingram?"

"Yes."

"This is Katie Bonner over at Artisans Alley. May I speak to Vance?"

"He's not home yet. Did he just leave? I thought he was supposed to be there until closing."

"Um . . . yes," Katie said, thinking fast. "I couldn't find him here and assumed he'd gone home early. Perhaps you could tell him I called."

"I'll do that."

"Thank you. Good-bye."

Katie hung up the phone. So Vance's wife thought he'd spent the entire day at Artisans Alley. He'd been unavailable on the evening Ezra died, too. Why was he being so secretive? What did he have to hide? Infidelity—or did he know more about Ezra's death than he'd been willing to admit?

She really needed to talk to Vance, and maybe it wouldn't be a bad idea to get Detective Davenport in on the conversation, too.

Katie grabbed a pile of papers from the floor, flipping through them before straightening them to put away. A wave of shame coursed through her. Where did she get off judging Vance Ingram and contemplating telling Detective Davenport to lean on him for information? Vance's private life—however he lived it, with whatever moral code he lived by—was really none of her business.

She'd ask him why he hadn't shown up and if he didn't want to tell her—well, that was his business. But she did want to pin him down to a time when he could teach her what she needed to know about the mechanics within Artisans Alley. And unfortunately that was all she could expect from him.

Still, a man who'd lie to his wife about his whereabouts could lie about other things . . . including murder.

Katie's already weakened sense of security ebbed that much more.

"It was a good thing you offered to drive," Rose said as Katie steered her car onto the expressway entrance ramp. "I've lost my nerve for city driving—especially at night."

Katie had to smile since they'd never actually ventured into Rochester proper. The sheriff's substation was located in one of the western suburbs. The fingerprinting had gone smoothly, and Katie had let them take hers as well. It was likely the technical team that had dusted her office earlier had found just as many of her own prints as Ezra's.

"Are you okay, Rose?" Katie asked.

"It wasn't as bad as I thought it would be," the older woman said with most of the usual good cheer evident in her voice. "Just like something off a TV show."

"I wouldn't worry about it," Katie said. "Now that they've got what appears to be the murder weapon, I'm hoping they'll figure out who killed Ezra so we can all feel safe again."

"Amen," Rose said.

"I'll drop you off at Artisans Alley to pick up your car," Katie said, "but do you mind if I stop at Ezra's house to feed his cat first?"

"Ezra had a cat?" Rose asked.

Katie nodded, keeping her eyes on the road. "I didn't know about it until yesterday. The poor thing was half starved."

"I guess there was a lot about Ezra that none of us knew," Rose said.

"I knew very little about him. Like, was he ever married?"

"Oh, yes. Almost forty years to Dorothy Johnson." Rose laughed. "Funny how you always remember your friends by their maiden names, no matter how long—or how often—they've married. Dorothy had heart problems, poor thing. She died about ten years ago."

"How sad they had no children," Katie said.

"Oh, but they did. A son, Ronnie."

So that's who the person in the framed photo in her office was.

"He owned his own business here in McKinlay Mill," Rose continued. "Ronnie was a tree surgeon. Seems to me he died about five years ago now."

"That's terrible."

"Yes. They say he never worked alone—it was too dangerous. But that day he was on a job all by himself. It was hours before anyone found him, poor man."

That was a year before she and Chad had come to McKinlay Mill. Had Ezra looked at Chad as some kind of a replacement for his son? And if Ezra was all alone in the world, it made sense that he'd prepay for his own funeral. How sad.

Then again, now that Chad was gone, Katie was all alone. She'd struggled to pay for Chad's funeral, and had no funds to pay for her own—at least, not if she still hoped to buy the English Ivy Inn.

"Then was Ezra to be buried in a family plot?"

"I guess so. I was surprised there was no graveside service. I just assumed that was what Ezra wanted."

Katie took the Lake Ontario State Parkway exit west, putting on her high beams, and hoped the local deer population had bedded down for the night.

"I didn't know Ezra well, but he didn't seem to want for female companionship. I mean, he seems to have been friends with Mary Elliott at

184

the tea shop, and before that Nona Fiske."

"Nona was a possessive shrew," Rose said with contempt. "She wasn't at all good for Ezra."

"How about Mary?"

"She was a lot younger than Ezra. I suppose if someone hadn't hit him with the pink quartz, she'd have killed him in bed."

So Rose wasn't fond of either Mary or Nona. What would Detective Davenport make of that information? Katie decided to push just a bit further. "I take it Ezra didn't let Nona down gently?"

"No. One day he just took up with Mary."

"Did he ever have a showdown with Nona?"

"Not that I heard. But you can understand her distress when that hussy Mary moved in on her territory."

Hussy? Territory? What were Rose's feelings for Ezra?

Katie's gaze stayed fixed on the road. "Did Mary pursue Ezra or did he go after her?"

"Oh, it had to be Mary. Ezra wouldn't have done anything to actually hurt Nona."

But he had, if he'd just taken up with Mary with no explanation to his former lady friend. And that didn't make sense either. There had to be more to the story than Rose either knew or was willing to repeat.

Katie took the Walker Road exit and headed for Ezra's house. "It'll only take me a minute or two to feed the cat. She's a pretty little tabby. You wouldn't happen to want a furry companion, would you?"

"No, thank you," Rose said. "I was badly scratched as a child. I can't abide the things."

Katie's stomach tightened. She'd always loved cats and had never been without one. Illogical though it might be, Rose had just dropped a peg in her estimation.

She pulled up Ezra's driveway and parked beside the darkened house. "I'll only be a minute," she said, and climbed out of the car.

"I'll be fine," Rose assured her, and folded her hands on her lap to wait.

Katie climbed the steps to Ezra's back door, and fumbled to find the keyhole. Maybe she should have a motion detector sensor installed on the outside lamp so that she could see to get in the house after dark. She opened the door and once again the little tabby was ecstatic to see her. The cat wound around her ankles as Katie flipped on the outside light switch. Nothing happened. Probably a burned-out bulb. She'd have to replace it.

A minute later, the sound of the pull-tab lid coming off the cat food can had the cat dancing in circles around Katie's ankles.

"Tomorrow I'll call the village vet and see if we can't find out your name, little girl. I haven't found you a home yet, but I haven't given up either."

Katie set the food bowl on the floor, changed the

water, and then attended to the litter box. She felt bad to leave the cat in the dark, and turned on the stove light.

Locking the door behind her, Katie headed for her car. She opened the driver's door to get in, but found the car was empty. She straightened and spoke to the darkened sky. "Rose? Rose, where are you?"

Panicked, Katie peered through the darkness, but couldn't see a thing. She groped under the car seat, came up with the flashlight Chad had insisted she carry, and prayed the batteries hadn't died. The thin beam of light did little to dispel the gloom.

The grass under her feet was long and wet, the ground beneath it uneven. Katie headed for the only place Rose could have gone—Ezra's barn.

Peter Ashby's SUV was parked by the door. Light glowed faintly from inside the structure.

"Rose?" Katie hissed. "Rose!"

"Over here."

Katie crept around to the back of the barn to where she'd heard the voice and found the old lady standing on tiptoe, looking through one of the dirty windows.

"What are you doing?" Katie whispered.

"There's a reason Ashby won't tell anyone where he gets his merchandise. He's making it himself."

Katie squinted through the window to see Ashby moving around inside. His nose and mouth were covered by a filter mask. He poured a white viscous liquid into a rubberized mold that stood in some kind of wooden frame. Behind him were examples of cemetery art—but were they copies or the originals?

Katie grabbed Rose's arm, pulling her away from the window to head for the car.

"Katie!" Rose protested.

"Shhhh!"

After they were in the car, Katie started the engine.

"I wanted to see more," Rose complained as she buckled her seat belt.

"So, we know where he gets his stock from. Big deal," Katie said, relief flooding her—thank goodness Ashby hadn't caught them spying on him.

"It *is* a big deal," Rose insisted. "If his master copies are stolen!"

Twelve

"Stolen?" Katie echoed, momentarily tearing her gaze from the road.

Rose nodded. "Selling stolen cemetery statuary is big business."

"But Ashby isn't selling the real thing. He's selling copies," Katie exclaimed.

"And where did he get his prototypes?" Rose asked.

That was a very good question.

"Have you heard of any local cemeteries being vandalized?" Katie asked. The thought of someone possibly tampering with Chad's grave filled her with anger and disgust.

"No, but that doesn't mean it hasn't happened. Mount Hope Cemetery in Rochester is one of the best examples of a Victorian cemetery in the whole country. Buffalo's Forest Lawn is another fine example. Both have exemplary statuary, as well as being the final resting places for the famous and infamous. There're books available on the subject—take a look at the local-interest shelf next time you go to the mall bookstore. But my guess is Ashby went out of state for his master copies."

Rose was quiet for a moment. "Seems to me that

when Peter first came to McKinlay Mill, his car had Ohio license plates. I'll bet he vandalized some cemetery back there—and maybe still does."

Katie kept her eyes riveted on the road, sickened by what Rose had just said. Ashby had told her he had new merchandise arriving. If he was making copies—where *had* the originals come from?

"What should we do about it?"

"Ask the police to send out an APB—or whatever it is they do when they suspect someone of a criminal offense," Rose declared.

An all-points bulletin was hardly appropriate for this situation, but Detective Davenport might be interested in this little development. Of course, if Rose was right, if Ezra *had* discovered what Ashby was up to—on his own property—maybe it would be worth the risk for Ashby to silence someone who had that knowledge.

Say Ezra confronted Ashby in Ashby's booth at Artisans Alley, and then headed down the stairs to call the police. An angry Ashby could have grabbed one of the rocks from Rose's booth, smashed it against Ezra's skull, and then left him for dead. Ashby would have had to replace the pink quartz —no doubt wiping it clean of fingerprints first— then emptied the cash drawer to make it look like a robbery.

It all fit perfectly.

Too perfectly. Or at least Davenport would think so. Although he hadn't actually said so, Katie knew the detective considered her suggestions and offered tidbits of information more a hindrance than help to his investigation.

"Slow down," Rose cautioned, just before Katie would have missed the Victoria Square entrance.

Katie made a sharp right turn, grateful there'd been no car behind her or in the oncoming lane. McKinlay Mill's streets were virtually empty— even though it was just seven thirty on a Wednesday evening. Pulling up alongside Rose's little red car, she eased the gear shift into park.

"I know you're not scheduled to work tomorrow, but we had two no-shows today. Is there a chance I could impose by asking you to—"

"Of course I'll come in, dear," Rose said, her smile bright. "A widow has plenty of empty hours to fill."

Katie pursed her lips. Did Rose hate going home to an empty bed as much as she did?

Rose unbuckled her seat belt as Katie switched off the engine. "What are you doing?" she asked.

"My office is still a terrible mess. I thought I'd take an hour or so to finally clean it up."

"Oh, no you don't," Rose said, her voice filled with maternal indignation. "I'm not leaving you here all alone with a murderer running around loose. Especially not at night."

Rose did have a point.

"I suppose I could come in early tomorrow," Katie said.

"Yes, you can," Rose said. "Go home and get a good night's sleep. You have to promise me, now."

A smile tugged at Katie's lips. "Okay, I promise."

"All right, then. I'll see you tomorrow. And thank you."

"For what?" Katie asked.

"For taking me to the police station."

Katie had almost forgotten why they'd been out together.

"And for making an old lady feel worthwhile again."

The poor lighting made it hard to see if there were tears in Rose's eyes, but her voice betrayed the depth of her feelings.

"You're very welcome," Katie said, and she meant it.

Rose got out of the car and Katie waited until she'd gotten safely into her own vehicle, started the engine, and pulled out of the lot.

Katie started her car, put it in gear, then steered for the exit. As she passed Angelo's Pizzeria, she caught sight of Andy Rust's unsmiling face peering out through the large plate glass window. She sketched a quick wave, but he turned away.

Katie drove on, feeling as though she'd just been snubbed. But that couldn't be. They'd had a pleasant conversation at lunch and had parted under good terms. At least, she thought they had. Or maybe she just *hoped* they had. She liked Andy Rust. A lot.

She also liked Seth Landers, who hadn't

called her back, she noted. But then, she couldn't remember if she'd switched on her cell phone.

"It's too soon after Chad's death to think about other men," she chided herself as she pulled into her apartment's parking lot. "Much too soon."

She parked the car, sorted her door key from the others on the ring, and opened the driver's door. Almost immediately a figure got out of a car across the way.

"Hey, lady, you hungry?" came a familiar voice.

"Seth, is that you?" Katie called, squinting in the lot's wan lamplight.

He caught up with her. "I've been waiting for almost an hour. I was about to give up."

"I was expecting a call, not a visit," Katie said, nonetheless flattered by his attention.

"Could I interest you in dinner? McKinlay Mill hasn't got much to offer, but the meatloaf at Del's is pretty good. If they've got any left."

Katie glanced at her watch. Her poor cat, Mason, had been alone all day. But she was hungry and still hadn't made it to the grocery store to refill her empty cupboards.

"Great," she said, and let the lawyer escort her to his car.

Much too soon, her inner voice scolded again. But dinner was only dinner—not a lifetime commitment. Still, she wished she was wearing her blue business suit. That would've looked smarter. More sophisticated.

Oh, what the heck, they were only going to the diner!

Seth opened the passenger door of his car, and Katie sank into the comfortable leather seat. Seth slid behind the wheel and the Mercedes's powerful engine purred to life. He gave her a quick smile as he shifted into reverse. Katie smiled back but thought of Andy Rust's dour expression as she'd left Artisans Alley, and wondered what it was he'd been intent upon.

"What's my civic duty?" Katie asked, and took a sip of Del's house wine. Not bad—and neither was the company. She'd ended up dominating the conversation, telling Seth about the problems at Artisans Alley, and how she wished Ezra had left the business in better shape—as well as her plans to remedy the situation, hardly giving him a chance to reply—until now.

"You could tell Detective Davenport that Ashby *may* have stolen statuary in his possession. It'll be up to him to look into it," Seth advised.

Katie nodded, glanced down at the remnants of her dinner, and then pushed it aside. The meatloaf had been pretty good, she admitted to herself, but the portion was overwhelming.

"Do you want dessert?" Seth asked.

"Only if you do."

He smiled. "I'm partial to cherry pie."

"À la mode?" she asked.

"Is there any other way to eat it?"

Betty, the night waitress, cleared away their plates, boxed up Katie's leftovers, offered coffee, and took their dessert orders. Katie went with the peanut butter mud pie. If she was going to be bad, she decided, she may as well do it with panache.

"How are you getting along with your artists? Have they calmed down since Saturday?" Seth asked.

"Pretty much. In retrospect, I'm surprised some of them voiced their concerns so passionately. There seems to be an enormous sense of apathy among them—no doubt brought on by Ezra's stringent rules and regulations. Still, I seem to spend a good portion of my day suspecting just about every one of them of murder. Peter Ashby's got my vote this evening. By tomorrow, who knows? What about you?" *About time you stopped talking about yourself,* Katie's inner voice chided.

"Small-town lawyers don't lead very exciting lives," Seth admitted.

"You were in court today," Katie reminded him. "That sounds riveting."

He shook his head. "It was a civil suit, not the stuff of movies or TV dramas. They decided to settle during recess. My client made out quite nicely."

"Have you always practiced law here in McKinlay Mill?"

"After I passed the bar, I spent a couple of years with one of the big firms in Rochester. In those days, I specialized in real estate law. Not very interesting. My father convinced me to take over his clients when he retired. I still do house closings, but more like two or three a month instead of one or two every day."

"Then you're a McKinlay Mill native?" Katie asked.

"Through and through. I was born in a hospital in Rochester, but my parents adopted me when I was three days old. Except for college, I've lived here all my life."

"Then I suppose you know all the local gossip?" Katie said.

"And a lot of privileged information," Seth agreed.

Elbows on the table, Katie leaned forward and rested her head on her hands. "What do you know about Andy Rust?"

"Angelo's Pizzeria," he said and frowned.

Betty returned with their desserts and filled their coffee cups before retreating to the kitchen.

Katie picked up her fork and scraped a minuscule layer of chocolate onto it, sampled it, and savored the exquisite flavor. "Mmmm," she sighed, then turned her attention back to the subject at hand. "I was curious about Andy's arrest record."

"What I know is hearsay. It happened when I was still in college," Seth said. "Apparently he stole a couple of cars and got sent to reform school."

"Andy said he didn't go to jail," she said,

remembering her conversation with the pizzamaker.

"He probably spent a night or two in the county juvenile hall before he was shipped off to The School for Boys at Industry. It used to be the local kid crime deterrent."

"I don't suppose you remember whose cars he stole?" she asked, taking a bigger bite of her sinful indulgence.

Seth swallowed, looking thoughtful. "That was years ago. But it seems to me one belonged to a teacher at McKinlay High School and the other was the coolest car in town: Ezra Hilton's classic Porsche."

Katie's fork dropped to the table with a clatter. "Andy stole Ezra's car?"

Seth nodded. "Not just *any* car. A nineteen fifty-nine Porsche three fifty-six A Convertible—sixteen hundred super."

Katie could only blink at his enthusiasm. She'd never considered a car anything more than a tool to get from Point A to Point B. "Is that a good car?"

"One of the best." Seth sighed, growing wistful. "It was silver with a red leather interior. Everything a teenaged boy—and a grown man—could lust after. Ezra bought it from a wrecker and he and his son spent years, and tons of money, restoring it."

"How do you know so much about it?"

"For years my dad tried to buy it from him. Ezra wouldn't sell."

"And Andy swiped the car?" Katie asked.

"He and a friend. They messed it up pretty bad," Seth said, taking a bite of his pie.

Andy hadn't mentioned that little piece of news. "Did Ezra press charges?" Katie asked.

"Against Andy? Yeah. I don't know about the other kid. Ezra was determined to teach Andy a lesson in responsibility. Funny, I haven't thought about all this in years."

But Katie wasn't listening. Her brain was whirling, too busy with possibilities. "What if Andy resented that lesson? What if—"

"Are you thinking maybe Andy Rust killed Ezra?" Seth shook his head, cutting another piece of pie with his fork. "Why would he wait for a decade and a half for revenge? And besides, Andy's owned the pizza parlor for over a year now. I know, because I represented him at the closing. If he held a grudge, and I don't think he did, why would he wait a year before killing Ezra?"

"To avert suspicion?" Katie asked.

"You've been watching too many TV cop shows," Seth said, amused.

Katie scraped another thin layer of chocolate and peanut butter onto her fork, trying to prolong the culinary decadence. "I did warn you I've spent the last few days thinking everyone's a murderer."

"You might be looked at as a suspect yourself," Seth admonished.

Katie gaped at him. "Me?"

"You had the most to gain. Or at least that's the

way Detective Davenport's going to look at it."

"Me?" Katie echoed again.

"Think of it from a police perspective. Because of Chad's ten percent investment, when you inherit half the business, you'll have a majority interest, meaning you get to call the shots. You got to quit a job you didn't like, and as the owner of your own business you get more respect, more prestige. People have been killed for a lot less. I wouldn't be surprised if Gerald Hilton hasn't already mentioned all this to Detective Davenport. Your favorite cop may also think you're feeding him all your suspicions to throw him off the track."

"That's ridiculous. I could never kill anybody. And my behavior has not been suspicious. I'm trying my darnedest just to keep Artisans Alley afloat. If you want suspicious, why hasn't anyone seen Gerald Hilton in town since last Saturday?"

"I have."

"When?" Katie demanded.

"This morning—he came to my office. He wants me to persuade you to sell the land to the hotel chain."

"And you didn't tell me?" Katie asked, forgetting about dessert and setting her fork aside.

"How is it relevant?"

"Oh, Seth—it proves he's got a motive for getting rid of his uncle. You said Ezra changed his will in a hurry. Had Gerald been the sole heir before that?"

Seth nodded. "I see what you mean." He polished

off the last of his pie. "I wouldn't worry about any of this, Katie. Stay focused on keeping Artisans Alley open—if that's what you want."

Katie digested that piece of halfhearted advice. "I have to save Artisans Alley to keep Victoria Square viable." She told him her plans to sell Artisans Alley and acquire the English Ivy Inn at the east end of the Square. "Selling the Artisans Alley's land for a hotel would kill the Square. McKinlay Mill needs Victoria Square if it's going to become a booming tourist mecca."

Seth gave her a funny, crooked smile. "You're forgetting about all the investments at the new marina."

"It doesn't hurt for a small town like McKinlay Mill to have more than one tourist attraction," she countered. And then proceeded to tell him exactly why. Funny how in only days, revitalizing Artisans Alley, and her plans to get it back on track, had become Katie's newest favorite subject. It was only Seth's stifled yawn over a third cup of decaf that finally shut her up.

"I'm sorry, Seth. You've had a much longer day than me," she apologized.

"Maybe, but I've enjoyed this evening. Perhaps one day I could take you out to a real restaurant for a gourmet dinner."

Their gazes locked. "That would be nice."

Seth reached for her left hand, covering it—and her wedding band—with his own.

"Real nice."

Thirteen

The afterglow from her dinner with Seth stayed with Katie through the night. Her sleep was dreamless and restful. She awoke, showered and dressed, and then searched her cupboards for apple or cherry pie filling and found none. It was just as well—pies were better made from scratch, and she'd missed cherry season by at least two months. Maybe she'd bake something else for Seth to show her appreciation for all his kindnesses. She'd have to think about it.

It would be a busy day at Artisans Alley. Katie had arranged with two of the artists to help her spruce up the outside of the building, and so she'd dressed appropriately in jeans and a sweatshirt. Fred Cunningham had also promised he'd come by to inspect the retail space. Katie hadn't looked at the locked rental spaces near the building's main entrance, and had no idea what state they might be in. She might have to tidy them up, as well. Still, she was determined to take in stride anything the day offered.

Her euphoria evaporated, however, when she returned from feeding Ezra's cat to find Gerald Hilton on Artisans Alley's doorstep. A solemn-faced uniformed man of about sixty—with gray hair, a trimmed, gray mustache, and a clipboard in hand—stood beside him.

Katie got out of her car, balancing a Tupperware container of home-baked oatmeal-raisin cookies fresh from her freezer, her purse, and the morning paper. She picked through her keys as she approached Artisans Alley's main entrance. "Good morning," she said, and managed to at least sound civil.

"Hi. I'm Ed Davis," the stranger said in introduction, holding out his hand. "McKinlay Mill's fire marshal."

Oh. Swell.

Katie set her purse down on the ground so she could shake hands, and then glanced at Hilton's smug face, fighting the urge to smack him.

"I hope I haven't kept you waiting long," she told Davis.

"As a matter of fact, you have," Hilton said. "I want my own set of keys. I do own forty-five percent of this operation."

Katie forced a smile. "Not until after probate." She picked up her purse, her own keys jangling as she opened the lock. "I assume this is a sneak inspection?" she said to Davis.

"Sort of, ma'am. Mr. Hilton here was concerned—"

"Yes, I'll bet he was," Katie said, cutting him off.

The two men followed her inside, waiting for her to hit the master switch that would bathe Artisans Alley in light.

"This looks old," Hilton said, tapping a knuckle against the dented gray metal circuit box. "Is it up to code?"

"Probably not," Davis said, "but then, an old building like this would be grandfathered in. As long as we find no blatant safety violations, Artisans Alley can continue to operate as usual."

Hilton frowned. It was just like him to try to get Artisans Alley shut down, Katie thought.

"How can I help?" Katie asked Davis, wanting to cooperate fully.

"I'd prefer to just wander around by myself, if you don't mind. We can talk after I've made my inspection."

"That would be fine." Katie led them through the lobby to the French doors of Artisans Alley, and unlocked it. Davis nodded and proceeded into the Alley. Hilton started to follow, but Katie grabbed him by the shoulder. "I'm sure Mr. Davis is capable of doing the job by himself."

"Oh, yes," Davis called over his shoulder. "I've been here many times before."

Hilton's glare could've singed Katie's eyebrows, but she managed to smile until Davis was out of earshot, then turned on her unwanted business partner.

"Go ahead, try to shut us down. But I will *not* sell

the building or the land until I'm good and ready to. I'll drag us both into bankruptcy before I do that."

"That's what you say now. But you'll cave. Everyone does eventually."

Katie straightened, stepping into Hilton's personal space. "Mr. Hilton, my ancestors were Scottish. My maiden name was MacDuff. A Scot never bluffs about money. And a Scot never backs down from a fight. If you want a fight over this, I'd be more than happy to give you one."

Their gazes locked for long, painful seconds. It was Hilton who looked away first.

"You won't be talking so tough after the inspection," he grumbled, turned, and plunked down on one of the folding metal chairs that had been in the lobby since the after-funeral gathering. Hilton opened his briefcase, took out his cell phone, and began to text, ignoring her.

Katie stormed off for the tag room; she'd had enough of the pompous little jerk. Anger pumped adrenaline through her. Her oatmeal breakfast lay heavy in her stomach. Okay, maybe she was bluffing. She had no intention of filing for bankruptcy —if she could possibly help it, that is. But Hilton didn't have to know that.

She tossed her coat at the rack in the corner— and missed. "Damn!" Kicking it, she snatched up the coat, slinging it over a peg before heading for the side entrance, to open it for the artists who might come in early to restock their booths. She abandoned the cookie container in the lounge and made coffee before finally making it to her office. Turning on the desk lamp, she was again confronted with the remaining mess from the break-in. Right now she wasn't up to a prolonged battle with Hilton. Right now she wished she could jump into her car, push the accelerator to the floor, and escape to the mountains, to the beach, anywhere but McKinlay Mill—a far cry from the woman who had stood up to the arrogant bully only moments before.

Chad's face, smiling at her from the framed photo on her desk, annoyed her. "*You* should be taking care of all this—not me," she growled. Then, feeling angry with herself for blaming him for this whole convoluted mess, Katie brushed her fingers against the pewter frame. She'd handle Hilton and whatever news the fire marshal gave her.

She would, because she had to.

Katie bent to pick up a stack of old receipts. Dated a decade before, they weren't worth keeping. She tossed them onto the already overflowing wastebasket, which toppled and fell.

Sighing, Katie picked up the mess and took it to the Dumpster that held recyclables out back. Back inside, she found Ida Mitchell, still clad in her raincoat and scarf, in the vendors' lounge standing near the coffeepot, contemplating one of the cookies. "Good morning, Ida," Katie said, forcing herself to sound cheerful.

Ida glared at her for several long seconds before turning her attention back to the container of cookies.

Katie shrugged and sailed past her, but was taken aback when she found another unwelcome visitor in her office, poking through a file folder marked "Rents." "Can I help you?" she snapped, not sounding at all helpful.

Peter Ashby whirled. "Do you always sneak up on people like that?"

"Well, you are in *my* office."

"And you invited me," he reminded her.

So she had, albeit for the previous day.

"Have a seat," Katie said, dropping into her chair.

Ashby remained standing, crossing his arms over his broad, sweatered chest. "What do you want for the barn rental?"

"To tell you the truth, I haven't given it any thought. First of all, I need to inspect the property and I can't. You have it locked. If the roof leaks, I'll get it fixed. That would protect your property and improve the quality of mine."

"Then you could ask for a higher rent."

"That, too," she conceded.

Ashby towered over her, his expression thoughtful as he considered her proposal.

"I don't think I want to continue renting the property. I'll need a couple of weeks so I can find another place to store my merchandise."

Katie nodded. "Fine. I'll charge you the same as

your regular per-week booth rent here at Artisans Alley."

"That's unfair. That's—"

"Probably a lot less than you were paying Ezra, and you know it."

Ashby didn't deny it. Still, he let out a harsh breath. "How's a guy supposed to make a living in this business with money-grubbers like you putting on the squeeze? Ezra did just fine, and you could, too. In fact, you ought to drop the booth rent now that you're letting low-end crafters in."

"Why?"

"Because by allowing them to sell new, made-in-China merchandise we've lost our prestige—our cachet."

Katie bristled. "I will not allow any vendor to bring in commercially made products. And do I need to remind you that you're selling resin statuary—copies of other people's work? That doesn't qualify as all that artistic in my book."

"The work is classic. Resin is just a modern medium."

"They're not your original work. I'm surprised Ezra even let you into Artisans Alley. And you always have the option of leaving."

Ashby's gaze hardened. "I may just do that."

"Fine. I've already got a waiting list of crafters eager for booths. Just give me a week's notice before you vacate," she said, and bent to pick up another stack of yellowed papers.

Ashby stood there for a moment, fists clenched, looking ready to explode, then abruptly turned and left the office.

Jerk.

It was then Katie noticed Ida still standing in the vendors' lounge, nibbling on a cookie. Had she heard the entire conversation? Did it matter? She was years behind in her rent—and a prime candidate for eviction. Witnessing Katie's conversation with Ashby might drive home the point that vendors who didn't pay couldn't stay. Instead of looking embarrassed at being caught eavesdropping, Ida continued to stand there and blankly stare.

"Do you need some help?" Katie asked, perhaps more sharply than she'd meant to.

Ida shook her head and scurried away.

Katie turned her attention back to her desk. She needed to calm down, and reached across the desk to turn on the radio. Was that Hank Williams, Sr., accompanied by twangy steel guitars, belting out a song of love gone wrong? Where had Ezra ever found an oldies country station?

Twirling the dial of the antique receiver, Katie found the local classical station. A mournful dirge that she couldn't identify filled her office, reflecting her mood, and for a moment she reconsidered her choice. Instead of changing it, she went back to the task of picking up and sorting the debris from her office floor.

Now Katie had another dilemma. Should she call

Davenport and tell him what Rose suspected about Ashby and the possibility of stolen cemetery art, or would it sound like sour grapes, considering the conversation she'd just had with him?

As soon as she thought she could string a rational sentence together, Katie picked up the phone and punched in Davenport's number. For once, she was happy to get his voice mail instead the man him-self. She recapped Rose's suspicions with an invitation for him to call if he had any questions. She knew he wouldn't.

The music had done its soothing trick, and by the time Ed Davis popped his head around her office door some ninety minutes later, Vivaldi had cheered her, and all the papers were in neat stacks—albeit on every flat surface.

"Can I speak to you?" Davis asked.

"Sure," Katie said, dreading the conversation. Could this dour-faced man really shut down Artisans Alley?

"The bad news is I found six safety violations," he said, handing her a sheet of paper with check marks dotting the appropriate squares. "The good news is, they're easily fixed, and you have seven days to comply."

Katie let out a breath as she studied the list. "What does this mean, daisy-chained extension cords?"

"Come on, I'll show you."

Katie followed the fire marshal to Booth 20.

"See how this vendor has an extension cord

plugged into a strip plug and then an extension cord coming out of that? It could cause an overload. You don't want that in a tinder-dry old building like this."

Katie frowned. "Yes, I see."

"We recommend each wall plug have a surge protector, with a fuse. If there's an overload, the fuse will trip."

"Let's take care of this right now," Katie said, and unplugged the offending extension cord. She had to move the lamp, which had been plugged into the second strip plug. Its cord was much too short to reach the wall socket.

"This is the most common problem," Davis said. "There are three booths that need attention. Probably new vendors. That's what usually happens."

Katie nodded. "I'll make a point to stress safety. And I've already been thinking about upgrading the electric throughout the building." Although she didn't know where on earth she'd find the money to do that. "What about the rest of the items on the list?"

Davis explained what needed addressing and how it should be done. Katie agreed she'd make the work a priority. All in all she was actually glad the fire marshal had come. She had too much at stake to let a couple of artists' carelessness give Hilton what he wanted.

"Have you spoken to Mr. Hilton about this?" Katie asked.

"Not yet. I'm sure he'll be quite disappointed. He told me he wants to shut down Artisans Alley and sell the property as soon as possible."

Katie studied the man's face, noticing the kindness in his gray eyes. "And you wouldn't like that?"

"Ma'am, I've lived in McKinlay Mill all my life. I've seen a lot of changes over the years, but I'd sure hate to see it lose its small-town flavor. There're plenty of hotels in Rochester. Plenty of marinas in the area, too. Building those things here would just bring a lot of transient people—maybe the wrong element, if you see what I mean."

Katie nodded, not sure she approved of his reasoning, but agreeing with his conclusions.

"I know Ezra Hilton was murdered," Davis continued, "but that was the first killing in McKinlay Mill in over forty-five years. I wouldn't want that to become commonplace."

"Amen," Katie agreed. She walked with Davis toward the exit. "Thank you for coming. And I'll see you on November fifth."

Davis nodded and stepped into the lobby. Hilton was on him like a pit bull. Katie abandoned Davis to his fate, unwilling to get into another verbal tussle with her soon-to-be partner.

Rose had arrived and was already stationed at the cash checkout, her ever-present romance novel open. "Vance is looking for you," she said without looking up from the printed page.

"Thanks, Rose."

Katie wandered back to her office, didn't find Vance there, and took a walk around the ground floor. Sure enough, Vance was at his own booth, straightening up after the previous day's customers.

"You wanted to see me, Vance?" Katie asked.

He turned smoldering eyes on her. "Why did you call my house and upset my wife yesterday?"

Taken aback, Katie could only stare at him. "Excuse me for calling the only living person who knows how Artisans Alley's mechanics work. I own it now, and I need to know, too. I didn't lead your wife to think you were here all day. I covered for you!"

It was Vance's turn to squirm. "Sorry. I didn't mean to jump down your throat. But Janey's a worrier, and she doesn't need that kind of stress."

What kind of stress? Katie was tempted to blurt out. *That she suspects her husband of cheating on her?* She decided to try tact first. "I'm sorry to hear about your wife's medical problems, Vance. But please don't use me or Artisans Alley as your alibi for whatever else you do in your personal life."

Vance's eyes bulged. For a moment he looked on the verge of erupting, then he took a breath. "You're right," he said, his voice tight. "It's just that the police harassed Janey to tell them where I was the night Ezra died. I . . . I didn't tell her."

"Did you tell Detective Davenport?"

"I had to."

Katie waited. Would he confide in her? Did she really want to know what he'd been up to?

Yes! If Vance had been where he belonged, helping Ezra close Artisans Alley, Ezra might still be alive! So many people's lives had been disrupted because of some thing—some act—Vance was too ashamed to admit.

Vance remained tight-lipped, standing rigid before her.

"I'm free all day," Katie said, trying to keep her voice neutral. "Can we set up a time to go over how things operate around here?"

"Let me finish tidying my booth, and then I'll meet you back in your office."

"Thank you." Katie turned.

"Wait."

Katie paused, looking over her shoulder.

Guilt and confusion paraded across Vance's worry-creased face. His expression said he wanted to unburden himself, yet he looked away.

"Whenever you're ready," Katie said, leaving it an open invitation to talk—on any subject.

Vance nodded, and then turned away to resume straightening his booth.

Katie strode away, heading for her office.

Back in the large showroom, Gerald Hilton stood at the main cash desk, his pudgy face flushed in anger.

"I told you, I don't have any say in how Artisans Alley is run," Rose said. "And if I did, I certainly wouldn't side with *you*. *You* want to close us down!"

Anger propelled Katie across the floor to face Hilton. "What do you think you're doing, badgering one of my vendors?"

"I'm simply trying to get her to see the logic in selling this fire trap."

Heat burned Katie's cheeks. "You are not to refer to Artisans Alley in that way."

"You can't tell me what to do," Hilton snarled.

"I just did."

Whoa, girl, something inside Katie warned. She took a breath to calm herself. It didn't work.

"Mr. Hilton, if Artisans Alley is hit by fire, flood, or locusts, you can bet I'll do everything I can to see that the person responsible rots in jail forever.

"As a future partner in this business, you'd be better off encouraging me to make it a success. You'll be entitled to almost half the profits without lifting a finger to help. Right now there are no profits. Maybe by the time probate is finished, there will be. In the meantime . . ." Katie paused, running out of steam. "Just go away."

Hilton bristled. "I—I . . ."

"Good day, Mr. Hilton." Katie turned on her heel and strode away.

"You haven't heard the last of this—or me!" he shouted.

Of that, Katie had no doubt.

Fourteen

It took a good ten minutes for Katie to calm down a distraught Rose, who'd been rattled by Hilton's fervor. By then, Katie's volunteer force of two, Dan Amato and Ed Wilson, had arrived to spruce up the outside of Artisans Alley. She dispatched them to the tunnel by the side entrance, where they were to pick up their tools. Meanwhile, Katie grabbed a box of heavy-duty black plastic garbage bags from her office, donned heavy work gloves, and, rake in hand, exited the building to join them.

Across the Square, a familiar car was parked outside Nona Fiske's quilt shop. Though white and unmarked, the Crown Victoria may as well have had a neon sign, strobe lights, and the siren going full blast, for it screamed COP CAR, and, of course, meant Detective Davenport was somewhere around Victoria Square. A thread of unease wriggled through her, which was ridiculous. She'd been complaining the detective wasn't taking Ezra's murder seriously enough, and now that he was, she felt uncomfortable.

Katie shook the thought away. "Okay, guys, let's get started." Armed with loppers and pruning sheers, Dan and Ed attacked the overgrown bushes, while Katie raked last fall's rotting leaves from around the landscaping that surrounded the front of the building. She had quite a pile accumulated when she looked up to see Detective Davenport and Gerald Hilton standing in the middle of the parking lot. Hilton was gesticulating wildly, pointing in Katie's direction, while Davenport scribbled notes in his pocket notebook.

Katie remembered her conversation with Seth the night before. Did Davenport really believe she might have killed Ezra to take over Artisans Alley for some kind of profit? Right now, she wasn't certain she could even pay herself a salary. Still, she didn't doubt Hilton was making a good case for Davenport to come right over and arrest her on the spot.

A suddenly nervous Katie fumbled for a black plastic bag and tossed the wet, gummy leaves into it. She willed herself not to look up again until the bag was nearly full to bursting. The two men still stood in the parking lot, deep in conversation. Katie's cheeks flushed as the worry grew inside her. She turned away, and dragged the heavy trash bag to the Dumpster out back, straining her muscles to heft it in.

When she returned to the front of the building, she saw Hilton's car was gone and found Detective Davenport conversing with Dan and Ed. They all looked up at her approach. Was it her imagination, or were the two Artisans Alley vendors look- ing at her in a much more critical light? She swallowed hard and willed herself to buck up. After all, she *knew* she hadn't killed Ezra Hilton.

"Good morning, Detective," Katie said, hoping she sounded welcoming—and not at all guilty.

"I have a few more questions for you, Mrs. Bonner." Did his voice sound just a little bit sinister?

Katie forced a smile. "I'd be glad to answer them." She gestured toward Artisans Alley's side entrance. "Shall we talk in my office?"

He nodded, and headed for the door.

"You're doing a great job, guys," Katie said—trying to sound enthusiastic, instead of terrified—before taking leave of her helpers. Once inside the door, she put the rake away and peeled off the gloves from her shaking hands, wondering what else she could do to stall for time before the detective began his inquisition. She paused in the vendors' lounge and checked the coffeepot. It was full—someone must have just made a fresh pot. The Tupperware container she'd brought in from home was nearly empty. The cookies had gone over well; only two remained. She wrapped them in a napkin and approached her office.

Davenport stood over her desk, studying the contents strewn across it.

"Sorry about the mess," Katie said. "I still haven't had time to clean up since the break-in on Sunday. Would you like a couple of oatmeal cookies? I made them myself. And I can get you a nice fresh cup of coffee to go with them."

Davenport straightened. "No, thanks, ma'am."

Katie managed not to cringe at that last word. "Sit down," she said, and gestured toward her office chair, taking the uncomfortable metal folding chair for herself. The tiny office really wasn't conducive to holding meetings. "What did you want to know?" she asked.

Davenport looked her straight in the eyes. "Your whereabouts last Thursday evening."

Katie hesitated. "I was home alone. I'd left my job at Kimper Insurance late and went straight home."

"Were there any witnesses?"

Katie shook her head, her stomach tightening.

"I spoke to your ex-boss." Davenport consulted his notes. "One Joshua Kimper. He didn't know what time you'd left Thursday evening."

"He was in Syracuse on business last Thursday. I locked up the office about seven o'clock and came straight home."

"Did you often work late?"

"Yes. We were a two-person operation. There was always work to be done, and I welcomed the overtime pay."

"Are you in financial trouble?" Davenport asked, his tone flat.

"No," Katie said, startled.

"May I ask why you needed the extra money?"

Katie sighed. "When my husband invested our

life savings in Artisans Alley, he left us flat broke. When Chad was killed several months later, I had no money to pay off his funeral expenses."

Again Davenport consulted his notes. "According to your bank, you paid off Collier's Funeral Home back in August. This is October."

What else did he know about Katie's financial situation? "I've been trying to shore up my savings."

"For a rainy day?"

"Something like that." She wasn't about to tell him that deep inside she still harbored the dream of opening the English Ivy Inn.

"Did any of your neighbors see you arrive home on Thursday evening?"

"I wouldn't know. I mean, I didn't speak to anyone."

Detective Davenport merely nodded. His cool-and-calm routine was really beginning to bother her.

"You could ask the management of the Winton Office Park to check their surveillance tapes," Katie suggested. "They might show what time I got into my car on Thursday night."

"I've already done that. I'm still waiting for that information," he said matter-of-factly.

Katie's throat constricted. Could he be seriously trying to pin Ezra's murder on her?

"Tell me again why you were here at Artisans Alley on Friday morning," the detective asked.

They'd already been over this at least three

times on Friday, but Katie dutifully repeated her story that she'd seen the police cars outside the building when heading for work that morning. Again, Davenport nodded. Wasn't he capable of showing any emotion? Or would that be even worse than his *I'm an android* personality?

"Look, Detective, I don't know what nonsense Gerald Hilton told you, but I had no reason to see his uncle dead."

"You did quit your job to take over the running of this place."

"I should've quit my job a long time ago."

"The timing does seem coincidental," Davenport insisted.

"Only to you and Mr. Hilton."

The detective consulted his notes once again. "What's the current value of Artisans Alley?"

"I have no idea. I've only briefly spoken to our accountant. I have an appointment for next week. The business has several loans in arrears. It looks like I'll spend the next couple of weeks just trying to keep us out of bankruptcy."

His eyes narrowed. "I understand there's an offer by a major hotel chain to buy the land Artisans Alley sits on."

"That's what I've been told. But I've found nothing to substantiate that claim."

"Who would have that information?"

"I have no idea. I've heard it might be the Radisson chain, but I have no proof of that."

Davenport grunted, closed his notebook, and stood. "Thank you for answering my questions, Mrs. Bonner. I'll be in touch."

Katie rose and followed him out into Artisans Alley, but Davenport retraced his steps to the side entrance, and left the building without another word. Katie stood in the open doorway and watched him go.

Dan and Ed had finished their pruning, and were filling more plastic bags with the detritus. The front of the building looked tidy and much more inviting, thanks to their efforts.

Detective Davenport climbed into his big white car, started the engine, and pulled out of the Victoria Square parking lot, leaving Katie nearly as rattled as Rose had been upon Gerald Hilton's departure.

Fred Cunningham called at nearly three o'clock to say he'd soon arrive with a measuring tape, his digital camera, and a stack of contracts to be signed, giving Katie and her two-man cleanup crew only enough time to pick up the worst of the rubbish left by former tenants. Katie left the guys to sweep the place and replace some fluttering fluorescent tubes. Within minutes of signing the contract, one of Fred's prospective clients arrived to inspect the empty retail space at Artisans Alley.

Katie found herself wringing her hands as Fred and the dancing school instructor wandered the space, talked about adding floor-to-ceiling mirrors, a ballet bar, new flooring, and upgrading the lighting, making Katie grateful such improvements wouldn't be her responsibility.

It was after five when the woman finally left, with no contract signed. By then, Katie had closed Artisans Alley and all her vendors had left for the day. She and Fred retreated to the vendors' lounge to talk.

"Well, what do you think?" Katie asked anxiously, and handed Fred the last, dregs-filled cup of coffee from the pot.

Fred accepted the cup, took a sip, and didn't wince. If nothing else, the man had intestinal fortitude. "She'll think about it overnight, and will be in my office before ten o'clock to sign the papers."

"You really think so?' Katie asked, already anticipating a new dribble of income for Artisans Alley.

"Not a doubt. Everything else she's looked at is substandard. You've got higher ceilings than most of the retail space in McKinlay Mill, giving her little ballerinas a lot more room to leap around."

"That's the first real piece of good news I've had since Ezra's death."

Fred smiled. "And it won't be the last. We'll have all that space rented by March, if not sooner," he said confidently.

March? That was five months away! How could Artisans Alley survive until then? How was Katie supposed to pay her bills without income? "That long?" Katie asked, her voice almost a squeak.

"I hope I can do it before then—but I don't want to mislead you either. It could take that long."

Katie's hopes sank.

Fred frowned. "Ezra left you a real turd, Katie, no doubt about it. But I know a good business-person when I see one. You'll turn things around in no time."

Businessperson? Oh well, at least Fred wasn't some misogynist brute. And Katie hoped he was right about her managerial skills.

"How well did you know Ezra?" Katie asked. "I mean, what if it wasn't just a robber who killed him?" Detective Davenport certainly didn't seem to believe that scenario.

Fred shrugged. "Ezra and I clashed on several occasions." He laughed. "We argued about that empty retail space on more than one occasion. I told him over and over again that I could rent it for him, but he always blew me off. He was too cheap to pay me a commission, and you can see how the place went downhill without that steady income."

Had Chad realized that simple truth, too?

Then what Fred said took on a more sinister meaning. They'd argued. For a full ten, foolish seconds, Katie wondered if telling Detective Davenport that tidbit would divert him from trying to pin Ezra's murder on her. Just as quickly, shame enveloped her. The commission on such a deal was hardly worth Fred's time—let alone risking his freedom for. In all her dealings with Fred during the time she'd hoped to purchase the old Webster mansion, she'd never had the feeling he was in business just for the money. He seemed to derive more pure pleasure in wrapping up a successful deal—any deal—than the income it produced, and she felt ashamed for even considering him a potential killer.

"What are you thinking, Katie?" Fred asked.

She took a deep breath and lied through her teeth. "I'm trying to imagine why anyone here in McKinlay Mill would want to see Ezra dead."

Fred laughed grimly. "The fact that he was a cantankerous bastard might have something to do with it. He pissed off a lot of people for a lot of years."

"He did?" That wasn't what Rose and some of the other vendors and Victoria Square merchants had said. They'd spoken about Ezra in reverent tones.

"Oh, sure," Fred said, and took a gulp of his coffee. "When his appliance store closed, he left a slew of creditors in the lurch. Same as when his hardware store went under. If he hadn't died last week, I'm betting Artisans Alley would've had to close before the new marina opens next summer. By now you've had a chance to look at the books, so wouldn't you agree?"

Katie nodded. "You're right. I'm not sure I *can* keep it open until then."

Fred smiled. "Then it seems I have more faith in you than you do."

Katie so wanted to believe him. "Really?"

His grin broadened. "Yes, really."

"I'm so glad you feel that way. It gives me hope. What I want to do is turn this place around so that I can buy the old Webster mansion. I've never given up hope that I can one day open the English Ivy Inn."

Fred's smile waned. "It might take a long time to do that."

"Maybe, but I'm nothing if not persistent."

Fred stared into his nearly empty cup, failing to meet her gaze. "I have every confidence in your abilities." He looked up. "I know you just quit your day job and are gambling on Artisans Alley to pay off for you, and I see success in your future. I never felt that way about Ezra, and believe me, Katie, I'm seldom wrong."

Katie felt a smile creep onto her lips, her hopes soaring once again.

Fred put his cup down and stood. "I'd better get going. And aren't you supposed to attend that emergency meeting of the Merchants Association tonight?" he asked.

Katie glanced at the clock. "Oh, gosh, I forgot all about it. And look at me—dressed in jeans and a sweatshirt."

"I don't think they'll care what you look like —they're eager for fresh blood."

"That sounds almost scary."

"A lot of the merchants are in almost as bad financial shape as the Artisans Alley vendors. Have you seen how many of the shops are empty on the Square?"

Katie had noticed, but it hadn't made that much of an impact on her until he'd mentioned it. Katie walked him to the door. "How did you know about tonight's meeting?"

"I know just about everything that goes on in McKinlay Mill," he admitted with a bit of a sly smile. He paused at the door. "Check my website when you get home. I'll have your retail space listed by then. And I'll really push it with my clients."

"I appreciate that, Fred. Good night."

She closed the door and thought again of calling Detective Davenport. If Fred really knew all the secrets in McKinlay Mill, he might know who held a grudge against Ezra and why.

But she didn't have time to do even that. As it was, she'd be late for the Merchants Association's meeting. Instead, she did a quick circuit around Artisans Alley, turning off the lights as she went, retrieved her coat, set the security system, and locked the vendor entrance. As she walked to her car, Katie looked over her shoulder at Artisans Alley, with its dual lampposts illuminating the entrance. Its tidied exterior did look more inviting, but all closed up and darkened, the sight of it made her shiver. Ezra had died inside. Someone had killed him. Someone she might even know.

That thought didn't make her feel at all secure, because whoever killed Ezra was probably still right here in McKinlay Mill, probably waiting to see if he or she would get away with it.

Fifteen

"Order. Let's come to order," Gilda Ringwald announced, banging her gavel on the Formica table. The chatter of voices quieted amid the clatter of cutlery on heavy restaurant china as Betty, the night waitress, finished clearing the table.

Katie glanced at the others surrounding her at the long table in the dreary, dark-paneled private dining room in the back of Del's Diner. Only the row of faux Tiffany lamps overhead broke the gloom. All ten of the surviving members of the Victoria Square Merchants Association gave Gilda their full attention.

Nona Fiske had deigned to honor them all with her presence, but she sat at the opposite corner of the table from her rival, Mary Elliott. Still, her frosty demeanor didn't put too much of a damper on the evening, and after an hour of polite conversation, Katie was pretty sure she could apply names to all the Association members' faces and identify their businesses.

Paula Mathews owned the Angel Shop—what Rose had described as a "death" store. Paula had opened her business, which was filled with angel figurines and items such as garden memorial stones, to help her through the loss of her mother after a long battle with cancer. Sue Sweeney owned Sweet Sue's Confectionary, the Square's candy shop, and often all of Victoria Square smelled heavenly of melted chocolate—that is, when it wasn't vying for prominence with the just-as-agreeable scent from Booth's Jellies and Jams, made by owner Charlotte Booth. Dennis Wheeler owned Wood U, a specialty shop that featured hand-crafted wooden products. Chad had bought Katie one of Dennis's oak-inlaid-with-maple jewelry boxes as a Christmas gift several years before.

"Our first sad duty," Gilda began, "is to elect a new president of the Association. Ezra Hilton's passing left a large hole in all our lives, but he would have wanted us to go on, to make Victoria Square the success we all know it can be."

"Hear, hear," said Conrad Stratton, owner of The Perfect Grape wine store.

"Any volunteers?" Gilda's gaze swept those assembled. Ten sets of guilty eyes darted away from her. "Surely someone must be interested?"

Katie tuned out the murmur of voices as Gilda cajoled each of the members, suggesting why they'd be perfect for the job, making Katie glad she was a newcomer. She traced her finger along the rim of her wineglass. The last thing she needed was yet another brick on her shoulders. She had a lot to learn, like the Association's rules, their long-term goals for promoting Victoria Square, and any marketing strategies that were already in place.

"Katie?" Gilda said.

Katie looked up. "Yes?"

Gilda's face lit up. "Then it's all settled. All in favor?"

Ten hands shot into the air.

"Wait a minute . . ." Katie protested, realizing exactly what Gilda had meant.

"It's unanimous. Katie Bonner is our new Association president." Gilda thrust the gavel at Katie, and then quickly took her seat.

Staring numbly at the wooden mallet in her hand, Katie found her throat closing. "No, I didn't understand. I wasn't paying attention. You can't ask me to—"

But Conrad was already on his feet, refilling the wineglasses. He raised his own. "A toast. May new blood bring us all success in the coming years."

New blood! Exactly what Fred Cunningham had said.

Katie stood on rubbery legs. "Uh . . . I don't know what to say. Except—I really don't think I'm up for this job."

"Nonsense," said Jordan Tanner, owner and chief pastry chef at Tanner's, McKinlay Mill's only bakery and coffee shop. "You were great at the vendors' meeting on Saturday. And I heard all about how you put Gerald Hilton in his place this morning."

Gossip sure traveled fast in McKinlay Mill.

Katie took a steadying breath. Okay, if they stuck her with this job, she wasn't going to wait to push the envelope.

"Thank you for this, uh, honor. However, I'm curious as to why one member of the Square has not been included in the Merchants Association. Can someone tell me why Andy Rust was never invited to join?"

The once-attentive faces found somewhere else to look.

"You're asking me to take on a lot of work. I won't do it if I can't at least expect honesty from my fellow association members."

Silence.

"Gilda?"

Gilda fiddled with a pink-stoned cocktail ring on the index finger of her left hand. "Pizza wasn't a staple of Victorian life. It just doesn't fit the image we want to project."

That sounded as phony as a televangelist's promise of salvation.

"Tracy?" Katie asked.

Tracy Elliott looked at Katie over the rim of her wineglass. "I wasn't a member when that decision was made."

"Well, surely someone was. Conrad?"

The wine merchant squirmed in the hot seat. "It's just that Mr. Rust is a convicted criminal. And the boys he employs are all local troublemakers.

We have to protect our businesses. Our insurance rates—"

"Are not influenced by Mr. Rust's business or his employees." Katie took in the guilty expressions on all the people at the table. "Won't somebody please tell me the truth? Otherwise, you're going to have to elect another president."

Nona Fiske's face was taut with disapproval. "Ezra did not want that—that criminal in our organization. And I can't say I blame him. That young hooligan stole and smashed Ezra's car!"

Katie's stomach tightened. "I did some checking the other day. Andy was sixteen years old when he stole Ezra's car. And he went to reform school for it. He also paid Ezra back and went to college. Fifteen years later, he hires kids who are at risk to keep them from making the same stupid mistakes he did. Andy votes and pays taxes and runs a profitable restaurant that makes a damned good pizza. Why *shouldn't* he be in the Merchants Association?"

Nona's eyes narrowed. "But Ezra said—"

"Ezra's no longer here," Katie said, her voice firm. "He may have held a grudge against Andy, but the man's done nothing to any of you. A lot of his customers are your customers. He's willing to pay his membership dues and become a contributing member of this association. Why can't you cut him some slack?"

Katie's gaze slipped across their guilty faces. What kind of control had Ezra exerted over these people? Had he kept them in line because he was an old curmudgeon, because his was the biggest, most visible business on the Square, making him the most powerful man in the Merchants Association?

Good grief, Katie realized with sudden insight, had they been afraid of Ezra?

Tracy Elliott broke the silence. "I move we give Mr. Rust a chance." Her gaze shifted to her mother, whose eyes flashed with disapproval, then back to Katie. "How about a six-month trial membership? If it works, he can become a full-fledged member."

"I suppose . . ." Gilda murmured. She, too, was looking at Mary.

"Let's put it to a vote," Katie said. "All those in favor, please raise your hands." She raised hers first; Tracy followed suit. Gilda, Conrad, Jordan, and his wife, Ann, raised their hands, too. After briefly hesitating, Sue, Dennis, and Paula followed suit.

Only Ezra's former lovers—Nona and Mary—hadn't voted to give Andy a chance. Of course, Tracy had voted in her mother's place. As partners in the business, would they have words about it later?

"Motion carried." Katie banged the gavel, momentarily enjoying her newfound influence. Yet it bothered her that Ezra had wielded his power over these people for his own selfish reasons. Chad's mentor had been just an ordinary man with foibles after all.

"Who's going to tell Mr. Rust?" Nona asked, her voice cold.

"I will," Katie volunteered. "Now, there's something else I'd like to discuss. Several lights in the parking lot are burned out. Whose responsibility is it to fix them, and how soon can we get it done?"

The strip of jingle bells rang cheerfully as Katie opened the plate glass door, but she wondered if she would be persona non grata as she entered Angelo's Pizza Parlor.

Wooden paddle in hand, a flush-faced Andy Rust looked up from the oven door he'd just closed. "Did you come in for a late-night snack?" he asked.

After the heavy meal at Del's, not even the aroma of pepperoni could entice Katie.

"Not tonight," she said, feeling better at his neutral greeting. Maybe she'd imagined the hostile look he'd given her the night before. Now he just looked harried. "Have you got a couple of minutes?"

"A couple," Andy said. Then to prove him wrong, the phone rang. While he took the order, Katie made herself at home on one of the green plastic patio chairs he kept for waiting customers.

Andy hung up the phone, grabbed a round of dough from the waiting rack, and then started making a pizza. "Two of my employees called in sick tonight. It's been a madhouse since five o'clock. What can I do for you?"

"I just came from the Merchants Association meeting. I have good and bad news."

Andy frowned.

"The good news is you've been accepted. The bad news is you have to pay your dues—by first thing Monday morning."

"They're not going to hose me, are they?" he asked, sounding less than thrilled.

"I convinced them to prorate it. Your first installment is for November and December. The organization collects dues for the coming year in January. They figure everyone has a good holiday season and can best afford it then."

Andy shrugged. "Makes sense."

"*You* got off easy. I got elected to take Ezra's place as head of the Association."

Andy's eyes twinkled. "How'd that happen?"

Katie told him, making light of the situation. What other way was there to look at it? Andy listened, his expression neutral. "You do seem to be living under that famous Chinese curse," he said at last.

Katie blinked in confusion.

" 'May you live in interesting times,' " he explained.

"You got that right. My entire life has turned around in the last week."

"Has it only been a week since old man Hilton was killed?" Andy asked.

Katie nodded. "Is that what you called him when you were a teenager?"

"Everybody did. He wasn't exactly the nicest man in town. At least from a kid's perspective. He never bothered me since I bought the shop."

"No, but I'm afraid it was Ezra who blackballed you from the Merchants Association. Apparently he held a grudge."

Andy shrugged. "There's nothing I can do about that now. But I can be an asset to the Association now that he's gone."

His words sounded so cold. But then, Katie reminded herself, she'd been looking for slights and grudges or anything else to explain why someone would kill the old man. She had plenty without suspecting Andy, too.

Time to drop the other shoe.

"There is kind of a catch," Katie admitted. "Your membership is provisional—on a six-month trial basis. I'm afraid not everyone in the Association was willing to welcome you with open arms."

Andy straightened, his expression hardening. For a moment Katie was afraid he might decide joining the group wasn't worth the trouble.

"Then I guess it's up to me to prove them wrong."

"Thank you," she breathed. "I was hoping you wouldn't let other people's pettiness drive you away."

Andy's smile was ironic. "It would take more than that to scare me off."

The phone rang again. Andy's plastic-gloved hands were covered in cheese.

"I'll get it," Katie volunteered, and darted behind the counter. Finding a pad and pencil, she took down the order, read it back, then looked at Andy for a time estimate.

"Twenty minutes pickup, an hour delivery."

She repeated the bad news. "Pickup!" she said, and thanked the customer for calling Angelo's.

"Not bad," Andy said, topping his latest creation with broccoli. "You any good at making pizza?"

Katie hadn't planned on taking a crash course in pizza construction, but by the end of the evening she could at least make a credible job of it. And she'd definitely cemented a friendship with Andy Rust. That, in itself, had made the evening a success. She'd been grateful for the time spent with him. The busywork had helped keep at bay the growing worry that Detective Davenport was spending a little too much time looking into her background and lack of a concrete alibi for the night of Ezra's death.

Though tired from her long day, Katie had lain awake for more than two hours, staring at the ceiling, thinking about the day's events, and wondering if Detective Davenport was planning to arrest her in the not-too-distant future. Meanwhile, Mason contentedly snoozed at her side. Though Seth was a general-practice attorney, perhaps she should ask him to recommend a good criminal attorney.

This was insane. Katie had never so much as run a stop sign, and now there was the possibility she could be arrested—albeit on only circumstantial evidence—for murder. How had her life degenerated so quickly in less than a week?

Artisans Alley was more of a liability than an asset, and perhaps she had been monumentally stupid to quit her job to take on the task of bringing it back to viability. Only an idiot would kill for such a sinkhole. Still, she knew she hadn't killed Ezra—was the Sheriff's Office so focused on a conviction that they didn't care whom they accused?

The sky was still dark when Katie visited Ezra's house to feed his cat the next morning. The little tabby had been ecstatic to see her, purring so loud and hard that Katie feared the cat would explode with joy. It almost broke her heart to leave the cat alone and head back to the Alley. Minutes later, she unlocked Artisans Alley's back door. She hadn't planned on arriving at the crack of dawn, but after tossing and turning for several hours she'd decided Mr. Sandman wasn't going to make a visit after all.

Despite her fatigue, Katie felt ready to start work and hit the light switch inside the back door, illuminating the vendors' lounge. Ezra hadn't made the room too hospitable, and maybe that was the point. If he was shorthanded, why make the lounge a comfortable respite? Still, surely Vance-the-woodworker could fix the rickety maple table with its six mismatched chairs that sat under the wan yellow light from a naked sixty-watt bulb. The hole of a room felt chilly, unwelcoming. Should she waste heat and turn on the blowers, or wait until opening and hope the body heat of her anticipated customers would warm the cavernous building?

Economics won out over personal comfort. Katie decided she'd activate the blowers ten minutes before opening. Tomorrow, she'd bring along an extra sweater.

Her office seemed even colder, even more unwelcoming. Of course, it was still Ezra's space. Painted a drab institutional green, it reminded Katie of a military prison—or perhaps a mental ward from the nineteen thirties. A warm peach color would lift her spirits. Yes, she'd paint it peach—and the file cabinets, too. And soon. And she'd brighten the north wall with one of Chad's big floral paintings.

Although it had been days since the break-in, Katie's office still looked like a disaster zone. Getting any work done during retail hours was proving difficult. She could see her day off—Monday—as the only time she'd ever accomplish anything of significance. So be it.

"I need caffeine," Katie told herself, remembering the coffeepot in the vendors' lounge. She secured water from the ladies' room tap, measured

Maxwell House's best into the filter basket, and hit the on switch.

Still reluctant to attack the mess, Katie decided to take a scenic tour of the place while the coffee dripped. Maybe she'd think of some inexpensive way of brightening the place. Threading her way through the darkened booths, with only the emergency lighting to illuminate the gloom, Katie groped her way to the main circuit box out front.

Why had Ezra enforced a policy that required all the booths to be the same drab brown? Well, that, too, would change. She'd give the artists a free hand in decorating their spaces. That would perk up the place and encourage sales. She'd call Edie Silver to see if she had any other ideas . . .

Katie opened the breaker box, throwing the master switch. The inside of Artisans Alley glowed. Light for heat was an acceptable compromise, although she'd literally pay for it when the electricity bill came.

Humming tunelessly, Katie turned and started back to her office along the main aisle but stopped abruptly, the breath catching at the back of her throat.

Peter Ashby lay on his back on the rumpled, dingy carpet, his dull eyes staring at the ceiling, his neck twisted at an impossible angle.

Sixteen

"I'm getting tired of driving all the way out here every day," a weary Detective Davenport said to no one in particular.

More than an hour had passed since Katie had called 911. Peter Ashby still lay on Artisans Alley's grubby carpet, still dead.

"I'm sorry to have inconvenienced you, Detective. This isn't how I planned to spend my morning either. And Artisans Alley will lose another day of revenue because of it."

Davenport frowned. "I wouldn't have thought you so coldhearted, Mrs. Bonner."

Katie blinked, ashamed at her thoughtless outburst. All the same, she hadn't liked Ashby, and the possibility that he might have vandalized graves still angered her. "I'm concerned for our artists," she amended. "Because now we'll have to close for the day."

"And reopen to hordes of morbid curiosity seekers tomorrow. Maybe you should hire a clown to entertain the folks." Davenport slapped his notebook closed and stepped away to speak with the medical examiner. "How long would you say he's been dead?"

The ME straightened. He looked like the

stereotypical nerdy scientist, complete with crew cut and Coke-bottle glasses. Katie wouldn't have been surprised if the man was named Poindexter. "Rough guess—between ten and twelve hours."

"And what would you say killed him?" Davenport asked.

The man squinted up at the rail above. "The fall. Broke his neck, as you've probably already surmised. The autopsy will make it official."

"And the classic question," Katie said. "Did he fall, or was he pushed?"

"There were definitely signs of a struggle upstairs," Davenport said, staring directly at Katie. "And you say you locked up about six last night?"

"Yes."

Davenport nodded. "Who else has keys?"

"Only me . . ." Katie let the sentence dangle. "Well, I'm not really sure. Vance Ingram might have a set. The photographer who rents the space above the lobby has a key to the main entrance, but shouldn't have one to Artisans Alley. Other than that . . ." Something cold clamped around her heart. "I really don't know."

"There were no keys on the body," the ME volunteered.

Davenport turned back to Katie. "Is Ashby's car in the lot?"

"I didn't see it," she said, "but I came in the back entrance; it could be in the Victoria Square lot. I didn't think to look."

"It might be a good idea to change your locks to keep anyone else from using the place after hours," Davenport advised.

She nodded. Why hadn't she thought of that herself?

Davenport stared at the body on the floor. "Is this the man you left the message about yesterday morning?"

"Yes. Have you had a chance to look into his background?"

"Not yet. It'll be on the top of my to-do list when I get back to the office."

Typical, Katie thought.

Davenport stared straight into Katie's eyes, and didn't even look at his notebook as he flipped it open once more. "Now, let's recap how you spent last evening."

Katie sighed, crossing her arms to hug herself. She never had gotten around to turning up the heat. "Fred Cunningham—he's looking for clients to rent out unused retail space for me—was here with me until about six o'clock. After he left, I locked up and then drove over to Del's Diner for a dinner meeting with the Victoria Square Merchants Association. It lasted until nearly nine thirty. I came back to the Square—"

"What for?" Davenport interrupted.

"To talk to Andy Rust at the pizza parlor."

"Did you see any lights on in Artisans Alley?" Davenport barked.

"I didn't look. If I had seen something out of the ordinary, I certainly would have checked up on it."

Davenport nodded. "You said you spoke with Mr. Rust," he prompted.

"He was shorthanded. I helped him make pizzas until after midnight."

"And you have witnesses who can corroborate all of this?"

"Of course—Andy and several of his delivery boys."

Davenport frowned. It seemed to be his normal expression. He took a couple of paces away from Katie, then turned back to face her. "Did Mr. Ashby have any enemies?"

"How would I know? I only met him six days ago—and I wasn't impressed by his charm or honesty." Katie's gaze drifted down to the dead man once again. In death, he didn't look half as hunky. She remembered that Ida Mitchell had heard her loud discussion with Ashby the day before. As Ida wasn't happy with her just now, it might be better if she volunteered that information.

Davenport listened—with no discernible expression on his unblinking face—to her version of what happened.

"Did you see Mr. Ashby after that?"

"No. He was so obnoxious I half expected it was Ashby who killed Ezra. He had the motive, the opportunity—"

"The motive?" Davenport asked, frowning.

"Well, maybe." Katie repeated Rose's theory that Ashby's resin copies of cemetery statuary could have been made from stolen originals—and suggested he check for reports of graveyard vandalism locally and in Ohio, where Rose thought Ashby might have come from. Although Davenport listened, he looked skeptical.

"Ma'am, please leave the speculation—and the investigation—on these deaths to us. Unlike the general public, we actually *do* know what we're doing."

Katie bristled under Davenport's accusing glare. "I beg your pardon, Detective. As Artisans Alley's manager I have a pretty good idea of what's going on around here. At least I've been asking questions, whereas you—"

Shut up. Shut up! Katie's better judgment screamed. Hadn't Seth warned her she could be considered a prime suspect? And now Detective Davenport had found her standing over yet another body.

"I'm sorry, Detective. I'm upset. I'm new to managing a business of this size, and Artisans Alley has a precarious bottom line. Two deaths in one week haven't helped."

Davenport simply stared at her, his pudgy, unattractive face and dull, shark-like eyes revealing no emotion. "I'm sure it's all been extremely upsetting to you, Mrs. Bonner. Why don't you just run along to your office like a good girl and let us professionals do our jobs."

The others all seemed to wince.

Run along? Good girl?

Katie clenched her fists. Of all the pompous, infuriating, condescending, male chauvinist pigs she had ever met—

Yet Katie also knew that annoying Davenport was not in her own—or Artisans Alley's—best interests.

Katie spoke through gritted teeth. "Maybe I'll just do that." Turning on her heel, she stormed off.

Squelching the impulse to slam her office door, Katie closed her eyes and counted to ten. That didn't work, so she counted to twenty. Looking around the room reminded her of the abundance of filing she still had to sort through. Frustration set in. What should she keep? What if she threw away important papers?

She sat down and sifted through the first pile, discarding anything older than three years. What she needed was a good cry.

No. That would be just what a man like Davenport would expect of a woman.

Barring that, what she needed was to blow off some steam. Maybe she could buy a punching bag. Could Edie Silver paint a reasonable facsimile of Detective Davenport's face on one? Inflicting a left hook and a right jab on a dummy might not teach the real imbecile a lesson, but it would sure make Katie feel better.

I'm only here because of the English Ivy Inn. I have to get through this in order to—she eyed the ugly khaki-colored walls and winced—*make this place a success so I can finally get what I want.*

That said, she still wanted to punch Davenport.

After a few minutes Katie felt rationality begin to set in once again. What she really needed was to talk. Only there were very few people in her life that she felt she could confide in.

And just whom should she trust?

Andy? Seth?

Katie liked both men—a lot. But what she needed now was a woman's perspective. Rose Nash had been great, treating Katie like a daughter, but Katie needed a younger, more businesslike confidant. Someone familiar with the kinds of problems she was encountering.

Tracy Elliott had gone against her mother's wishes by voting to let Andy Rust in the Merchants Association. Had Katie put her in an awkward position, or did that mean Tracy was serious about using every available resource—people and assets—to make Victoria Square an economic success?

It would probably be hours before the police and sundry professionals would pack up Ashby's body and leave, Katie realized. In the meantime, she decided to call a locksmith to make sure only she had access to Artisans Alley. After that, she'd head straight across the parking lot to seek out some woman-to-woman talk.

A knocking at the back door drew Katie's attention. She glanced at her watch. It was ten minutes past time to open Artisans Alley for the vendors who wanted to restock their booths. Why hadn't she thought to call those scheduled to work? Then again, when would she have had time to do that? As she got up from her desk, she figured she should make signs to tape on all the door to let them—and Artisans Alley's customers—know the store would be closed yet again.

The knocking at the back door intensified. Katie turned the bolt and opened the door. Ida Mitchell stood on the top step, bundled up in her raincoat once more, her hand poised to knock again. "Why are all the doors locked? Why are police cars taking up all the good parking spaces?" she demanded.

"There's been an . . . an accident," Katie said. "Peter Ashby was killed. We won't be open today."

"But we were closed on Tuesday, too," Ida said belligerently.

"I know. But the police said we can't reopen today."

"That's not fair," Ida cried.

"I'm sorry, but there's nothing I can do about it."

Ida pushed past Katie, barging into the vendors' lounge, where she pulled out one of the chairs at the table, and sat down. "I don't have anywhere else to go. What am I supposed to do all day?"

"I'm sorry, I don't know." Since Ida had decided to sit a spell, Katie decided she might as well ask her some questions. "Did you know Peter Ashby?"

"Who?"

"The man who was killed here last night. He was a vendor."

"What number was he?"

"Number sixty-four."

Ida nodded knowingly. "Resin statuary. He didn't get many tags, but when he did—they were whoppers. Hundreds of dollars." Did she know all the artists by their booth number and merchandise rather than their names? "He didn't talk to me much," Ida continued. "He'd come into the tag room and grab his tags before we were even closed. He never filled out a new sheet, and the rules were that if you took your tag paper before Sunday night, you had to put in a replacement page."

Okay.

"I don't understand why people can't follow the rules. There are reasons for rules, you know," Ida said emphatically.

She'd given Katie a perfect segue to talk about another important subject. "Speaking of rules," she began. "Ida, is there a reason you haven't paid your rent in almost a year?"

Ida looked up, surprised. "I rarely sell anything. How can I pay rent if I don't sell anything?"

"But it's important that you do pay your rent.

That is, if you wish to remain a vendor here at Artisans Alley."

Ida shook her head impatiently. "No, no. You don't understand. I had an arrangement with Ezra. He said I could stay as long as I took care of the tag room. I told you, I take that job very seriously."

"Yes, and you do it well. But . . . things have changed around here since Ezra's death."

"I don't understand."

"Ida, Artisans Alley is in deep financial trouble."

"How does that affect me?" she asked, totally without guile.

"I'm afraid we're going to have to come to a new arrangement, or I'll have to ask you to leave."

"What kind of arrangement would that be?"

Katie sighed, exasperated. "You're going to have to start paying your rent on a weekly basis, just like everybody else."

"But I'm on a fixed income. I can't pay rent every week."

"Then I'm afraid I have no alternative but to ask you to leave."

Ida's eyes widened in horror. "But I don't want to."

"I'm sorry. But it's not fair to the artists who *do* pay their rent. You see that, don't you?" she said in her kindest voice.

"No," Ida said adamantly. She jumped up from the table. "I think you're picking on me. You think I'm ugly and old and that you can single me out because of it. Well, I won't let you. You can't make me leave. Nobody can!"

And with that—she turned and stormed out of Artisans Alley.

"It was *her!*" Ida Mitchell proclaimed and pointed her right index finger directly at Katie, who suddenly felt like a felon in a lineup. In reality, she stood in the aisle where Ashby's body had lain just minutes before. Ida must've snagged Detective Davenport as he'd been about to leave the building and told him what she'd witnessed the day before.

Katie swallowed, determined to keep her cool. She didn't know what kind of hysterical report Ida had made—but at least she'd had a chance to tell her side of the story first. She could only hope Davenport would take her words at face value and dig to find Ida had a reputation as the Alley's resident kook.

"Thank you, Miss Mitchell," Davenport said kindly. "Deputy Schuler will walk you out to your car."

Schuler dutifully stepped forward and waved a hand in the direction of the exit.

Ida caught sight of Katie again. Her face twisted into an ugly sneer and she actually stuck out her tongue before she turned and stalked off.

It took all of Katie's self-control not to do likewise.

Davenport turned back to face Katie. "Would

you tell me again about that argument you had with Mr. Ashby?"

Katie nodded, resigned.

"Let's go sit down somewhere," Davenport said, and gestured in the general direction of the vendors' lounge.

Katie led the way. Once there, she pulled out a chair. Davenport took the one on the opposite side of the table. In the dim light, it might as well have been a stark interrogation room like the ones she'd seen in so many TV dramas. That made her even more determined to redecorate and make the room a much more cheerful place.

In the meantime, she met Davenport's dull eyes.

"About that argument with Mr. Ashby," the detective prompted.

Katie sighed. It had only been a few hours since she'd found Ashby, but it seemed like days. "I found him in my office, poking through my files," she began.

"And that made you angry?" Davenport asked.

He was leading the witness—not at all kosher in a court of law, but then, they weren't in a courtroom. Katie had no lawyer here to protect her interests. All she had was the truth.

"I was annoyed," she clarified. "Mr. Ashby was belligerent toward me—at the vendors' meeting on Saturday, when I found him at Ezra Hilton's barn on Tuesday, and then yesterday when he told me he would vacate that property within two weeks."

Davenport nodded, and consulted his notepad before speaking. "You said Mrs. Nash was suspicious of him and his merchandise. She's the one who owned the pink crystal, right—the rock that likely killed Ezra Hilton?"

Did Rose's suspicions make her look even guiltier? She hesitated before answering.

Davenport spoke first. "You realize none of this looks good, Mrs. Bonner."

"What are you saying, Detective, that you think either I or Rose Nash had a motive to kill Mr. Ashby? If so, what would it be?"

"It's not up to me to ascertain guilt or innocence. That's for the courts. It's my job to present evidence. Everything you and Mrs. Nash have told me could be nothing more than a carefully crafted story to divert suspicion."

"It's the truth."

"As *you* see it," he said.

Katie didn't bother to deny that. "I don't know how Peter Ashby got in here after hours. I don't know why someone would want to kill him. I didn't know him well, but I suspect he wasn't a man of good character. It's up to you to find out if that's true." She stood. "Now, unless you've got more questions for me, I have a business to run and you have an investigation to continue. I suggest we both get back to work."

Davenport stared at her for long, painful seconds, before he, too, rose and, without a backward glance, left the vendors' lounge.

Katie steadied herself against the table, afraid her knees might buckle if she moved too quickly. Had she helped her case or had she just made a really big mistake?

Seventeen

Stu Carter made the trip from Rochester with a truck full of everything needed to change all the locks in Artisans Alley. Only one lock escaped his attention, that of the photography studio above the lobby, and Katie would have to provide her tenant with a new key to the main entrance.

Katie winced at the grand total—including tax —at the bottom of Carter's invoice, but she wrote out a check and handed it to the locksmith before walking him to the main exit and throwing the brand-new dead bolt after him.

Lunchtime had been and gone, but she didn't feel the least bit hungry. It was human companionship she craved, and she knew just where to look for it.

Late-afternoon diners sipped tea from bone china cups, nibbling savory delectables as Katie entered the cheerful Tea and Tasties tea shop. Once again, the aroma of cakes, tarts, and fresh-baked bread nearly lifted her off her feet.

A ponytailed high schooler in a white skirt and blouse, her frilly apron piped in pink, looked up from her order pad, flashing Katie a braces-filled smile. "Have a seat. I'll be right with you."

"I'm not here for lunch. I'm looking for Tracy Elliott," Katie said.

"Oh, hang on."

The girl finished taking an order from two gray-haired ladies in printed silk dresses, then signaled for Katie to follow her through the small dining area into the kitchen.

Dressed in matching waitress garb, Tracy looked years younger. She turned, giving Katie a welcoming smile. Behind her at the center island, Mary's usually pleasant face collapsed into a glower.

Unnerved by Mary's reaction, Katie glanced back at Tracy. "I'm sorry to interrupt, but I was hoping you might have a few minutes to talk. I could use a sympathetic ear."

Tracy gave her a kindly smile. "I'm just about done with my shift. Let me take out this order, then Janine can finish up for me."

"Sure thing," said the young woman, no doubt eager to collect Tracy's tips.

Balancing three plates on her arm, Tracy headed back into the dining room.

Mary carefully arranged sandwiches on a plate, adding a parsley garnish, then handed it to the girl. "That tea will be stewed if you don't serve it soon."

"I'll be right back for it," Janine said, and started for the dining room.

Katie cleared her throat. "Hello, Mary."

"Good afternoon."

An arctic breeze would have been warmer than that greeting.

"I hear Peter Ashby's been killed," Mary said, her ice blue eyes boring into Katie's.

"It could've been an accident," Katie said, but even she didn't believe it.

Tracy reappeared, already untying the apron at her waist. She hung it on a peg on the wall. "I'm going upstairs to check the e-mail orders. Call if you need me, Mom," she said, and motioned a relieved Katie to follow her up the narrow back stairs.

Skylights helped brighten what could have been a claustrophobically small attic room. Pale pink walls and cozy, incandescent light blanketed the room in warmth. Katie's mouth dropped and her breath caught in her throat as she took in a painting of multicolored pansies that graced the south wall: no doubt about it, it was one of Chad's unframed canvases. And very much like the one he'd described in his journal. Something he'd said he'd planned to paint as a gift for Katie. She turned away, taking in the rest of the room.

In the middle of the finished space sat an old oak table, dominated by a computer and piled with papers, a coffee mug, and a haphazard stack of books. The north wall consisted of shelving segmented into pigeon holes, presumably crammed with orders, receipts, and other paperwork.

"Welcome to the empire," Tracy said with a flourish, and flopped onto the ergonomically correct padded office chair in front of her make-shift desk. Kicking off her thick-soled white shoes, she leaned her head back. "Thank God for high school co-op students."

Katie blinked, sinking into an overstuffed brown leather club chair directly in front of Tracy's desk.

"I still have to put in a couple of hours a day waiting tables," Tracy continued, "but since Janine came to work for us, I've been able to catch up on our Internet orders. You ought to get a high school kid to help out at Artisans Alley."

"I—I could sure use someone to help me wrestle Ezra's files into order. Thanks for the idea."

Tracy studied Katie's face. "Is something wrong?"

"No," she said, and half turned. "The picture—"

"I bought it at the Alley. Pretty, isn't it?"

"Yes. It—it was one of my late husband's."

"Really? He did lovely work."

"Yes, he did," Katie said, feeling foolish at her reaction to seeing the painting. He'd most likely sold it because it paid more than a week's rent. He probably figured he'd do another, similar picture and Katie would never know. Still, it was lovely, and he had originally intended it to be for her . . .

"But that's not what you came here to talk about, is it?" Tracy asked.

Katie shook her head. "I found Peter Ashby dead this morning."

"So we heard," Tracy said and shuddered. "Broken neck?"

Katie nodded. "He was my least favorite artist,

or at least one of them," she said, remembering her little altercation with Ida. "But good Lord, what a way to die."

"At least it was quick," Tracy said, sounding sensible, if not compassionate. "Do you think it was an accident?"

"The naive part of me wants to. The logical part of me says 'no way.' "

"Did the cops give you a hard time about it?" Tracy asked.

"Only one: Detective Davenport and I just don't get along. But I had no motive to kill Ashby."

Tracy's eyes widened. "I think he was hoping you did. That mean old goat grilled Mom and me for almost half an hour this morning when we really needed to be setting up to open."

Something in Katie's chest tightened. "He grilled you? About what?"

"You, of course."

Katie's mouth dropped open. "Me?"

Tracy nodded. "He wanted to know at precisely what time you arrived at Del's last night. What was your mental state? Were you flustered? When did you leave?"

"That's just swell," Katie groused. "He takes an active interest in the case only when he thinks he can pin the murders on me!"

"You wanted him to work harder at his job— you got your wish."

For a moment Katie wasn't sure if Tracy was

kidding or serious. "I barely knew either of those men. And Peter Ashby was not a nice person."

Tracy cocked her head to one side, her eyes flashing, her smile sly. "Do tell."

Katie did. In detail, answering all of Tracy's questions, wondering if her new friend had missed her calling to be either an investigative reporter or a prosecutor.

Eventually Tracy's mini-interrogation wound down and she frowned. "What you've told me sure paints Ashby in a bad light. But despite being disagreeable, it's unlikely he killed Ezra. His death is proof of that. So who do you think did it?"

Katie sank farther into her chair. "I haven't got a clue. And a week after Ezra's murder, I don't think the Sheriff's Office does either."

Tracy leaned forward, her eyes widening in anticipation. "Okay, spill the dirt—what was it like finding Ashby?"

"Besides scaring the hell out of me?" Katie shrugged. "He wasn't bloody or anything, just . . . dead. He'd been a damned handsome man. Too bad he had the personality of a shoehorn."

Tracy struggled to stifle a laugh, clearing her throat. "You noticed that, too?"

"How could I miss it?" Katie sank back in her chair, crossing her legs. "Hey, I wanted to thank you for supporting me last night at the Merchants Association meeting."

"You mean about Andy?"

Katie nodded, a sudden tightness creeping into her muscles. Something about the way Tracy said Andy's name—a certain familiarity—threw up a red flag.

"Ezra wasn't about to give Andy a break," Tracy continued. "He could be kind when he wanted to be, but I made up my mind a long time ago never to cross him."

"I didn't know Ezra well, but I guess he scared me a little, too." Did Katie dare press her new friend about the pizza man?

Why not?

"Until Davenport finds out who's killing people, I don't know who to trust. Is Andy Rust reliable? Do you know him at all?"

Tracy seemed to tense. "We were in the same graduating class. I guess I've known him since childhood," she said guardedly.

As evasive an answer as Katie had ever heard.

Tracy knew more than she was telling, but suddenly Katie wasn't sure she wanted to know how well the woman knew Andy.

And why should Katie feel possessive toward the newest member of the Merchants Association? She'd only met Andy some six days before. Yet spending several hours with him, working with him the evening before, she kinda . . . sorta . . . wanted to know him better.

Guilt pressed down on her once again. Chad hadn't even been dead a year. Despite their separation, they'd still been husband and wife, and close to a reconciliation. For the past week she'd done nothing but entertain thoughts of other men: Andy . . . Seth. What in the world was wrong with her?

Loneliness! some inner part of her wailed. She was so god-awful lonely she could scream.

"Yoo-hoo! Earth to Katie!" Tracy said, a crooked smile warming her lips.

"Sorry. I kind of zoned out for a minute there." Katie sighed, depression settling over her. "I haven't exactly been winning friends and influencing people this past week. Half the artists want to rub *me* out. I've alienated Detective Davenport, and your mother, too."

Tracy sobered. "Mom doesn't dislike you. In fact, she admires the way you've jumped in to save Artisans Alley. That's what Ezra would've wanted. It's just—" She stopped, exhaled, and looked away. "Mom gets upset when anyone defends Andy Rust."

"Because he stole Ezra's car all those years ago?"

Tracy met Katie's gaze. "No, because he divorced me."

Eighteen

Startled, Katie blinked at Tracy, her heart suddenly pounding. "Oh, I'm . . . so sorry."

"It's okay," Tracy said, waving a hand in dismissal. "I'm not as scarred by the ordeal as Mom thinks I am." She sighed, the corners of her mouth drooping. "Andy and I were married for three years. People say that a marriage license isn't important when you're in love—that it's just a piece of paper. But it *does* matter. It represents a lifelong commitment that Andy—"

"Couldn't accept," Katie finished.

"No. I was the one who wanted out. I was bored. I thought there might be someone better out there—somewhere—and I was right. I fell for a real outdoorsman, the antithesis of Andy, who was constantly holed up in a stuffy office in Rochester. After three years of marriage, Andy wasn't at all the man I thought I'd married. I dumped him so fast I don't doubt his head was spinning. But I really thought I'd met my Mister Right."

"What happened?" Katie asked.

"He died—the ultimate separation," she said with bitterness. "It was an accident. We'd had a fight the night before. We weren't even engaged and already we had in-law problems."

"Your mother?" Katie guessed.

"She wasn't happy, but it was his parental unit, not mine, who worked so hard to break us up. I wasn't good enough."

"What happened then?" Katie asked.

"I was pretty much a wreck. I turned to Andy, but he—my best friend—turned his back on me." Tracy sighed. "Well, what did I expect?" Regret shadowed her eyes.

Katie, too, had many regrets where Chad was concerned, but most of all she regretted that they'd never grow old together.

Katie cleared her throat. "I'm so sorry, Tracy."

Tracy's smile looked forced. "Hey, it's been a couple of years now. I'm a successful businesswoman; Andy's a successful business-man. It all worked out for the best."

Except they were both lonely people, pouring their souls into their separate businesses. What might they have accomplished together?

Katie stood. "I'd better be going. I've still got things to do over at Artisans Alley before I can go home for the day. Thanks for letting me vent."

"You're welcome—anytime."

Tracy walked Katie back down the stairs and into the kitchen. "We ought to get together to talk about our respective businesses—compare notes."

"Great idea. What's a good time for you?" They made plans to meet for dinner on Monday.

Mary listened, scowling with disapproval while

she rinsed dishes, then packed them into the industrial-sized dishwasher.

Tracy ushered Katie through to the now-empty shop. "Sorry about Mom. I'll talk to her—ask her not to let her dislike of Andy color her feelings toward you."

"I'd appreciate that. We'll be neighbors for a long time here on the Square. See you Monday."

Katie exited the shop and paused on the tarmac to take out her shiny new keys to Artisans Alley, wondering if her friendship with Tracy would interfere with cultivating a business relationship with Andy.

She swallowed. Yes. It would be just a business relationship. Nothing more.

Katie gazed with affection at the old Webster mansion to her left. If probate could be completed within six months, she'd be free to sell Artisans Alley. Yet the thought of all the business's debt threatened that scenario. Could she make a dent in all that red ink? And if she couldn't—

She watched as a car pulled up outside the mansion. A man in a tan raincoat got out and inspected the faded FOR SALE sign. How long had it been exposed to the elements? Five, seven years?

With a jolt, Katie realized she recognized the man, and started across the parking lot at a jog.

"Fred," she called. "Fred Cunningham!"

The lenses of Fred's glasses flashed in the

sunshine. He held out his hand as Katie approached. "Hey, good to see you again, Katie."

Katie took it, but wasted no time with other pleasantries. "Please don't tell me the old place has been sold."

The real estate agent looked chagrined. "The new owners signed the paperwork this morning. I just came out to put up the sold sign." There was no pleasure in his voice, and he tried not to look Katie in the eye.

"Why didn't you tell me this last night?" she cried, fighting tears.

"I couldn't. I mean, sometimes buyers back out at the last moment. If that had happened, I wouldn't have had to tell you at all."

"Thanks for sparing my feelings," she grumbled, her cheeks growing hot as she struggled not to burst into tears. "Who bought it? When did all this happen?"

"A couple came through about a month ago. I took them through two or three times. They made an offer on Wednesday and the estate accepted it."

"For a private home?" she asked, dreading the answer.

Fred shook his head. "No. A bed-and-breakfast, just as you envisioned. Of course, it'll take a lot of work—and a helluva lot of money—to restore it from apartments and into suites. But at least all the added plumbing will be put to good use in the bedroom suites."

A B and B. And someone who was *not* her was going to own and run it. Katie's breaths came in short gasps as she fought the urge to cry.

Fred frowned, his voice tinged with real concern. "I'm sorry, Katie. Until last night, I thought you'd abandoned all hope."

Katie swallowed. "I guess I'll have to now." She bit her lip and looked up at the building's roof, which needed replacement shingles. Hell, the new owners would probably have to replace the whole thing. Buying the mansion wouldn't have been enough. She would have needed enough capital to completely renovate the place, not to mention furnishing it in period style.

Katie let out a sigh as she looked back at the ugly hulk that was Artisans Alley. It was all she could do not to sob.

"I know your heart was set on opening a bed-and-breakfast," Fred said, "but it would've been an uphill battle, especially now that Chad's gone. Zoning laws, the County Health Department's rules and regs—they can make your life a living hell, even if you have someone to share it with. But alone . . ." He let the sentence hang.

Katie turned to stare at him, betting he hadn't mentioned any of the county's regulations to the new owners. Before she could comment, he spoke again.

"Yup. Retail's a much safer bet than hotel management. Especially if it's you who's collecting the rents and not depending on sales for your livelihood," Fred said with cheer and nodded sagely.

Katie blinked. "I . . . I guess I hadn't thought of it that way."

"If we can't rent all your available space, maybe you could open a little café inside, then you'd be sitting pretty. Especially once the new marina opens. People get bored sitting in their boats on a hot summer's day—*and* when it rains—and what with the price of marina gasoline . . . Mark my words, when you pull Artisans Alley out of the red, Victoria Square is going to be one terrific draw." He gave her a hope-inspiring smile. "I'd say you made the right decision, Katie."

Katie's cheeks didn't feel quite so hot anymore. She looked back toward Artisans Alley, realizing it was her only hope of survival—personal and financial. Was it possible she could grow to love the place like Chad had?

"Thank you, Fred. Thanks a lot."

An hour of uninterrupted silence would have been nice, but as soon as she entered her office, Katie found herself fielding calls from the press and declining interview opportunities. As decided at the Merchants Association's meeting the night before, Gilda Ringwald, the new PR director, agreed to handle all media inquiries into Ashby's death.

Katie had just changed the Alley's answering

machine's message when the phone rang again. "This is the last call I'm going to answer today," she vowed, then lifted the receiver. "Artisans Alley."

"Katie?" Josh prompted.

Katie's insides did a somersault as she recognized the voice as that of her ex-boss. "What do you want, Josh?"

"Uh . . . this isn't easy for me to admit, but . . . I want you to come back to the agency."

Katie said nothing for a long moment—contemplating slamming the receiver into its cradle. Then again, she almost wished she were recording the call—for Josh to make such a declaration was an historic occasion.

"Katie?" Josh prodded.

"What happened, Josh? Did the girls the agency sent over quit already?"

It was Josh's turn to be silent. Katie could envision his scowl. She wouldn't be surprised if steam was seeping from his ears.

"I heard on the news that someone else was found dead at Artisans Alley this morning. You can't tell me you feel safe in that crime-ridden place. Besides which, you'll never be able to salvage the business. Not with that kind of bad publicity."

"You don't think so?" Katie said, her hand clamping around the phone, her temper rising.

"No. So why don't you just admit defeat and—"

"Come crawling back to you?"

"Yeah," he said, cockiness returning to his voice.

"I'm willing to let bygones be bygones. I'll even sweeten the pot with a two percent raise."

Katie took a breath to quell her growing anger. "Josh, you could offer me a million dollars and I still wouldn't work for you."

"No need to get snippy," he said. "You're just upset because of everybody dying over there. Now, I'll see you in the office tomorrow morning—eight o'clock sharp. There's a lot of filing you need to catch up on. And then we'll talk about how you can take on more of the day-to-day responsibilities—"

"What?"

"I'll even give you the title of office manager. I can afford to be that generous," the little creep said.

Katie's hand tightened into strangulation mode around the phone. "Josh, drop dead!" She slammed the phone onto the receiver. Immediately, it began to ring again. She yanked the cord out of the wall, breaking the little plastic connector.

Swell.

It took an hour of blissful silence for Katie to calm down. She spent the time checking the dates on the old paperwork, and dumping them into the wastebasket while ruminating over Fred Cunningham's words of wisdom. Perhaps she had made the right choice to manage Artisans Alley. Maybe if she forced herself, she could even muster the shadow of a smile at the thought.

After an hour of concentrated work, Katie closed the file cabinet's top drawer, assessing the office's new sense of order. The room was tidy all right, but still dirty. She was about to gather cleaning supplies and give it a thorough going-over when a tap at the newly replaced window gave her a start.

Rose, her ever-present plastic rain bonnet tied beneath her chin, waved. Behind her stood Edie Silver, bundled up in a lilac ski jacket, and holding a large canvas tote bag—looking as formidable as ever. Rose pointed toward the back door and Katie hurried into the lounge to unlock it.

"The police shooed us away earlier," Rose said, "and then when we came back, you were gone."

"I needed to speak with one of the other merchants on the Square. I'm sorry, Rose, but we're closed for the rest of the day."

"We tried to call, but just got the answering machine; later, the phone just rang and rang. Can we tell you what our committee has decided?" Rose asked.

Katie blinked in confusion. "Committee?"

"At the meeting last Saturday you suggested a number of us get together to brainstorm ways to get customers to come visit Artisans Alley," Rose reminded her.

"And you've already met?" Katie asked.

Rose nodded, her eyes bright with pleasure, the ghost of a smile on her lips.

"We've got a whole list of ideas," Edie piped up with pride.

For the first time since finding Ashby's body,

Katie felt a surge of hope. "Please come in," she said, sweeping her hand to usher them inside.

The ladies bustled into the dimly lit, shabby space that passed for the vendors' lounge. Removing their coats, they took seats at the tippy table. Edie withdrew a couple of file folders from her bag, and proceeded to spread out handwritten sheets before her. She leaned forward and turned her steely gray eyes on Katie.

"Christmas," she began. "It's the hottest time of the year for retail. We've got to cash in on it. We've come up with two different scenarios. The first just involves Artisans Alley; the second involves all of Victoria Square."

"Let's hear them both," Katie said, intrigued.

"We're supposed to be an artists' enclave," Edie began, "so let's act like one and be a little more creative in our presentation—starting at the booth level. Instead of just numbers identifying our booths, we could have Vance cut painters' palettes out of plywood. I could paint them to look real, and then we could stencil the booth numbers in the middle. It would be really cute. Here, I have a mock-up." She pulled a colorful drawing from her folder and handed it to Katie, who studied the design. It *was* cute, and perfectly rendered, with little circles of different colors representing paint, and even a paintbrush set to one side.

"That sounds like an awful lot of work. We have about sixty booths—with more on the way."

"If you supply the materials—I'll take care of the painting. We can even do an extra ten or twenty. You've got a lot of booths to fill up in the loft and we can be ready to accommodate them."

Katie laughed. "It's a deal. What else have you got in mind?"

Edie leaned forward, her eyes twinkling with excitement. "Next, we hold a contest for all the artists, encouraging them to fix up their booths. The best-looking one wins a prize. To keep the peace, maybe a couple of the Victoria Square merchants could be impartial judges."

"Yes, let's see some Victorian decoration with paint and wallpaper," Rose piped up.

"Who pays for the paint and other supplies?" Katie asked. She couldn't bankroll something of that magnitude.

"It would be up to the individual artists," Rose said.

"That's the beauty of the contest," Edie continued. "The inside of Artisans Alley gets a face-lift, and the prize is one month's free rent. You could swing that, couldn't you?"

Katie struggled to stifle a smile. "I think I could manage that. Anything else?"

"We need a website. I can't think why we haven't already got one," Edie complained.

"I agree," Katie said. "Tracy Elliott has already offered to design one at a discount for us. I may take her up on it."

Edie shook her head. "My grandson will do it for free. He's learning this stuff in school and is looking for a project to do for college credit. I'll give you the URLs of his past work so you can check them out. And we may as well get Myspace and Facebook pages, too—they're free and we can have them up within an hour. Have you thought about Twittering?"

Katie gaped at the old woman, who didn't look at all computer savvy. "These are all wonderful ideas, ladies. Please, tell me more," she said, wishing she could have sat in on the brainstorming session.

"We can offer to hold receptions and maybe even cocktail parties here at Artisans Alley," Edie continued. "You know, to groups like the Rotary or the Elks, and maybe some nonprofit organizations. They could mingle, drink wine, eat cheese—and have the opportunity to shop here. Maybe we could issue ten-percent-off coupons to those attending. Either way, some of us would sell our wares, and Artisans Alley could rake in some money to pay down expenses."

"That sounds good to me," Katie said. "You mentioned your other ideas involved all of Victoria Square," she reminded Rose.

"That's right. Our other big idea," Rose began, "is to play up the Victorian angle. If we can interest the Merchants Association, we could stage a Dickens Christmas gala and involve all the businesses in the Square. Everybody could dress up in period costumes. We'd have music, food—make it a real old-fashioned extravaganza. It could draw people from the whole Rochester area—maybe even bus tours from Buffalo and Syracuse!"

"That sounds rather ambitious, considering Thanksgiving is less than a month away," Katie said, hating to squash their enthusiasm.

"Oh sure, for this year," Edie agreed, "but if we stage a miniversion, we could learn from our mistakes and build momentum for next year. We can use the spring and summer months to plan a much bigger celebration and next December we'd all make a killing."

"More important," Rose interjected, "we'd make people happy—the artists, the merchants, and all the customers."

Edie kept talking. Katie listened with growing admiration. Involving the entire Square would assure success and maximize their advertising dollars. Bringing Artisans Alley back into solvency was her chief goal—this might not do it, but it sure couldn't hurt.

"Ladies, you are amazing," Katie said, smiling.

"Not just us," Rose said, looking over at Edie. "There are five of us on the committee. We all contributed ideas."

"And they're wonderful. I'd be glad to take them to the Merchants Association. They're just as eager as we are to improve sales, so I don't believe it would be a hard sell."

The two older women beamed with pride.

"Come on into my office," Katie said with a wave in that direction. "Let's type your ideas into the computer."

"See you!" Edie called and waved as she headed out the back door. Katie threw the bolt on the growing darkness and went back to her office.

Rose sat bent over the imposing gray metal desk, red pen in hand. Before her were the scattered papers that had come out of the printer. "I can't believe how many typos I made. I should have run the spell check. I'm so sorry, Katie."

"Don't worry about it. We'll take a few days to polish up the proposal before we submit it to the Merchants Association."

They were good ideas, but Katie soon found her elation fizzling. She sat in her chair and stared out the window at the mercury vapor lamp that had just come on over the rusty old Dumpster out back.

"Are you okay, Katie?" Rose asked. "You always look so worried."

Katie glanced at the elderly woman. Something about the tilt of her head, the gleam in her eyes, reminded Katie of her great-aunt, who'd raised her after the deaths of her parents. She'd lost her beloved Aunt Lizzie MacDuff nearly eight years ago. Then, like now, she'd been thrust into the middle of settling an estate, selling off her aunt's possessions to pay off creditors. She'd felt overwhelmed then, too—by the task and by grief. Only weeks later, she'd met Chad . . .

Katie shook herself back to the present. "Despite all our best ideas, Artisans Alley's still got big money problems that only time—and expanding our clientele—can solve. I'm going on faith that I can pull us out of the threat of bankruptcy. In the meantime, Artisans Alley has three loan payments due within the next two weeks. I need to call my health care provider and see what I can do to arrange health insurance. My apartment rent is due on Sunday, and my car's leaking oil. All these expenses are going to stretch my savings to the limit."

Rose frowned, her wrinkled brow furrowing deeper. "Is there anything I can do to help?"

Katie smiled with affection at the old woman. "Help me get some of the deadbeat artists to pay their rent?"

Rose nodded. "Speaking of Ida, is it true you're throwing her out of Artisans Alley?"

Katie's mouth dropped. "I'm not throwing her out. I simply told her she'd have to pay her rent like everybody else or she'd have to leave. And how did you find out anyway? I just spoke to her this morning."

"She called me, and she was steaming—telling me how unfair you were, and what a witch you were. She even cried. Did you know Ida was one of Ezra's first artists? Her booth number is four."

Katie sighed, annoyed that she'd been portrayed as Ebenezer Scrooge before his conversion. She took a calming breath before speaking. "Ida's booth is nearly empty and it's in a prime location. I've already been approached by several artists, asking if they can have the spot."

Rose straightened with indignation. "Hey, I've been here since the beginning, too. I deserve that spot more than a lot of others who haven't been here as long. And I always pay my rent on time!"

Katie blinked at Rose's abrupt turnabout, but declined to comment about it. "I'm sorry Ida is upset about the situation, but I have to think about the good of the business as a whole if Artisans Alley is going to survive. That means bringing more money in than is flowing out—and that's not happening right now."

Rose nodded, straightening up the papers on the desk, her lips pursed. Why did the artists find it so hard to understand the cash flow problem?

If money was the root of all evil, was Katie selling her soul to keep this sinkhole afloat? Detective Davenport had said not to mention the outstanding loan, but what if Rose knew who'd borrowed five thousand dollars from Ezra? Or maybe Vance knew? Katie could do so much with that money . . . if she could wring it out of the deadbeat who'd signed and then defaulted on the loan.

No, Davenport was right. It might be dangerous to talk about the loan . . . if that was the motive someone had had for killing Ezra. And now that she'd decided to take a longer-term interest in Artisans Alley, she had another problem.

"Rose, what do you know about Gerald Hilton?"

"Next to nothing," she said offhandedly. "I think he was Ezra's brother's boy. He didn't come around much that I remember. I might've seen him two, maybe three times since we opened. That's going back ten or more years."

Not at all helpful.

Rose's eyes narrowed. "Why don't you talk to Mary Elliott. She knew Ezra . . . intimately," she said with scorn. "I'll bet she could answer a lot of your questions."

Yes, Mary probably could. But would she?

Nineteen

Though the business had closed several hours before, lights still glowed in the back of Tea and Tasties. Katie rapped her knuckles against the unyielding black-painted steel door and waited. Footsteps thumped toward her. She glanced at the peephole above her, feeling uncomfortable.

Long seconds later the handle rattled and the door was thrown open.

"Mary?" Katie asked the figure silhouetted before her.

"Tracy isn't here." Mary's clipped words sent a chill through Katie. "She went home about an hour ago."

That was odd. Only the day before Tracy had mentioned her misgivings at leaving her mother alone on Victoria Square.

"I was hoping I could speak to you . . . about Ezra and Artisans Alley," Katie began.

"Oh." Mary's rigid stance wavered until she seemed to sag. "Come in," she said at last, sounding suddenly exhausted.

Katie entered the immaculate kitchen, breathing in the yeasty scent of baking bread. Her stomach rumbled. "It always smells wonderful in here."

Mary ignored the compliment, instead turning to her flour-dusted bread board, which held a round of dough. She punched it down. "I've got a lot to do. What do you want to know?"

"For starters, why Ezra left me half of his estate." The statement came out sounding a lot more desperate than Katie intended.

Mary turned, her lips lifting into vague facsimile of a smile. "Because he knew you'd fight to keep Artisans Alley open."

"How could he know that when I didn't?"

"Ezra was an excellent judge of character," Mary stated, then immediately frowned. "At least . . . he thought he was." Her confidence seemed to falter. Did that mean Ezra had judged Katie wrong—or could Mary be thinking of her former son-in-law? Suddenly, Mary looked every bit her age. She turned watery eyes on Katie. "I'm sorry. I didn't mean to be rude to you just now. This past week has been . . ." She paused and took a shuddering breath. "Terrible."

"Yes," Katie agreed, "it has."

"I'm sorry. I've treated you shabbily, which is especially rude after you arranged for me to have a private good-bye with Ezra. It meant a lot to me."

Katie nodded, not knowing what else to say.

"Would you like a cup of cocoa?" Mary asked. "I could sure use something to warm me through. I've felt cold for days." Kindness tinged Mary's voice, something Katie hadn't heard from her in days.

"Yes, I'd like that."

"Why don't you go sit in the shop. I'll be there in a minute," Mary said as she took a carton of milk from the industrial-sized refrigerator, then filled a saucepan on the massive Vulcan stove.

Katie nodded and turned for the darkened room. She switched on the lights and took a seat at one of the oak tables in the cozy room. Scalloped pink paper placemats sat at each place, with a matching paper napkin folded to resemble a simple crown. Nice and neat. While she waited, Katie composed her thoughts. She wanted to get this right.

A few minutes later, Mary came through the door with a wooden tray laden with old-fashioned, thick white china mugs, freshly sliced bread still steaming from the oven, and a bowl containing whipped butter. She took the seat opposite Katie.

"When times were tough, my mother fed my three brothers and me on her homemade bread. Fresh-made bread, hot from the oven, always takes me back to those happy days."

Tough times—happy days?

"It smells wonderful. Thank you."

Mary sighed and set one of the mugs in front of Katie. "Now, what else did you need to know?"

Katie sipped her cocoa. "Tracy told me you knew Ezra well; what would he want me to do?"

Mary didn't hesitate. "He would have loved for you to make a success of Artisans Alley. It was something he struggled with. I swear he loved that old building more than he loved life. He looked forward to opening every day, and he didn't like to be away for even a few hours. I wanted to take a day trip to Toronto to see a big show, but he wouldn't go. You may think this funny, but he never even invited me to his house. We only ever saw each other at Artisans Alley or at the Merchants Association meetings."

Then they hadn't been lovers? And no wonder she hadn't known about Ezra's cat.

The wistful look in Mary's eyes reawakened Katie's own sense of loss. She cleared her throat, trying not to think about Chad. "Seth Landers told me Ezra changed his will only weeks before he died. I assume he originally intended his nephew Gerald to inherit his entire estate."

"That's right," Mary said, slathering a generous layer of butter on her still-warm bread. "With Ronnie gone, Gerald was the only living relative Ezra had. But he decided to change his will when Gerald told him he wasn't going to repay the loan."

Shocked, Katie leaned forward. "Gerald owed Ezra money?"

Mary nodded, took a bite of bread, chewed, and then swallowed. "Five thousand dollars. I know that's not a lot, especially with the Radisson chain offering Ezra over a million for the Artisans Alley site, but it was the principle of the thing. Gerald had promised to pay Ezra back. He begged and pleaded for the cash last year to pay off his credit card debt. Then when Gerald made money on a stock deal, he went right out and bought a new car instead of paying back Ezra. Well, you can understand how that didn't set well with Ezra."

"I don't imagine it did," Katie said, following her hostess's lead and applying a thick layer of the sweet creamy butter onto a slice of bread. "The police think the outstanding loan might be a motive for murder."

Mary gaped. "Gerald a murderer?" She laughed. "He hasn't got the guts."

"Would he have the guts to ransack Ezra's office looking for proof of the loan?"

Mary gazed at the steam curling from her mug of cocoa. "Yes, I'll bet the little weasel *could* do that. In fact, it would be just like him."

"That still doesn't explain why Ezra left me half his estate."

"Don't think me bad for saying this, but Ezra had a bit of a mean streak, although I'm sure he would've called it a sense of justice," Mary said, a hint of laughter entering her voice. "I think he knew that you'd give Gerald a fight. He didn't feel it was right for open hostility to break out between family members, and he felt deeply about preserving family relationships. Ezra also knew that Gerald would never honor his wish to keep Artisans Alley alive. But he guessed right that you would."

"I didn't know Ezra well. Hardly at all," Katie admitted. "I'm really doing this for my late husband, Chad." Okay, that wasn't the *total* truth, but it was more socially acceptable.

Mary smiled. "I think Ezra realized that would be your motivation . . . but I also think it was his last chance to annoy Gerald. And he would have been proud of what you've already accomplished."

Which seemed to be damned little in Katie's estimation.

"I need that five thousand dollars to keep Artisans Alley going. I'll call Seth Landers first thing in the morning to find out how I can collect it."

"You do that," Mary encouraged. She'd lost all her former air of animosity. Katie wondered if she would antagonize Mary once again by bringing up Andy's name. There was only one way to find out.

"Tracy told me about her marriage to Andy. It's sad they weren't able to patch things up."

"Katie, I was raised a good Catholic. You don't leave your husband, and you never get divorced. At least, that's the way it used to be. After Tracy and Andy separated, I wanted to believe it was all Andy's fault. I'll never understand why Tracy found marriage to be such a trap."

"Do you think they'll ever get back together?"

"No," Mary said with certainty. "And it doesn't do to hold grudges. I'm afraid I let Ezra influence me there. He couldn't forgive Andy for crashing his beautiful car. I think Andy reminded Ezra of his son, Ronnie—a bit of a hellion with a reckless nature in his teenaged years. Of course, Ronnie straightened out—even owned his own business. I thought one day he might even be my. . . ." Her voice faltered.

Mary buttered another slice of bread. "Ezra was so proud of Ronnie, but I think he probably meddled too much in his son's life. Above all, Ezra wanted Ronnie to be a successful businessman. He never thought any girl was good enough for Ronnie, and he broke up every serious relationship the poor boy had."

It wasn't Ezra's dead son Katie wanted to talk about. "Why didn't Ezra leave anything to you or any of his other friends?"

Mary shrugged. "None of us really needs anything. You did. You needed a reason to start living again. And now you have one."

Halloween dawned gloomy with gray clouds and intermittent rain. Another perfect day for retail, Katie told herself. After a makeshift breakfast of dry toast and tea, she headed for Ezra's house to feed the little tabby, chiding herself for not yet calling the local vet. She was getting fond of the fur ball and, truth be told, had more or less decided to keep her—based on the vet's report, of course. She'd make that second on her list of things to do today. Getting back in her car, she headed for Artisans Alley.

Once in her office, Katie picked up the phone

and dialed Seth's work number. As it was Saturday, she expected to reach a switchboard and leave a message, but instead his secretary answered, and put her right through.

"Wow, I wasn't expecting to actually talk to you. I thought I'd have to leave a message."

"You've become my most important client," Seth said, sounding quite happy about it.

The warmth in his voice sent a glow through Katie. "I wish I could say this is strictly a personal call, but I need some professional advice." Katie told Seth about the loan agreement, that it was Gerald who'd signed it, and asked what she could do about it.

"That's easy. Gerald owes the estate that five thousand dollars and he has to pay before probate can be settled. Since the debt is already due, the estate—that's you—may collect any way you see fit. You can take it out of any future profits, or you can go to court to attach his other sources of income."

"I need that money *now* just to keep Artisans Alley afloat."

"I'll write him a letter advising him to pay up. It won't be worth court costs for him to try and fight it."

"Does it make me look cowardly, not calling him myself?"

"Not at all," Seth assured her. "I'm an officer of the court. This is a legal matter. It's really the most efficient way to remind him of his obligation. Of course, I'll need a copy of the loan agreement."

"Uh . . . I only have a copy. Detective Davenport has the original. In fact, he told me not to tell anyone about it. In case the loan was the reason someone killed Ezra. We both thought whoever owed Ezra the money probably broke into Artisans Alley's office on Saturday night or Sunday morning looking for it."

"I see." Seth was quiet for a moment. "Why don't I give Detective Davenport a call. It's only natural that you would consult your attorney on this. He can confront Gerald, then I'll send the letter. That would solve both your problems."

"Thank you, Seth. You always have a way of making me feel better."

"I'm glad to hear that. Any chance you're free tonight? I promised you dinner in a real restaurant."

Katie hesitated, enjoying the smile that tugged at her lips. "I'd love to."

"Great. You can give me a copy of the loan agreement when I pick you up at your apartment. How about seven o'clock?"

"That would be lovely."

"See you then."

Katie hung up the phone, savoring her sense of elation. A real date. Her first in ages and she had absolutely nothing to wear.

She frowned. Swell.

• • •

"Her name is Della," said the vet tech on the other end of the line. "She's three years old, and she's up-to-date on all her shots, including feline leukemia. We've got her down as being an indoor cat, so she should be safe to bring into your home. Did you want us to add her to your records?"

"Yes," Katie said.

"Fine. We'll send you a reminder when it's time for her rabies booster," the woman said and ended the call.

Katie hung up her phone. Della? Now, wasn't that a coincidence? Chad had named their cat, Mason, after guitarist Dave Mason, but Katie had secretly thought of him as a diminutive Perry Mason in a dark furry suit. Now she'd have to introduce Mason to his new companion . . . Della Street? The thought brought a smile to Katie's lips.

"Excuse me," said a vibrant female voice.

Katie looked up at the stranger framed in her office doorway. Although the lines around her eyes suggested she was older than Katie by a good ten or fifteen years, the woman was still a knockout dressed in a low-cut, form-fitting red dress that seemed more appropriate for a cocktail party, or maybe a stint at the Grand Ole Opry, than an excursion to an artisans' arcade. Her long lacquered nails and big, perfectly coifed honey blond hair reminded Katie of a certain well-known country-western singer.

"Katie Bonner?" the woman asked.

Katie pushed back her chair to stand. "Yes. Can I help you?"

"Where's my husband?" she snapped.

"I'm sorry?"

"Vance Ingram. Where is he?"

"Uh . . . I don't know. Why do you think he's here?"

"Because his truck's parked out back. He told me he'd be here all day. He told me *you* needed him."

This was not the frail, MS-afflicted woman Katie had envisioned. In fact, despite her age, Janey Ingram still looked like a bombshell. And a jealous one at that.

"I'm sorry, Mrs. Ingram, but I haven't seen Vance in two days. I really have no idea where you can find him."

Janey's chin jutted out. "Oh yeah, we'll see about that." She turned perfectly, steady on her stiletto-clad feet as she stalked off.

Katie followed the woman through Artisans Alley's main showroom to the front of the store.

Rose was already stationed behind the register. Her face lit up as she recognized the woman advancing on her. "Janey! It's been ages. You're looking well."

Janey stopped dead. Hands on hips, she regarded the older woman with disdain. "Cut the crap, Rose. Where the hell is Vance?"

Rose blinked, taken aback. "He hasn't been here in days. Isn't that right, Katie?"

Katie hooked her thumbs through the belt loops of her jeans, thinking how dumpy she must look in her sweatshirt, crummy old pants, and scuffed-up sneakers. "That's what I told her."

Janey turned back to Katie. "Page him."

Katie shrugged, stepped over to the phone on the wall, and pressed the intercom key. "Vance Ingram, please meet your party at the front desk. Vance Ingram." She hung up the phone.

Janey surveyed her surroundings, throwing her chest out until her breasts looked ready to pop out of her push-up bra.

"I don't mean to intrude, Mrs. Ingram, but I understood you were ill," Katie said.

Janey frowned. "I've been in remission from MS for ages. Is that the line Vance has been feeding you—that I'm feeble and helpless?"

"No, it's just—"

"I take damn good care of myself and my family, and I won't stand for a sexy young widow going after my man."

Katie blinked, tempted to look around to see who the woman was referring to, then realized with a start: "You mean me?"

"Who else am I talking to?"

Katie looked to a puzzled Rose, then back to Janey, then laughed. "Me? And Vance?"

Janey's eyes blazed.

Katie cleared her throat and sobered as Edie Silver approached the front cash desk. "I'm sorry, Mrs. Ingram, it's just that Vance doesn't even seem to like me. I can't imagine he'd—"

"All I've heard for the last week is 'Katie this' and 'Katie that.' Now I demand you tell me where my husband is!"

"He ain't here, that's for sure," Edie said. Everyone turned toward her. "I saw him pull up in his truck about an hour ago when I was unloading my stock. A car was waiting for him. He got in, then he and a woman drove off."

"A woman!" Janey shrilled. "Who?"

Edie shrugged. "Beats me."

"What kind of car?" Rose asked.

"It was blue. I don't know the make and model." Only the radio playing a Faith Hill tune being broadcast over the PA system broke the quiet. Janey's Iron Woman facade slipped. Her lower lip trembled, her eyes growing moist.

Katie fought the urge to hug the poor woman, deciding Janey probably wouldn't appreciate her concern. "I'm sure when Vance gets back, he'll have a perfectly reasonable explanation."

Janey took a breath, straightening. "He'd better. I'm not leaving here until he shows up. Even if it takes all day." Squaring her shoulders, she stomped off in the direction of Katie's office.

Katie glanced at Rose and Edie and shrugged. "Swell."

Twenty

"What a way to increase business," Katie murmured as she closed the spreadsheet program on the computer. Despite being closed for two days, Artisans Alley took in more money than it had during an average week before the murders occurred. Ezra's and Ashby's deaths had sure pulled in the ghouls—but at least they'd dropped some cash during their gawking.

A heavy sigh from the chair three feet away reminded Katie of her not-so-welcome visitor. Janey Ingram stared morosely out the newly replaced window, her gaze riveted on Vance's pickup truck.

Why, Katie wondered, had she allowed the woman to camp out in her office?

She had a lot to do in the next couple of days, including making the flyers for the improve-your-booth contest. Putting together a list would keep her from forgetting every little task. She opened the desk drawer to grab a pad of paper and saw the journal she'd avoided reading. Had Chad ever mentioned his impressions of Vance in it? Katie risked a glance at Janey. There was no time like the present to check it out.

She withdrew the book, flipping through the pages, her gaze settling on an entry just a week after their breakup.

December 20th

The lack of enthusiasm around AA seems to be contagious—and Ezra is responsible. The lack of Christmas cheer is depressing. The old man shelled out for a wreath on the front door, but I couldn't convince him to put up lights. He says it's too late this season. Of course it is—they should have gone up in early November.

I've been kidding myself that I could ever change Ezra's mind about the way he runs this place. I risked—and probably lost—not only my investment, but my marriage, and for what? A penny-ante wanna-be gallery. My God, we've even got a booth with nothing in it but strips of yellowing lace. It would take a lot of work to get this place in shape, but it might really be worth the effort. If I could just convince Ezra to listen and accept even some of my ideas, I could have my investment back in a couple of years. As it is, the concept of the place is great —but the execution is mediocre at best.

Katie frowned. Would Chad have welcomed crafters into the Alley as opposed to artisans? Hadn't he said something about scouring the Clothesline

Art Show and the Corn Hill Arts Festival to look for new vendors? He'd never had the opportunity.

She flipped through a few more pages, her gaze settling on a date six weeks before Chad's death.

January 26th

Vance and I loaded the software for the new computer. Ezra didn't want to spend the bucks on the more advanced version, but we can better sort the sales and it should cut down on vendor complaints.

Ezra said if he didn't have to spend money on such foolishness he'd be paying me back faster. I keep telling him I don't want the money. I'd rather keep a stake in Artisans Alley. I know Katie wouldn't want to hear that, but I also know that with just a few more improvements this place could really take off. Ezra's already assured me that if something happened to him he wanted Artisans Alley to go on—and that he'd take care of me in his will.

I believe him, but if something isn't done to change the way this place is run, it'll go down the tubes long before that happens.

Chad would never have believed that he, the much younger man, would have died first.

Katie skimmed the next passage, but there

was no further mention of Vance. Flipping pages, another entry caught her attention.

March 8th

At last, Ezra finally allowed me to accompany him to the monthly Merchants Association meeting, stressing that as senior partner he's the only one who gets to vote. I can't say I'm impressed—at least with the Association as a whole. Nona Fiske looks at Ezra with cow eyes and would rubber-stamp approve everything he says. Some of them hang on Ezra's every word, and nod agreement when he squashes any suggestions he doesn't agree with. Then again, most of them just looked exhausted. Running a business seven days a week can sure kill your spirit—especially if you're fighting just to keep it alive. From what I can see, the most successful people on Victoria Square are Gilda, Conrad, and the Tanners. It's too bad none of them are running the Association, then at least Victoria Square might have a fighting chance of success.

The group is only planning to devote five thousand dollars for advertising for next year's Christmas season. That won't buy many ads. They ought to target different demographics, use print, radio, and TV ads. Every time I tried to bring up the subject, Ezra shot me down. Sometimes I get so angry at that old coot.

Katie's marketing degree would sure come in handy right now. If only I could interest her in all of this. Then again, she works herself to death for that bully at Kimper Insurance. And without the English Ivy Inn, she has no stake in the Square. I sure killed that incentive for her.

Yes, he had.

Still, maybe I'll bring it up to her the next time we talk.

Katie remembered him briefly mentioning the meeting during one of their conversations, but she hadn't given the subject much importance at the time. She shook her head. And now she was he head of the organization. How times changed.

Katie closed the book, swallowing down a pang of regret. She couldn't keep doing this to herself. Most of what Chad had written—his frustrations —mirrored her own thoughts. Only now she had the authority to implement Chad's ideas. Maybe they'd work and maybe they wouldn't. She'd read the rest of the journal and try to adopt whatever suggestions seemed viable.

Katie put the book into the desk drawer. Until she figured out what else she might want to do with the rest of her life, the whole Artisans Alley experience would at least be a managerial entry on some future résumé.

She pushed back her chair and rose. "I think I'll go see if the mail has arrived."

Janey's only reply was another bored sigh.

Katie escaped the office to wander through Artisans Alley's main showroom, her attention caught by a display case filled with Rose's jewelry. It really was depressing to walk past the poorly lit booths. It amazed her that the vendors ever sold anything. Somehow she had to find the money to upgrade the whole building's electrical system. And before the day ended, Katie vowed she'd complete the booth decoration contest flyer and place a copy in every vendor's mail slot. That would be a good start. And maybe after that she'd approach Edie Silver to ask her to hold a workshop for the other vendors to show them how best to set up a display.

Rose finished ringing up a sale as Katie sidled up to the cash desk. A neat pile of envelopes and circulars sat on the back shelves that housed "hold" items and reshops—articles customers had decided against purchasing.

Katie picked up the mail and flipped through it. Bills, bills, and more bills. No, she did not believe Ezra was a finalist in a million-dollar sweepstakes. And being deceased, he didn't need another credit card either.

Seth's law firm's return address on one of the envelopes drew Katie's attention. She ripped it open, leaving a jagged tear in the top, and then removed and unfolded the crisp linen stock paper. As her eyes scanned the page, her body tensed until fury made her wail in disgust.

Storming over to the first cash desk, Katie waved the paper under Rose's nose. "Do you believe this?"

Rose took the sheet, her gaze darting back and forth as she read the long list of expenses. "Oh, my."

"I thought he was just being nice," Katie ranted. "When he took me to Del's Diner, he not only charged me for his time—he charged me for the meatloaf, too! Plus the flowers at the funeral home, and every phone call, too!"

"Lawyers do have that reputation," Rose said, handing back the page. "But I never would have thought that of Mr. Landers. He always seems so nice."

Of course, Katie wasn't about to mention that Seth had also kissed her—twice—reinforcing her mistaken notion. Seth had made it seem like he'd wanted to be with her, to get to know her.

"How could he?" Katie muttered, the hurt bubbling up until she thought she might choke.

Rose blinked watery eyes. "You were kind of sweet on him, weren't you?"

Katie's throat tightened, and her bottom lip trembled. Had everybody guessed?

"Real life bears so little resemblance to the stories I like to read," Rose said, patting the cover of her romance novel. "I know what it's like to think a man might care for you, then find out he doesn't."

Katie swallowed, still unable to say anything without blubbering.

"It happened to me some forty years ago," Rose admitted. Her eyes darted left and right as she looked around, and when she saw no one nearby, she continued. "I worked in accounts at a big department store in downtown Rochester. It was March, nearly spring, when a big storm blew in off Lake Ontario. The roads were terrible. My car died just a mile outside the village. I thought I could make it home on foot, but my poplin coat was more fashionable than warm."

"Rose, you don't have to—" Katie started to say, but Rose waved a hand to interrupt her.

"My legs were frozen. I couldn't even feel my feet. I cried with relief when I saw the lights on in the local appliance store. The doors were locked, but I hammered on them until someone came to let me in." She held her thumb and forefinger an inch apart. "I came that close to dying."

"Rose—" Katie said again.

The old woman's eyes were wistful once more. "The owner took me into his office in the back, pulled out a bottle of Four Roses whiskey from his desk drawer, and said it would warm me right up. He took care of me," she said, her voice strained. "He helped me out of my wet clothes, put them on the radiator to dry—and let me wear a store apron and a baggy sweater he kept on hand. The wind howled outside, and the snow kept falling. There was no way either of us could leave. So we talked and drank and talked and . . . somewhere in the middle of the night, we made love. Just like in one of my novels. It was beautiful." Rose took a shuddering breath.

Katie stared at the weathered face before her, unable to picture the faded beauty that hid behind the wrinkles creasing the old woman's cheeks.

"He was married," Rose continued, "and had a child. There was no way we could ever be together. I suppose that's why I never told him about . . . our baby."

"Oh, Rose," Katie said. Suddenly her embarrassment over Seth seemed minuscule in comparison to the old woman's decades-old heartache. "I'm so sorry."

Rose shook her head. "I went away. I told everyone I was visiting a cousin in Pittsburgh. That's what women did back then. At least, I did. I never even saw my child after the birth. He was put up for adoption. When I met my Howard, I never told him about my shame. He always believed he was the first . . . my only . . ." Rose pulled a tissue from her skirt pocket and wiped her nose.

"It was all so long ago, but I've hardly slept for days worrying the police might find out about my shame and make it public. That pink quartz was mine—it came from my booth! They might think

301

that if I had one incident from my past to hide, I might have others. I would never have hurt anyone. In my own way, I loved Ezra. He was my friend. But Howard was the love of my life."

Katie patted the woman's bony back, not quite sure what to make of her last few sentences. "I'm sure you don't have anything to worry about."

"I've never told anyone in McKinlay Mill about this until now. But it's weighed so heavy on my soul I had to tell someone."

Katie fought tears and could only nod, totally at a loss for words.

An overweight, balding man in a too-tight Bills sweatshirt walked up to the register, clutching a dog-eared magazine. "Any JFK memorabilia in this place?" he asked.

Rose wiped her eyes and brightened, turning on the charm, chatting with the customer while she rang up the sale. Okay, maybe Rose didn't like cats, but by sharing her heartbreak she'd endeared herself to Katie.

Something registered in Katie's peripheral vision, and a figure in the doorway captured her attention: Vance Ingram.

Adrenaline surged through her, and Katie bolted to head the man off. "Vance, your wife is in my office. She got here just before we opened. She's in a terrible snit, and—"

"Where the hell have you been?" Janey Ingram demanded from across the Alley's showroom. Her eyes blazed and her ample bosom heaved as she glared at her husband. At last, she charged forward.

Bug-eyed and wary, Vance backed up a step, his eyes darting from his wife to Katie. "At Mindy Shaffer's house," he blurted out defensively.

Janey's dilated eyes narrowed in anger, giving her a decidedly sinister appearance.

"I was remodeling her kitchen," Vance explained lamely.

"Like hell you were," Janey hollered, coming up short in front of him.

"Wait, wait," Katie interrupted, seeing customers craning their necks to watch the show. "Give Vance a chance to explain," she said in a low tone, hoping Janey would take the hint and pipe down.

Vance gave Katie a look of thanks, turning to his wife. "I only told you I was here because . . . because I didn't want you to know where I'd be."

"Of course you didn't!" Janey yelled. "You cheating, lying son of a—"

"Janey—Vance! Can't we take this discussion into my office?" Katie begged.

Janey turned on her, with as malevolent a glare as Katie had ever received. Then the Dolly Parton look-alike transferred her weight from one hip to the other, exhaling impatiently as she turned back to glare at her husband. "Well?" she demanded of Vance.

"Go on, Vance," Katie said, throwing her hands up into the air and giving up.

"It's our twenty-fifth wedding anniversary in two weeks," Vance explained. "I needed the money to take you on a second honeymoon."

"Oh, yeah?" Janey challenged, her scorn almost palpable.

"Yeah," Vance said, reaching for his back pocket. Taking out his billfold, he showed a cluster of crisp, one-hundred-dollar bills safely tucked inside. "I got paid in full today. There's enough for us to go to Branson. Take in all the shows, and to go to—"

"Dolly Parton's Dixie Stampede Dinner and Show?" Janey squealed, as though she'd recited the words a thousand times before.

"And now you've ruined my surprise," Vance complained as Janey threw her arms around his neck, nearly knocking him over.

"Oh, sweetie pie, you've made me the happiest girl in the whole USA."

Katie scowled, vaguely remembering an old country tune by the same name—and not sung by Dolly—but decided not to mention it.

"Isn't that romantic," Rose said and sighed, clasping her romance novel, a sappy grin plastered across her wrinkled features.

"Ezra knew what I was up to," Vance admitted, guilt shading his voice. "He covered for me. I was at Mindy's the night he was murdered. How could I know someone would rob the place and kill him?" he said, his voice cracking with emotion.

How indeed?

Vance turned to face Katie. "I'm sorry I didn't tell you, Katie. I wanted Janey to be surprised, and I figured if even one other person knew, it would get back to her and ruin everything."

"You surprised me all right," Janey said, her grin so wide it threatened to crack her cherry-colored lips.

"And wait till you see Mindy's kitchen," Vance said. "It turned out great."

"Show me now, Vance," Janey said, wrapping her arm around his and dragging him toward the door.

"See you tomorrow, Katie," Vance called over his shoulder.

Katie gave them both a feeble wave. "Ciao."

With the show now over, the customers went back to browsing. Katie moved to stand beside the cash desk.

"I'm so glad Vance wasn't fooling around on Janey," Rose said, picking up her romance novel and extracting the bookmark. "It restores my faith in *man*kind."

"Yeah, me, too," Katie said, doubly relieved that Vance hadn't had anything to do with Ezra's death.

A customer holding a large pottery vase walked up to the register. "Wow—lots of drama in this place." His voice was familiar.

Katie squinted at the man. "Deputy Schuler?" she asked. He looked different out of uniform and dressed in jeans, boots, a Buffalo Bills jacket, and a Mets ball cap. "What are you doing here?"

"Shopping," he said, and put the vase down on the cash desk. "Boy, is this thing heavy. Think my wife will like it? It's her birthday tomorrow."

"I think she'll love it," Rose said, peeling the adhesive price tag from the front of it. She turned to her register to ring up the sale.

"Who's out protecting us if you're off duty?" Katie asked.

"Don't worry, McKinlay Mill is covered, and I'll be back on duty later this afternoon," Schuler assured her.

"I'm glad to know I can count on you—even if I can't count on Detective Davenport," Katie said.

Schuler frowned and shook his head sadly. "That poor guy."

"Poor guy?" Katie repeated. "I admit, investigating deaths all day can't be a fun job, but he could at least appear to be interested in solving his cases."

"He's got a lot on his mind. His wife died two weeks ago, and he's got three teenaged kids to look after, two of them girls."

"His wife died?" Katie asked, suddenly feeling like a heartless harpy.

Schuler nodded. "The whole family's pretty shook up. I was surprised he came back to work so soon. I don't think I could have."

"H-How?" Katie managed.

"It was sudden. A traffic accident."

"Like my husband," she murmured, her heart suddenly filled with compassion for the poor man. No wonder he'd found it hard to concentrate on Ezra's case with his own loss so fresh and painful.

Rose had wrapped the vase in tissue, bagged it, and handed it back to Schuler. "I hope your wife likes it."

"I'm sure she will," he said and smiled.

Katie fumbled for something to say. "Uh . . . thank you for shopping at Artisans Alley."

Schuler gave her a smile. "Christmas is coming. I'm sure I'll be back." He nodded a good-bye and headed for the door.

"That poor Detective Davenport," Rose said, shaking her head in sympathy.

Much as Katie wanted to be angry at Davenport, she now found she couldn't. How awful it must be to be thinking of death day and night—at home *and* on the job. Ezra had been dead a week and a day—that really wasn't an awful lot of time. She knew from reading books, newspapers, and magazines that murder investigations usually took months—sometimes much longer—to solve. She'd have to cut the detective some slack and let him heal—and do his job in his own way, in his own time. What else could she do?

Then Katie's gaze wandered back to Seth's bill still clenched in her hand, the sight of it reigniting her anger. She wanted nothing more than to yell, to throw something breakable against the wall, to release her ire, but she didn't want to air her grievances in front of the vendors or Artisans Alley's customers. She glanced at her watch—it was just about lunchtime. Tracy would no doubt be waiting tables and unavailable to talk. That left only one other person Katie could think of to talk to.

The door to Angelo's Pizzeria was locked. A CLOSED sign hung from a little suction cup on the plate glass door, but Katie pressed the doorbell anyway. Cold fat raindrops plopped from the edge of the gutters, splashing onto Katie's head. Since the last time she'd visited, something new had been added below the soffit on the ends of the building and along the peak: white-painted, wooden gingerbread accents. When had Andy had time to do that?

Plop! Katie moved aside only to be hit by another fat drop of water. She rang the bell yet again.

Andy came out from the back room, his Buffalo Bills sweatshirt dusted with flour, his hands covered in plastic gloves. His annoyed expression melted to mild interest as he moved toward the door, peeling off the gloves as he went.

"What's up?" he asked, letting Katie inside.

She indicated the additions just visible through the plate glass window. "Very nice."

Andy's smile was genuine. "I decided I should try to have my shop blend in with the rest of the neighborhood. I'm glad you approve, but that's not why you came to see me, is it?"

"No. I remembered you said you came in around noon to get your dough started. Would you have time to talk while you work?"

Andy studied her face. For a moment she thought he might refuse, then his expression softened. "Sure."

Katie followed Andy to the back room, stopping short at the sight of an enormous mechanical mixer with an evil-looking hook that stretched sticky dough inside a gigantic stainless steel bowl. Racks of finished dough, in premeasured sizes, stood against the opposite wall to rise.

"Wow," Katie said, breathing in the same yeasty smell she'd encountered in Mary's kitchen the evening before, only this was dough production taken to the max. "Will you use all this up tonight?" she yelled over the *wunk wunk wunk* of the mixer.

"That and more," Andy hollered. "What did you want to talk about?"

"Can we go back in the shop where it's quieter?"

Andy shook his head. "I'll be done with this in a minute. Then we can talk."

As if on cue, the machine abruptly quit. Andy donned a new pair of plastic gloves and raised the mixer's safety guard. Katie watched as he disentangled the dough from the hook, then moved the bowl to an adjoining worktable and began shaping gobs of the stuff into circular mounds, all the same size.

"Isn't there a machine to do that for you, too?" Katie asked.

"Yeah, but I like the feel of the dough," he said. "Now, what did you want to ask me?"

"I need a man's opinion."

Andy looked up, but continued to work. "About what?"

Katie hesitated. "Signals."

This time, Andy paused in his dough manipulation, raising an eyebrow in interest.

"The kind of signals a man gives a woman when he's interested in her," Katie explained.

Was that a look of panic in Andy's eyes?

"I don't think I've been giving you signals," he said, sounding alarmed.

Katie frowned. "Not *you,* someone else."

"What kind of signals?" he asked suspiciously.

"Oh . . . affectionate kisses. Holding hands. Little favors. That kind of thing."

"Sounds pretty tame to me," Andy said with relief, turning his attention back to the dough.

"I suppose it does," Katie admitted.

"Just who's been sending you these signals?" Andy asked, his tone now amused.

"Seth Landers."

Andy looked up, his eyes narrowing. "Seth Landers the lawyer?"

"Yes, why?"

"Katie," he said, his voice tinged with exasperation. "Didn't you know Seth Landers is gay?"

Twenty-one

Katie's throat tightened. "Gay, as in happy?"

Andy shook his head.

"I didn't think so," Katie said, suddenly feeling ten kinds of foolish. "How do you know he's gay?"

Andy shrugged. "Gaydar. A man just knows these things. But if he *has* been flirting with you, you have to ask yourself, what did he hope to accomplish by taking you in?"

Katie thought about it for a moment. Just what *had* Seth been up to, kissing her, holding her hand? She swallowed down a walnut-sized lump in her throat. "Gerald Hilton said the Radisson Hotel chain offered Ezra a million dollars for Artisans Alley site."

"The Radisson?" Andy repeated and laughed. "Hardly. It was Motel Six. Their lawyers talked to me about it, too."

"Did they?" she asked, surprised.

He nodded. "I own the tip of the tract of land they've been after. They wanted me to convince Ezra to sell."

"That wouldn't have worked. Were you willing to sell?"

"I considered it. But the charm of this place is

311

its location. I wasn't eager to be the cause of Victoria Square's downfall." Andy smiled, resuming his work. "Besides, I didn't stand to make half the money Hilton did either. And it wasn't anything like a million. Maybe Hilton told his nephew that just to piss him off."

"If he did, it worked. I know Gerald told Seth about it. He said Gerald wanted him to convince me to sell."

"Hand me that flour bin from the shelf, will you?" Andy said. "What did you tell Seth?"

Katie passed him the canister. "That I wasn't interested in selling."

Andy sprinkled flour on the gummy mass before him. "And Seth's reaction was?"

Katie shrugged. "Just that I should concentrate on keeping Artisans Alley open—if that's what I wanted."

Andy filled the first tray with rounds of dough, setting it on the rack and reaching for another. "What brought this whole Seth thing to a head anyway?"

"This," Katie said, pulling out the by-now crumpled letter from her jacket pocket. She held it for Andy to read.

"I'd say Landers blew it. He had to know this was going to make you mad. Unless it's a mistake."

"A mistake?"

"Sure, maybe he's got an overzealous secretary looking for a raise. It's the end of the month. She probably sent out bills to all his clients. See the signature? She signed his name, then initialed it."

Katie squinted at the letter. She'd been too angry to notice that before.

"Okay, but that still doesn't explain why a gay man has been coming on to me."

"Are you sure he was coming on to you, or was it just wishful thinking?"

Boy, that stung! But could it be true? Katie had been out of circulation for a long time, and these last few months had been the loneliest of her life.

Maybe Seth *was* just trying to be kind.

"What are you thinking?" Andy asked, scrutinizing her face.

"That maybe I *am* in over my head."

"Then take your time, look at all the possibilities before you make any major decisions. Whatever's going on, stall. The more time you have to think, the better. Don't let anyone bamboozle you, Katie. Not Seth, not Gerald. Not Rose, not Tracy. Nobody." He smiled and winked. "Not even me."

Back at Artisans Alley, Katie stared at her office phone, brooding for a good ten minutes before dialing Seth's office number. The line rang and rang. Finally, voice mail kicked in.

"The law office of Seth D. Landers, Esquire, is now closed. Our hours are—"

Katie hung up, and then consulted her address book before punching in Seth's home phone number. It, too, rang and rang. She was about to hang up when Seth answered the phone. "Hello?"

"Seth, it's Katie."

"My favorite client," he said, a gentle softness in his voice.

"Thank you for the compliment," she said, trying to keep her tone level. "I received your bill for services rendered in this morning's mail."

"You don't sound happy."

"I'd heard an attorney's billable hours are all important, but I didn't know you were on the clock when we ate at Del's the other night."

"I wasn't," he said.

"According to the bill I received this morning, you were. I also didn't realize just how much we'd talked during—and outside of—office hours."

"I document all my client phone conversations," he explained, his tone growing distant. "Linda, my secretary, goes through my personal calendar when she prepares the monthly billing. I probably jotted down that we talked about Ezra's estate during our dinner. She shouldn't have billed you for that."

"There's the flowers for the funeral as well. I didn't authorize you to send them."

"You're right. That was also a mistake. I'll speak to Linda and have her send out an amended bill on Monday."

"Thank you," Katie said, her voice still chilly.

The silence between them lengthened.

"Does this mean you won't have dinner with me tonight?" Seth asked.

"What's the point? I mean, I'm really not your *type,* am I?"

More silence. Then, "I'm sorry if you misinterpreted my offer of friendship, Katie. And I guess I misjudged you. Somehow I thought you'd be more open-minded."

"I'm very open-minded. I just don't like to be misled."

The silence that followed that statement was painful to endure.

Finally, Seth spoke. "I'll make sure Linda sends out that amended bill on Monday. I'm sorry if I've said or done anything that hurt your feelings or offended you, Katie. And I'll be glad to recommend another attorney for you. Good-bye."

"Seth, wait—"

But the connection was severed.

Katie hung up the phone, feeling like the worst kind of hypocrite. She hadn't thought of herself as bigoted. She'd just been . . . lonely, and now disappointed. She had liked Seth—a lot. And the fact that he could never be interested in her as a romantic partner . . . Well, what was wrong with friendship anyway?

She glanced at Chad's smiling picture on the desk in front of her. "Look at all the trouble I'm in. If you hadn't gone and gotten yourself—" She stopped, once again ashamed of herself.

That's right, blame Chad for everything. Like he'd planned on skidding into a tree and dying on that snowy winter night the previous March.

Katie glanced at her watch. It was less than an hour before Artisans Alley closed.

A long Saturday evening stretched before her—and now she'd have to fend for her supper, too. Cooking was the last thing she felt like doing. And, she reminded herself, it was Halloween. Maybe she'd get an assorted sub at the grocery's deli. Mason loved it when she tore off shards of ham to share with him. And she had to get Halloween candy anyway.

Saturday night—the loneliest night of the week. Maybe the trick-or-treaters would cheer her. Katie got a kick out of seeing the kids dressed as ghosts, goblins, and NASCAR heroes. And if there was any candy left over, well, it wouldn't be her first sugar binge. She'd buy plenty of Snickers bars to be sure she could indulge.

Katie straightened up her already tidy desk, then looked around her grubby office. Tomorrow she'd scrub the room. Monday, when Artisans Alley was closed, she'd hit Home Depot early and buy a couple of cans of paint and begin the process of making the room truly her own. She'd lost the English Ivy Inn. She'd lost Seth's friendship. Artisans Alley was just as good a place as any for a new start.

• • •

The "twenty-minute warning," as Katie liked to call it, had already been issued, letting customers know that Artisans Alley would soon be closing. She wandered up to Cash Desk 1, where Rose was taking care of a customer. Katie recognized the woman as the shopper who never spent more than five dollars.

"And what treasure have we found today?" Rose asked.

The woman frowned. "Are you making fun of me?"

Rose blushed. "No, of course not!"

"I've heard what some of you people say about me," she said with an edge to her voice.

"That you're one of our most valued customers?" Katie prompted.

The woman looked up sharply. "No, that I'm cheap!"

Katie did her best to appear shocked.

"Who are you?" the woman asked.

"Katie Bonner, Artisans Alley's new manager, and I'm very upset to hear that you've been insulted by one of my vendors," she said sincerely. "How can we make your shopping experience better?"

The woman's frown deepened. "You could spiff the place up. And offer stuff that regular people can actually afford."

Katie noticed the booth number on the tag of the hand-knitted dishcloth belonged to Edie

Silver. The item's cost: two dollars. "As you can see, we do have a few vendors with inexpensive items. And we'll be bringing in more in the next couple of weeks. They'll be in our newly expanded loft. I hope you'll continue to visit and patronize Artisans Alley during the holiday season."

The woman's expression softened. "I like to come here and shop. Thanks for telling me about the new vendors. I'll let my friends know."

Rose finished ringing up the sale, and then bade the customer good-bye, adding a cheerful, "Have a nice evening." She waited until the woman was out of earshot to speak again. "Gee, you saved us with that one."

"Bad word of mouth can cost us an awful lot of customers," Katie said. "I guess I'd better draft some rules of conduct for the vendors. I don't want any other customer to feel they aren't welcome here." She glanced down at the chipped coffee mug that was nearly overflowing with price tags. "Will you give me a small bag? I'll take these in to Ida. Maybe she can catch up on a few before she goes home," Katie said. She emptied the mugs from both cash desks and headed for the tag room.

As anticipated, Ida sat hunched over the little table, intent on straightening up the piles of paper before her. She'd divided them into stacks of ten, laying them out before her on the table, making it easier to find each individual sheet, which corresponded to each vendor's booth number.

She sorted through the tags, putting them in groups of tens, and then adding them to the appropriate sheets. She'd lined the tags up like soldiers on review. She really did take the job way too seriously. But then, maybe that was all she had in her life.

How sad to have no other purpose.

Katie knocked on the doorjamb so as not to startle the old woman. "Do you have a minute to talk, Ida?"

Ida raised her head, but didn't turn to look at Katie.

Katie entered the small room, drew up one of the folding chairs, and sat at the opposite side of the card table from Ida. "I wanted to let you know that I've had several requests from other artists who want to take over your booth. I've had to make a very hard decision. I'm sorry, Ida, but if you can't pay the back rent you owe by Monday, I'm going to have to ask you to vacate your booth."

A fat tear rolled down the old woman's cheek. "You can't do that to me," she said, her voice quavering.

"I'm afraid I can. The plain fact is, Artisans Alley can't survive without more income. Everyone has to pay their way."

"I don't have the money, and I can't leave. The only friends I have are here. What will I do? Where will I go during the day if I can't be here?"

"I'd like to suggest a compromise. You don't

have a lot of stock in your booth. If you're willing to take a shelf in one of the new display cases in back, I'll only charge you ten percent on anything you sell. That way you won't have to pay rent, and if you want to continue to be the tag room manager, you can. And you can come to Artisans Alley and work as much or as little as you like. Does that sound reasonable?"

Ida wiped another tear from her eye. "I—I could do that."

Katie gave the older woman what she hoped was an encouraging smile. "Good. Now, why don't we plan to move your lace to one of the display cases on Monday morning? I'll help you with it, if you'd like."

"Thank you," Ida said.

Katie stood, realizing she still held the little paper bag full of tags. "I almost forgot to give this to you." She handed it to Ida.

"I'll make sure I finish these off before I leave tonight," Ida said enthusiastically.

Katie looked at her watch. "We'll be closing in a few minutes. Why don't you save them until tomorrow?"

"Okay. Thanks, Katie," Ida said, and even managed a weak smile.

Katie gave the old woman a wave and exited the cramped little room. It was with a tremendous feeling of relief that she sidled past the line of customers at the cash registers and headed back to her office. At least she'd done one thing right today, grateful she hadn't made an enemy of Ida. Still, her misunderstanding with Seth continued to gnaw at her thoughts. She'd thought they were friends. Had he been trying to manipulate her all along? Had all his encouragement for her to keep Artisans Alley open been a sham? Lawyers were known to be cunning, and Seth was certainly no slouch.

Katie sank into her chair and leaned back, thinking about all her dealings with the attorney, all the things she'd learned in the last week, her mind roiling with suspicion.

She caught sight of Ronnie's photo on her desk and picked it up. He'd been a handsome young lad. The picture had to have been taken some twenty years before. No one had told her how old Ronnie would have been had he lived. Thirty-five? Forty? Older? Katie wondered what he would've looked like as he'd matured. In fact . . .

Katie studied the picture for a long time, trying to envision a much older Ron Hilton. Finally she got up from her chair and took the photo over to the tabletop copier. She changed the setting to LIGHTEN to compensate for the richness of the color hues, and hit the start button. A copy slid out the side a few seconds later, landing in the tray. She took the picture back to her desk and sat down, grabbing a dull pencil and adding some shading around the eyes, drew in a few wrinkles here and there, and—

With a jolt she realized just who this handsome young man looked like.

"Katie?"

Katie's head snapped up to see Seth Landers standing in her doorway, with his hands thrust into the pockets of his damp raincoat. She quickly turned the paper over and swallowed. "I didn't expect to see you again."

"I didn't want to leave things as they were on the phone." Although his voice was gentle, a thread of worry curled through her.

"I'm glad of that," Katie said. "Can we talk?"

"That's why I'm here," he said.

"Will you give me some straight answers?"

Seth gave a snort of laughter at her choice of words, but nodded and closed the office door. He looked at the top of the file cabinet, brushed away the dust with his hand, then leaned his elbow against it. "Shoot."

"Why did you kiss me? Hold my hand?" Katie asked, her voice wavering. "Why—"

"I like you, Katie. The fact that we could never be lovers has nothing to do with the affection I feel for you."

Katie felt her cheeks grow warm. "I've been doing a lot of thinking. Certain things just don't add up. But then, a lot of things have suddenly become clear."

Seth's gaze narrowed. "Why don't you tell me what you think you know."

"You said you were adopted. That you'd been going through your father's legal files. Everything sort of fell into place when I looked at this."

She gave him the doctored picture of Ezra's son. "Are you Ronnie Hilton's brother?" she asked.

Seth exhaled a long breath, fixing his gaze on Katie. "You're probably the only person in the village with guts enough to ask. Everyone else just whispered about it—that is, until Ronnie died, then they seemed to lose interest."

"Did you know?"

"I suspected. I knew I was adopted, but I never saw my birth certificate until my dad died. Then I knew for sure. How did you guess?"

"Rose Nash told me of her brief affair with a married man. She didn't say who, but she did say it was with the owner of the local appliance store. I guess she didn't realize I knew Ezra owned such a business some forty or fifty years ago. Rose said she put her child up for adoption. You're the right age, and you were adopted."

Seth's mouth drooped. "When I confronted him, dear Ezra denied it. He never would admit to making a mistake. But you're right, Rose Nash did list him on the birth certificate. And as you can tell, there's a definite family resemblance."

Katie felt her insides squirm. "Are you planning to have yourself declared his direct heir? Sue the estate, sell off the land Artisans Alley sits on . . ."

Dear Lord, she realized with horror, *could Seth have killed Ezra?*

"Hold it—hold it," Seth said, exasperated. "Where did you come up with all of this?"

"You knew the land Artisans Alley is on was worth a lot of money. As Ezra's heir you could—"

Seth's mouth dropped open, his eyes narrowing. He stared at Katie for long seconds, then his lips curled into a smile. "You really think I want his estate?"

"It's a logical assumption."

Seth started to laugh.

"It's not funny."

"Oh, yes, it is," Seth said, trying his best to stifle his amusement. "Katie, it's really none of your damned business, but I'm not some maladjusted adoptee who went looking for his birth parents. I happened to have loved the people who adopted me very, very much. And they also happened to have left me a very rich man. I'll say one thing, I probably inherited some of my business acumen from Ezra, but unlike him, I'm a lot more successful."

Katie decided to blast ahead with both barrels. "What percentage of the marina do you own?"

Seth's eyes widened in admiration. "Very astute."

"I figured you did more than just real estate closings at that big firm in Rochester—before you took over your father's practice. And you haven't answered my question. What percentage of the marina do you own?"

"Almost half."

"I suppose you've been quietly buying up land for the past couple of years," she said. "And you wanted this place, too."

"That's where you're wrong," Seth said, sobering. "Honey, I own three parcels of land that would make much better locations for a hotel site. I've been negotiating with the Motel Six chain for the past four months. We'll probably close the deal before the end of next week. And then there's the new water park. Big things are about to happen in the township, but Victoria Square will still be a big draw. I'm betting it'll keep those hotel rooms filled to at least fifty percent capacity during the winter months when the marina is closed. Why would you think I'd want to kill a cash cow?"

Katie hadn't considered that. But then, she'd only harbored her harebrained theory for a matter of minutes.

"I suppose I look pretty stupid, what with all my wrong conclusions, and then thinking you were coming on to me."

Seth took the chair near her desk, leaned forward, and took her hands in his. "Sweet Katie, I think you're a woman who's had a hell of a lot to adjust to in the past week. Thanks to Ezra's murder, you've been tossed into quite a traumatic situation. You quit your job. You've been vandalized. You found a dead body, and have even been overcharged by your overbearing lawyer. I think any mistakes you've made this week can be entirely forgiven. They would be, at least, by a friend."

Katie's bottom lip quivered. "I feel like such a fool."

"Why? Because you're human?"

She nodded, avoiding his warm brown eyes.

With one finger, Seth tilted her chin upward. "I'm offering myself in the role of big brother . . . if you'll accept me."

"I never had a big brother."

"And I've never been one. What do you say we struggle through it together?"

Tears burned her eyes, but Katie managed a smile. "I accept."

"Then are we still on for dinner?" Seth asked.

Katie sniffled. "I forgot it was Halloween. I'd kind of like to see the kids all dressed up in their costumes. How about a rain check?"

"How about tomorrow night?" Seth asked.

"Sounds great. I have a lot of stuff to tell you. And I've got that copy of the loan agreement Gerald Hilton signed that you wanted." She got up, fumbled in the file cabinet, and extracted the paper. She folded it into thirds and stuffed it into a business-sized envelope from the box on the top of the cabinet. Seth took it and thrust it into his raincoat's inner breast pocket. Again, he took both Katie's hands in his own. They were warm and dry, the touch giving Katie a feeling of security—something she hadn't felt since Chad's betrayal almost a year before.

"I guess I'll see you tomorrow, then," Katie said.

Seth leaned forward and gave her a quick, brotherly peck on the cheek. This time, it made her happy. "See you then," he said.

With both her purse and Chad's journal tucked under her arm, Katie turned the key in Artisans Alley's back door lock.

"Happy Halloween!" Rose called brightly as she headed for her car.

Katie waved, and then hurried through the drizzle to her own car. Rain on Halloween was just plain no fun. She felt sorry for all the little kids in their soggy costumes, their wet paper sacks dragging on the ground until they tore, leaving a trail of candy treasure behind them. She got in her car, tossed the book and her purse onto the passenger seat, buckled up, and then started the engine. The windshield wipers thumped as she headed for the parking lot's exit. She paused behind Rose's car, which was turning left.

Katie looked over at the pizzeria on her left, saw Andy in the window, and waved. He tossed pizza dough in the air and waved back, which messed up his timing. The dough came down on the brim of his baseball cap and tore in half. Katie laughed, feeling better than she had in months, then pulled forward, and checked oncoming traffic before she turned right.

Daylight was quickly fading as she headed east on shiny streets for Ezra's house. She'd have to stop at the grocery store on the way home to pick up Halloween candy. Her apartment complex was a favorite spot for McKinlay Mill's kid population. Many doors in a small area expanded the potential for chocolate bars, peanut butter cups, and other sweets.

Katie pulled into Ezra's darkened gravel drive. How had he ever gotten out of it in the winter when lake-effect snow pummeled the region? She turned off the engine. Only the sound of raindrops tapping on her car roof broke the silence. Fingers clutching the door handle, she hesitated before opening it. Why hadn't she changed that burned-out bulb over the house's side door? And why hadn't she left a light on in the house for Della when she'd left that morning? No other cars lurked in the drive or out by the barn. Had Detective Davenport been out to check on Ashby's merchandise? She really should check on that herself, but not tonight. Suddenly every nerve in her body was on alert.

Ridiculous! There's nothing to be afraid of, she told herself. Except that two people associated with this property had ended up murdered.

Katie switched on the car's dome light and sorted through the set of keys Seth had given her. On impulse, she grabbed Chad's journal. Maybe she'd spend a few minutes with Della, getting to know her better, and read a few more passages. And maybe she wouldn't feel so alone and skittish in the strange house if she had Chad by her side. Well, what was left of him anyway.

Clutching the book and her purse, Katie bolted from the car, dashing for the back door. Her hand trembled as she fumbled to insert the key into the lock. She practically fell into the kitchen, slamming the door and locking it in one fluid motion.

Della was waiting and launched herself at Katie, purring and meowing at once—happy, yet scolding Katie for being late.

Katie turned on the kitchen lights, then dropped her keys and purse on the counter. She stooped to pick up the empty kitty bowl from the floor. "I'm going as fast as I can," she told Della, swishing the bowl with a wet paper towel. She opened another can of food, dumping it into the bowl. "You're going to a new home on Monday, little girl. You'll probably have to live in the spare room while I'm at work—at least for the first week or so. But you won't be stuck out here all alone anymore. I don't know how your new brother will feel about that, but we'll manage somehow, won't we? Hey, we'll both have new big brothers," she said, smiling, the thought warming her.

Della wound around and around her ankles, more interested in dinner than talk of her new living arrangements.

As she attended to the cat's needs, Katie wondered if she ought to start calling estate liquidators. There was no sense in waiting. Maybe Rose or one of the other Alley artisans knew of someone who did that kind of thing. She'd have to ask. Of course, the house was probably filled with items Ezra would not like to see on the auction block. Photos, personal mementos, the family Bible . . . She'd have to let Gerald go through the house and take what he wanted in the way of personal effects. That was the decent thing to do, even if Gerald hadn't acted decently himself.

While Della, nose buried in her dish, happily lapped up her food, Katie grabbed Chad's journal from the counter and wandered into the living room, turning on lights as she went.

She sank into Ezra's easy chair and opened the book. What had Chad's last recorded thoughts been, she wondered, flipping to the last few pages of entries.

March 14th

She came to see me again today, making sure he saw her first, of course. I don't want her here. If Katie saw her hanging around, she might think I was interested, and I don't want anything to interfere with us getting back together.

Katie blinked. She? Who? Her gaze dipped back to the journal.

Katie's the best thing that ever happened to me. We talked on the phone for a while tonight. She said Mason misses me. I miss him, too. But not as much as I miss Katie.

Katie well remembered that conversation. It had been their last. And they'd said good night on good terms. But whom had he written about?

She read the next entry, written only two days later.

March 16th

Damn that woman! I swear it was her car that nearly ran me off the road last night. I confronted her this afternoon, but she swore up and down she was home—that it couldn't have been her.
Yeah. Right.

Katie's stomach tightened. Someone had tried to run Chad off the road only days before he died? Was that possible? Could someone—some woman—have actually tried to kill him? What for? Who could it have been? Another teacher at the school? She hadn't heard from any of Chad's colleagues that he'd had a problem at work. But if he'd turned down someone's advances, could the spurned woman have been angry—humiliated— enough to take revenge?

331

No. That was silly. That was impossible.

Then why did her stomach feel so tense?

Was there a pattern to the deaths? Chad? Ezra? Ashby?

A lake-effect snowstorm had hit that March afternoon. Chad had stayed late at school finishing a lesson plan. At least, that's what the police had told her. Could someone have lain in wait for him?

No. The police said Chad lost control of his car on the icy road. Nobody mentioned any other tracks or skid marks.

Katie sprang to her feet, jostling the chair-side table, knocking over one of Ezra's framed photos, dropping the journal on the floor. Her paranoia was definitely getting out of control.

With unsteady hands she retrieved the photo, setting it back on the little yellowed doilies. Too many pairs of dead eyes stared at her from the faded photos around the room.

Katie was drawn to the framed snapshot she'd just set down. Ronnie, holding a chain saw in one hand. It was the tool of his trade, she remembered. Had Ezra sat in his worn recliner, night after night, brooding over the picture? Maybe, but then, Ezra hadn't been entirely lonely these last few years. First he'd sought companionship from Nona Fiske, and more recently Mary Elliott.

Della sauntered into the room, then jumped on the back of the shabby recliner, the first stop to her perch atop the bookshelf, where she began to groom her paws.

Katie looked back at the snapshot, squinting under the inadequate lamplight. She thought again how handsome Ezra's son had been—like Seth— and noticed that the photo inside the frame looked bunched on one side, as though it had been folded over. On impulse, she slid off the frame's backing, took the photo out, and unfolded it.

Katie gazed at the picture, her face going lax as snatches of conversations filled her head. Gossip, innuendo, and all the myriad pieces of information she had gathered during the past week suddenly fell together, and she thought she knew just who had murdered Ezra, Peter Ashby—and probably Chad, too.

Twenty-two

Katie stared at the photo still clutched in her hands. Okay, so she had a good idea who *might* have killed Ezra. But what was the motive, and how could she prove it? And how in the world would she ever convince Detective Davenport to accept it?

She let out a breath, feeling deflated. Davenport already thought she was a borderline crackpot, and possibly his prime suspect. He wasn't likely to believe her newest wild theory. But somehow it all made sense . . . in a weird, convoluted way.

As she placed the framed picture back onto its crocheted tidy, she heard a knock at the kitchen door and glanced at her watch. Could it be trick-or-treaters?

Katie hurried to the back door, again wishing she'd had time to change the damned burned-out bulb over the back door. The man in the dark raincoat who peered up at her from the middle step was the last person Katie expected to see.

She unlocked the heavy wooden door, more annoyed than frightened. "What are you doing here, Gerald?"

"I followed you," he said, brushing past her and entering the kitchen, dripping onto the linoleum.

"What for?"

"To talk—away from Artisans Alley. You're too emotionally involved with that place. I hoped you'd be more rational in another location."

Fat chance, Katie wanted to blurt out, but that would only support his argument. She folded her arms across her chest. "I don't have time for this right now, Gerald. I need to get home. Couldn't we talk about it tomorrow morning? Maybe we could have brunch at Del's Diner to discuss—"

"No! I want to settle this tonight. You've been obstinate and damned self-centered. You haven't taken me into account in any of *your* plans. Uncle Ezra left me half the estate's assets. Artisans Alley is only one part of it. I want what's rightfully mine. I want—"

"You'll get what's rightfully yours, but you can't have it now. My God, Gerald, Ezra's only been in his grave four days. It's going to take months, maybe even a year, before either of us sees any money. Can't you get that through your thick head?"

Hilton glowered at her, a puddle forming around his wet shoes. "I'm running out of time. Can't you see I've got to—"

He stopped, and suddenly it wasn't greed that seemed to shine from the man's eyes, it was something else Katie well recognized: desperation.

"You borrowed five thousand dollars from Ezra last year. Why?" Katie demanded.

Hilton's eyes blazed. "How do you know about that?"

"I found the original agreement you made with Ezra. Did you think I wouldn't?"

"I . . . I hoped you wouldn't," he said, sounding embarrassed.

"Is that why you broke into Artisans Alley and ransacked Ezra's office?"

Hilton said nothing.

"Paying back that five thousand dollars could help keep Artisans Alley in business."

"I don't have the money. I—"

"Of course not," Katie shot back, her own anger getting the best of her. "You paid off your credit card debts, but you didn't pay back Ezra. Instead you spent money on a new car."

Hilton let out a breath. "I needed that car. I have to drive—"

"Where? To the nearest mall? Or how about a casino?"

"I don't know where you got your information on me, Mrs. High-and-Mighty Bonner, but it sounds like you only got half the story!"

"Then why don't you fill me in."

Hilton tore his gaze from Katie's, letting out a ragged breath as his anger dissolved. "You don't bring up your children to be drug addicts—but it doesn't take much experimenting before they're hooked."

Katie's breath caught in her throat, as though

he'd punched her in the gut. "Drugs?"

"Our HMO decided my daughter Miranda only needed two months of outpatient treatment." Hilton's laugh of derision sounded more like a strangled sob. "Seeing her so close to the edge—and being told they won't do anything more . . . I did max out my credit cards. Do you think I would've asked that miserable old skinflint for cash if I hadn't been desperate?"

"But you bought a new car," Katie protested.

"My fourteen-year-old station wagon died. How else was I going to get to work?" Gerald pushed himself away from the stove, his eyes shadowed with misery.

"Why didn't you tell Ezra you needed the money for your daughter?"

"My uncle believed drug addicts come from broken homes where there's little or no parental guidance, but it can happen in any family. Miranda was an honor student—had never been in trouble—before her sophomore year."

Oh dear, Katie thought. No wonder Hilton had been in such a state.

Then Andy's words came back to her: *"Don't let anyone bamboozle you, Katie. Not Seth, not Gerald. Not Rose, not Tracy. Nobody."*

Was Hilton lying? Was he only giving her a sob story to gain her sympathy?

She studied Hilton's eyes. No one could fake such desolation. "Ezra lost his only child—*your* cousin Ronnie. Didn't it occur to you that he might have wanted to help your child?"

"When Ronnie died, Uncle Ezra's compassion died with him. He wouldn't have—"

"How could you know for sure? You never gave him a chance."

"*You* didn't know him like I did."

Katie motioned him to follow her into the living room. She marched to the end table by Ezra's chair, grabbed the photograph she'd returned to its frame only minutes before, and shoved it under his nose. "A man who lacks compassion wouldn't keep pictures of his dead child on the walls and every flat surface to remind him of his loss."

Hilton stared at the picture of his dead cousin, his eyes shining. "I never heard the old man speak of Ronnie after the funeral. He never let on that he—"

"What? That he missed his son? Oh, Gerald . . ." Instead of anger, Katie could only muster sympathy for the pitiable man in front of her. Her next news would depress him more. "I have some bad news. The motel offer has been rescinded."

Hilton's head snapped up. "You're lying."

Katie shook her head. "They've chosen another parcel of land midway between the new marina and the village. The deal will be completed by next week."

"Who told you that?"

"Seth Landers. He said he'd be glad to talk to you about it, too. And by the way, it wasn't the high-end Radisson chain that wanted the land—it was Motel Six, a lot further down on the hotel scale, and their offer was nowhere near a million dollars."

Gerald paled, turning away. "My God, I'm ruined. I was counting on that money to help Miranda, to—"

"There are other options," Katie said, "but selling Artisans Alley should not be one of them. Victoria Square is on the verge of a real breakthrough. It would be better for McKinlay Mill—better for you and me—to give it a fighting chance to survive. We could sell this house, the barn, and the acreage—they've got to be worth a couple hundred thousand at least—that would keep you afloat for a while. You can have it, Gerald. You can have all this. I won't allow a child to suffer in order to keep Ezra's and Chad's dream alive. But let me try to make a go of Artisans Alley. Don't you see, if I can bring it into solvency, it could be a constant stream of income for both of us."

"I'd like to believe you, Mrs. Bonner. I—"

"Call me Katie."

"Katie," Hilton said, and for the first time there was no hint of animosity in his voice.

"Will you come back to McKinlay Mill tomorrow? We can talk this through. We should make plans for the future. There have got to be ways we can make this work—for both of us."

For a long time Hilton said nothing. Then, grudgingly, "Okay."

Katie offered her hand. "Partners?"

Hilton stared at it for a long moment. Finally he reached out, took her hand, and shook on it.

"How touching," came a sour voice from the open doorway. Katie hadn't heard the side door open, hadn't heard the intruder come into the kitchen.

"It's too bad neither of you will live to see a penny of Ezra's estate."

Slowly, Katie turned to face Ezra Hilton's killer.

Twenty-three

Katie eyed the intruder, apprehension growing within her. "Hello, Tracy."

"What's she talking about?" Hilton asked, looking puzzled.

"Yes, Tracy, why don't you explain," Katie said, sounding calmer than she felt. "You can start by telling us why you killed Ezra."

Hilton's eyes widened with alarm.

Katie glanced at a scowling Tracy. Her dark eyes were hard. Funny Katie hadn't noticed that before.

"It would only be a waste of time," Tracy said. Reaching into her denim jacket, she withdrew a snub-nosed revolver.

Katie looked at the barrel, then back to Tracy's cold brown eyes. *Keep her talking,* she told herself. "Then why don't I tell Gerald."

"What do *you* know?"

"Quite a lot, it turns out. You left Andy for Ronnie Hilton, but Ezra broke you up. He didn't think you were good enough for his son."

"He didn't think *anyone* was good enough for Ronnie."

"But there was more to it than that, wasn't there?" Katie asked.

Tracy glowered at her.

"Ezra knew you were trouble, because you'd been in trouble years before."

Tracy said nothing, her grip tightening on the revolver.

"It wasn't only Andy who got caught for wrecking Ezra's car. He had an accomplice. The person Andy tried to cover up for. The person who actually drove the car that night. The one who smashed it up."

Tracy's lips curled into a snarl. "How would *you* know?"

"I worked in the insurance business for years. I know how to get information on past driving offenses."

Tracy still said nothing.

"You killed Peter Ashby, too, didn't you?" Katie asked, playing for time. "You already had keys to Artisans Alley—you took them from Ezra the night you killed him."

"Ashby saw me leave Artisans Alley the night Ezra died—he tried to blackmail me," Tracy admitted. "We made a deal. I'd give him money for his silence. I was to pay him the first installment on Thursday."

"What did you do, ask Ashby to Artisans Alley—lure him to his own booth, then push him over the balcony rail?" Katie asked.

"He put up quite a struggle," Tracy admitted, amused, the gun still trained on them.

"You're going to kill us anyway, why not tell us the *real* reason you killed Ezra," Katie demanded.

Hatred twisted Tracy's pretty face into a grimace. "That creepy old man came after my mother! He wanted *her* money to save Artisans Alley. He asked her to marry him! She wanted a companion—a replacement for Dad. She *likes* older men," Tracy nearly spat. "She was actually going to give him the money. Money *I* earned. *I* turned that business around. It was my efforts on the Internet that finally turned a profit for Tea and Tasties. Mom had no right to promise Ezra my money, and I wasn't about to let him have it."

"So you killed him." Not a question—a statement.

"I would've done anything to keep him away from my mother and our assets."

"But Ezra wasn't your first victim. It started with Ronnie, didn't it?"

"If Ronnie hadn't been preoccupied by our break-up, he wouldn't have gotten killed by that falling limb. Just because I happened to be there doesn't mean I was responsible. That old man ruined my life once. I wasn't about to let him ruin it again." Tracy waved the gun. "Put your hands up."

Katie and Hilton obediently raised their hands.

"Ronnie's 'accident' wasn't pure happenstance, though, was it?" Katie asked.

Tracy raised an appraising eyebrow.

"Did Ezra suspect you had something to do with his son's death? Did he accuse you of being responsible for what happened to Chad, too?"

Tracy said nothing.

"Did you kill my husband?" Katie tried again, louder.

"What is your appeal with men?" Tracy asked with a sneer. "All Chad would talk about was getting back with"—her voice dropped to a simper—"his dear sweet Katie."

"You stole the painting that hangs in your office," Katie cried. "Was that before or after you threw yourself at him?"

Tracy's glare smoldered, but she didn't bother to refute either statement.

"You weren't interested in Chad anyway. You only wanted to make Andy jealous. You knew Chad was living at Artisans Alley. You made sure Andy saw you cross the parking lot to visit Chad."

"What of it?"

"So why kill Chad? Because he didn't fall for you?"

"*Real* men pay attention to me," Tracy stated. "Chad wouldn't. And he had to pay."

"But why get rid of us?" Hilton asked, panicked.

Tracy moved farther into the living room, her back to the bookcase, forcing Katie and Hilton to step back.

"I don't care about *you*," Tracy grated. "But

now Katie's got what I want—and I won't let her have it."

"I don't know what you're talking about," Katie said, confused.

"Andy."

"Are you crazy? I only met him a week ago."

"He likes you. Since our divorce, he told me he'd sworn off women. But he likes you. I saw the two of you in the pizza joint the night Ashby died, laughing, making eyes at each other. I've seen the way Andy looks at you—lusting after you."

Katie had to restrain herself from laughing. "I helped him make pizzas because he was shorthanded. That's all."

"Liar!" Tracy brought the gun up in line with Katie's chest. "If I can't have him, I'm certainly not going to let *you* have him. So I called Ezra's nephew and told him I was with the McKinlay Mill Town Development Association. I got him all worked up about how you were responsible for holding up the hotel deal, convinced him you were going to blow it for the whole town, knowing he'd confront you. I even told him he should get you on your own to talk."

Katie shot a look at Gerald. "There is no McKinlay Mill Development Association."

He shrugged. "How was I to know that?"

"I couldn't believe it when Hilton actually showed up in Artisans Alley's parking lot. I sat in my car and waited, then followed him straight here to you. Now I'll arrange for a fitting end—for both of you."

"What kind of end?" Katie asked, fear turning to panic.

"Murder-suicide. Everyone knows you two have practically been at each other's throats. Dear sweet Rose has been telling half the town about it for days. Mom told me Hilton owes Ezra's estate money he can't pay back. Yes, I'll make it look like he killed you—then himself."

"My wife will never believe it," Hilton said.

"It doesn't matter. That clod of a detective investigating Ezra's death will believe anything."

Katie's fingers began to tingle from lack of circulation. Her gaze strayed to movement behind Tracy.

Tracy glanced over her shoulder, then back to Katie. "What are you looking at?"

"Nothing." Katie's gaze returned to the gun.

Then, in a flash of fur, Della jumped from her perch on the bookcase, landing with claws sinking into Tracy's scalp.

Tracy screamed, arms flailing as she swatted at the cat.

The gun fired into the ceiling. A shower of plaster and lath rained down on all of them.

Katie grabbed Hilton's sleeve. "Come on!"

Scrambling into the kitchen, Katie yanked open the door and barreled through it as feline and human screams echoed from the living room.

More gunshots reverberated through the frame house, but Katie was already out the door, tripping down the wooden steps.

Tracy's Chrysler Sebring blocked the end of the driveway.

There were no houses in sight; only barren fields surrounded the property.

There was only one place to hide.

Katie sprinted for the barn, which was just a silhouette against the cloudy sky.

"Gerald!" she hollered, looking back. Hilton shambled behind her, his left hand clutching his sagging right shoulder.

Katie fumbled to open the barn door's hasp. The deputies must've cut off Ashby's lock.

Hilton caught up, breathing hard. "She—she shot me."

Katie yanked open the door, pushing Hilton inside. "Find a place to hide." She slammed the heavy wood door behind her, found the inside bolt—and threw it.

Oh, swell—now they were trapped, she realized. Tracy could shoot through the wooden barn, but Katie was willing to bet she hadn't brought much ammunition. At least, she hoped so.

"What do we . . . do now?" Hilton puffed, leaning against the back wall. His face was shiny with sweat and pale in the wan light.

"I don't know. I left my cell phone in my

purse on the kitchen counter, along with my car keys. I don't suppose you have a phone?"

Hilton shook his head. "I had to give it up—couldn't afford it."

"Katie!" Tracy yelled. "You're only making it harder on yourself."

Think! Katie's brain demanded.

Sudden light shone in through the barn's dirty window. Katie risked a look. Tracy had switched on Katie's car's headlights. Katie ducked back, afraid Tracy might see her and take a potshot.

"You can't wait in there all night," Tracy taunted.

"Oh, yes, we can," Hilton hollered.

Frantic, Katie glanced around the dim barn. There had to be something she could use against Tracy, but what? A gun had a longer range than the spades, shovels, and other gardening tools that hung neatly on the walls. And Katie couldn't lob old bricks, cans, and bottles out the window. Ashby's graveyard statuary stood on tables and on the concrete floor. Dropping a smiling cherub on Tracy would be a satisfying but an unlikely way out of their situation.

"What are we going to do?" Hilton hissed, crouched next to a trough-like sink with a hose connected to its faucet. Underneath sat a bulky machine.

A glimmer of hope raced through Katie. She peeked out the window, looking for Tracy.

Tracy fired.

A window shattered.

Katie ducked the flying shards of glass, and dashed across the barn to the sink.

"Think about it, Tracy," Katie yelled, connecting the end of the hose to the rectangular machine. "You kill us and there'll be questions. Davenport isn't as dumb as he looks—he'll link you to us."

"I'll take that chance, bitch!"

"What are you doing?" Hilton grated, his face drawn, his fingers slick with blood.

"Trying to save our necks." Katie fumbled to plug in the machine's power cord into a wall socket. "Keep her talking."

"Uh . . . I'm gonna sue you, young woman," Hilton stammered. "For . . . uh . . . grievous bodily harm."

Katie rolled her eyes but continued to work. "Keep talking—we've got to lure her in here."

"Are you crazy?" Hilton demanded. "She'll kill us!"

Katie duckwalked across the floor to the barn door, pulled back the heavy bolt, pushing the door open a crack.

"Come on out, Katie," Tracy called. "It'll be easier if you do this my way."

"You'll have to drag us out," Katie yelled, rushing back to the sink. She turned on the water. The hose grew rigid.

"I'll burn you out!" Tracy threatened.

Hilton's eyes widened in panic. "I *told* you!"

Katie uncoiled the hose. "She's bluffing. She'd need an accelerant."

"There're three cars out there full of gasoline," Hilton hissed. "All she's got to do is park one of them against the barn and shoot the gas tank. And then—boom—we're fried!"

Momentary panic ripped through Katie. Presumably Hilton's keys were in his coat pocket, and Tracy wouldn't sacrifice her Sebring and implicate herself. But what about Katie's keys? She'd left them in the house.

"She's bluffing," Katie said again.

"Katie!" Tracy hollered.

"Go to hell!" Katie shouted, hitting the button, powering up the machine. A rumbling growl drowned out the heartbeat thumping in Katie's ears.

An engine roared to life. The nearest car was her own—Tracy *did* have her keys!

Light and shadows shifted as the car rolled forward.

"She's gonna crash through the wall!" Hilton yelled.

But the car didn't crash. Instead the barn was doused in blackness.

Katie jumped to her feet, heading for the broken window, yanking the heavy box and hose behind her. Looking out, she saw that the car's front bumper touched the barn.

Tracy opened the car door—stepped out, turned, and aimed her gun at the gas tank.

Katie broke another, lower pane, shoved the plastic-and-metal three-foot wand through the jagged opening, and pressed the trigger handle. Her hands jerked as a geyser of water exploded from the pressure washer, the force knocking Tracy flat on the ground.

"Gerald! Get out there, get the gun away from her!"

"I can't—my arm is numb!" he cried.

"Then get over here and keep her pinned on the ground!"

Hilton struggled to his feet, staggered as he made his way across the dark barn.

"Lean against the wall for support," Katie ordered, thrusting the power washer's handle into his sticky hand, folding his trembling fingers around it. "Don't faint on me!"

Hilton nodded, swaying, his breaths quick and shallow.

Katie dashed for the barn door, threw it open, and ran across the rain-slick grass toward Tracy. She dived for the gun still clutched in Tracy's outstretched hand. Hilton caught her with a jet of freezing water, knocking her down, leaving her gasping for breath.

A car pulled up at the end of the drive, stopping behind the Sebring.

"Hey!" a male voice called.

Tracy staggered to her knees. The water caught her in the back, slamming her facedown into the muddy ground once again.

Katie threw herself on Tracy, grappling for the gun. They rolled over and over, needles of icy water drilling into them.

"Hey, stop!" yelled the familiar voice.

The torrents of water suddenly ceased, and a sneakered foot clamped down on Tracy's outstretched hand.

Frigid, muddy water dribbled down Katie's chin as she looked up into Andy Rust's face. He smiled. "I thought you might need my help," he said. "But it looks like I was wrong."

Twenty-four

"And you just showed up?" Detective Davenport asked, incredulous. Why did he look so disappointed?

Andy nodded, folding his arms across his beefy chest. "I saw Hilton pull out of the Victoria Square parking lot right after Katie. He turned right just like she did. Then I saw Tracy head out after them. It didn't feel right, but I kept working. Then the more I thought about it, the more it bothered me. I was married to Tracy for three years. I *know* how nasty she can be."

Still huddled under a scratchy wool blanket she'd found in Ezra's linen closet, Katie squinted up at Andy, grateful he'd been concerned for her welfare.

"I knew Katie had gone to feed Ezra's cat," Andy continued, "and it didn't feel right when those two followed her. So, I left one of the boys in charge of my shop and jumped in my car to see if I could catch up with them."

"How far behind were you?" Davenport asked.

"Five—maybe ten minutes," he said.

"And what did you find?"

Andy grinned, glancing over at Katie. "That Mrs.

Bonner is quite capable of taking care of herself."

It had taken almost an hour for Davenport to show up at the scene, but Deputy Schuler had gotten things well in hand. He'd shown up before the ambulance arrived, taking custody of Tracy. Suffering from blood loss, Hilton had been taken to the nearest hospital in Rochester, although the paramedics didn't seem to think he was in any immediate danger.

Davenport glared at Tracy. "What's your side of the story?"

Huddled under a matching wool blanket, Tracy glowered at the Detective. "I'm not saying a word until I have a lawyer present."

Davenport nodded at Tracy. "Get her out of here."

Deputy Schuler stepped forward and pulled a handcuffed Tracy to her feet. "Come on. There's a nice warm cell, complete with dry clothes, just waiting for you in the Monroe County lockup." He pushed Tracy toward the kitchen, where two uniformed deputies waited to escort her to the Sheriff's Office cruiser parked in the front yard.

Once they were out of earshot, Davenport spoke again. "It looks like Mrs. Nash was right about Ashby. I made inquiries yesterday, and just this afternoon got a report from the Cleveland PD. Seems Mr. Ashby was wanted for desecrating cemeteries in more than one county in Ohio, and he had a string of aliases as long as his arm, only he wasn't very clever. He was also called Ashly, Ashland, Ashburger—and probably a lot more. It won't be hard backtracking his movements."

"Surely he couldn't have made a living just selling copies of his cemetery art," Katie said.

"I wouldn't bet on that," Davenport continued. "He had a website advertising his wares. We'll be talking to PayPal to find out just how many sales he's made in the last year or so, and we'll be impounding everything in the barn out back."

"You're welcome to it," Katie said, and shivered. She studied the detective's face. She'd originally thought the dull look in his eyes came from disinterest in his work, but now she could see it was something that had been reflected in her own eyes after Chad's death: loss. She wanted to say something, to apologize, to offer her condolences, but thought better of it. He might not be happy that Deputy Schuler had even mentioned his wife's death. So instead she said, "I'm cold." Her damp clothes were still plastered against her like a clammy second skin. The only part of her that wasn't frozen was where the purring cat sat curled on her lap. Katie scratched the fur around Della's ears. The little tabby seemed none the worse for wear after her tussle with Tracy. "Can we go home now?"

"We?" Davenport asked, looking at Andy with a jaundiced eye.

"Della and me. She saved our lives when she jumped from her perch on the bookshelves and onto Tracy," Katie said. Della purred even louder at the praise.

"I suppose I've got everything I need for now," Davenport said. "But you and Mr. Rust will both need to sign statements in the morning,"

"I'd be glad to," Andy said, and winked at Katie.

Katie put Della on the floor and stood, pulling the blanket closer around her shoulders.

"What do you think Ashby used the power washer for?" Andy asked.

Katie shrugged, heading for the kitchen. "Probably to smooth the rough edges off his statue copies," she said, gathering up cat food, bowls, and a few of Della's cat toys, plopping them into a paper grocery sack. "Or maybe the force of the water helped 'age' the statues. I'm just glad it was sitting in the barn."

"It wasn't smart of you to confront Ms. Elliott," Davenport admonished.

Katie rounded on him. "I didn't have a choice, Detective. She showed up here—held us at gunpoint. I don't know what else I could've done."

"Next time, please call the Sheriff's Office." A couple of days ago, Katie might have taken offense at these words, but now she realized he really was worried for her safety.

She smiled. "Thank you, Detective Davenport. If I'm ever in the same situation, I'll do just that."

With a good-bye nod, the detective headed for the door.

"Need a ride home?" Andy asked Katie.

"I'd love one, but I'll need my car in the morning. Could you wait while I put Della in her carrier? Then maybe you could carry her stuff to the car for me."

"Sure thing."

Unlike Mason, who suddenly developed a dozen legs—with claws as wicked as machetes—when confronted with his cat carrier, Della settled down as soon as Katie closed the Pet Taxi's door.

Andy grabbed the bag of cat supplies and Katie's purse, then waited for her as she turned off the last of the lights and locked the door to Ezra's kitchen.

The rain had stopped and the sky was clear. Moonlight bathed the yard, and stars twinkled above them as they walked in silence through the dewy grass to where Tracy had left Katie's car. Katie placed the cat carrier on the back seat, setting the bag of cat supplies on the car floor. She shut the door. "It's been quite a night."

"In more ways than one," Andy agreed. "I've known Tracy almost my whole life. I knew she could be spiteful, but I never thought her capable of murder. Four people—my God. And to think I once loved her."

Katie nodded. "I just have one question. Wednesday night around seven thirty, I dropped Rose off at Artisans Alley to pick up her car. I saw you looking out your shop window and waved, but you just glared and turned away. I thought maybe I'd offended you."

Andy looked puzzled. "Wednesday?" He thought about it. "Oh, Wednesday. Yeah. Tracy had just paid me a visit. I suppose I was glaring at her shop."

"What for?"

"She came over, wanting to talk. About us getting back together. I asked her to leave."

"She's the one who suggested we let you join the Merchants Association."

"And don't think she didn't call to let me know it."

Katie smiled. "Well, I haven't said thank you for showing up like you did tonight."

"What're friends for?" he said, reaching for her hand. "Besides, you didn't need me. You had everything under control."

"I hate to think what might have happened if you hadn't come by." She squeezed his warm fingers. "It's been a heck of a day. I don't think I'll ever get to sleep tonight."

"Then why don't I bring over a pizza later?"

"Oh," Katie said, surprised. "That would be nice."

Suddenly Andy leaned forward, planted a brief kiss on her lips. He pulled back. "I'm glad you're safe."

They stared at each other for a long moment, and then Andy dropped her purse to take her face in his hands. He caressed her cheeks and then, unlike Seth, gave her a kiss that was anything but brotherly.

Twenty-five

Twinkling white lights brightened the buildings surrounding Victoria Square, complementing the glow of the newly refurbished gaslights. A dusting of snow had transformed the Square into a winter fairyland. Katie pulled the heavy wool shawl tighter around her shoulders, grateful for the full-length skirt and warm petticoats beneath it.

Nearly the whole village, as well as tourists and shoppers from Rochester, had turned out for the grand opening of the first annual Victoria Square Dickens Festival.

"Hurry up, Katie," Rose Nash encouraged, almost giggling as she tied the ruby red ribbon beneath her chin. She'd traded her plastic rain bonnet for an old-fashioned black felt hat decorated in period style. Edie Silver had hot-glued silk flowers and sewn on fancy colorful ribbons to an array of plain-looking headgear, outfitting all Artisans Alley's female artists and the Square's shopkeepers, adding millinery to her long list of creative talents. All the men sported rented top hats.

Katie and Rose started across the Square, heading for the large Norway spruce that had been put up at the end of the parking lot in front of the old

Webster mansion. By next year, it would be a bed-and-breakfast. Katie allowed herself a wistful sigh. She'd made her choice to quit a dead-end job and manage Artisans Alley, and it had been a good one, but somehow she knew she'd always mourn what could have been had she had a chance to open the English Ivy Inn.

Katie paused, deeply inhaling the crisp, cold air. "Can you smell those roasted chestnuts?"

Rose nodded, pointing ahead. "Look at the kids in their choir robes. Aren't they adorable?" She closed her eyes, listening. " 'Silent Night' has always been my favorite carol."

Vance and Janey Ingram stepped out of Gilda's Gourmet Baskets. Janey had traded her usual Dolly look-alike outfit for a hooped skirt and bustle, her blond hair hanging in tight ringlets beneath her pink satin hat.

"Are you ready to throw the switch, Katie?" Vance asked.

"It's quite an honor," she said, giving him a smile. Despite her protests, the other merchants had insisted that Katie and her enthusiasm were responsible for the rebirth of Victoria Square.

"Stand aside, stand aside," Vance bellowed cheerfully, clearing a path for Katie and Rose.

Katie took her place on the podium, gazing over the assembled crowd. Gilda Ringwald stood next to Conrad Stratton, owner of The Perfect Grape wine store, her arm entwined around his.

He looked dapper in his stovepipe hat and tails. Gilda's smile was turned up to at least a thousand watts. Nona Fiske stood off to one side, her thin lips drawn into a straight line. She'd adopted the look of a fussy schoolmarm rather than a Victorian lady.

Naturally, Mary Elliott was among the missing. After Tracy's arrest, she'd closed Tea and Tasties. Fred Cunningham had erected a FOR SALE sign only days later. Already an offer had been made and accepted on the property. However, it looked like Tracy's legal bills would soon eat up whatever capital Mary could raise. Mary, too, faced legal problems, as she'd lied to give Tracy an alibi the night Ezra Hilton died. Seth predicted she'd only receive probation, as she'd never been in trouble with the law before.

Mary had rebuffed all Katie's—and the rest of the Victoria Square merchants'—offers of sympathy. The entire situation left a bad taste in all their mouths.

Edie Silver joined Rose in front of the podium, the formal lines of her tailored costume lending her an air of maternal grace—something modern clothes had never done. The look of pride in her eyes at the sight of Victoria Square outfitted for the season brought a lump to Katie's throat. Edie and Rose deserved most of the credit for planning the celebration.

Scanning the crowd, Katie caught Gerald

Hilton's wave. His shoulder must have healed completely, for the sling was gone and on his arm was his seventeen-year-old daughter, Miranda. Though still in therapy, she was doing well. Hilton and his wife, who also flanked the girl, were hopeful their daughter would fully recover.

Seth, too, stood in the crowd, giving her a triumphant victory sign. If Rose was aware that Seth was her biological child, she hadn't let on. But Katie noticed that when Seth came to visit Artisans Alley, he made a special point to speak to Rose.

At last, Katie saw Andy making his way through the crowd. Although he still wore a modern jacket over hisT-shirt and jeans, he'd donned a bowler hat and scarf and, as promised, had left his pizza ovens long enough to witness the lighting of the great tree.

Vance twisted the knobs of the makeshift sound system, then shoved the microphone in front of Katie. She tapped it and a squeal of feedback made her jump. Frowning, Vance played with the dials once more, then gave her a thumbs-up.

"Thank you all for coming to Victoria Square's first annual Dickens Festival. I won't bore you with a long speech—"

"Hooray!" came a voice from the crowd, followed by a ripple of laughter.

"But I'd like to thank all of Victoria Square's merchants, and Artisans Alley's vendors, for making this celebration possible. And I'd like to invite the architects of this gala to help me light this magnificent Christmas tree. Edie Silver and Rose Nash, please step up to the podium."

Even in the dim light, Katie saw the ladies blush as they bustled through the crowd to join her. Vance helped them up the steps to stand beside Katie. Placing their hands on top of Katie's, all three pressed the oversized button. The Christmas tree blazed with more than a thousand sparkling colored lights, and high atop the tree, a gold star blinked.

The crowd erupted in cheers and applause, and Katie swallowed back a pang of regret. Despite Nona's earlier protests, Katie knew Ezra would have loved the festival. Chad would have, too. The memory of those missing made it a bittersweet moment, yet seeing the smiling faces of her new friends—and the warmth in Andy's eyes—Katie knew she was ready to embrace the future.

She smiled, whispering to herself, " 'God bless us, every one.' "

Katie's Recipes
Chocolate Chip Cookies

2 ¼ cups all-purpose flour
1 teaspoon baking soda
½ teaspoon salt
1 cup (½ pound) butter, softened
¾ cup granulated sugar
¾ cup packed brown sugar
1 teaspoon vanilla extract
2 eggs
2 cups (12-ounce package) milk chocolate or
    semisweet chocolate chips
1 cup chopped walnuts (optional)

Preheat oven to 375°F.

Sift the flour, baking soda, and salt into a small bowl. Cream the butter, sugars, and vanilla in a large mixer bowl. Add the eggs one at a time, beating well after each addition; gradually beat in the flour mixture. Stir in the chocolate chips and nuts. Drop by rounded tablespoon onto ungreased, foil-lined baking sheets.

Bake for 10–12 minutes or until golden brown. Let stand for a couple of minutes, and then remove to wire racks to cool completely.

MAKES ABOUT FIVE DOZEN COOKIES.

Aunt Lizzie's Scottish Shortbread

2 cups sifted all-purpose flour
¼ teaspoon salt
1 cup unsalted butter
½ cup granulated or confectioners' sugar

Preheat oven to 325°F.

Sift together the flour and salt. In a large mixing bowl, cream the butter and sugar together until they look almost white. Slowly add the flour mixture, mixing well. Press into an 8 x 8 x 2-inch pan until level and smooth. Using a fork, prick the entire surface. Bake for 30 minutes or until just starting to get golden brown. While still warm, cut into 2-inch pieces.

MAKES 16 BARS.

Raisin Scones

2 cups flour
¼ cup sugar
2 teaspoons baking powder
¾ teaspoon salt
3 tablespoons unsalted butter, cold
¾ cup milk
1 egg

½ cup raisins, sultanas, or currants
1 egg yolk
2 tablespoons cold water

Preheat oven to 350°F.

Sift the dry ingredients together. Using a pastry blender or two knives, cut the butter into the dry ingredients until the mixture resembles crumbs.

Beat the milk and whole egg together. Pour into the dry ingredients and stir until well blended. Add the raisins, stirring until well mixed.

Sprinkle the flour over a flat surface. The dough will be rather wet and will absorb the flour. Briefly knead the dough (once or twice) and pat down until the dough is 3/4-inch thick. Cut out the scones with a biscuit cutter and place on a greased cookie sheet.

Beat the egg yolk with the cold water. Brush glaze over the scones. Bake for 25–30 minutes or until golden brown.

Serve hot or cold with butter or clotted cream and jam.

MAKES 10–12 SCONES.

Oatmeal Raisin Nut Cookies

¾ cup butter, softened
¾ cup sugar
¾ cup packed light brown sugar
2 eggs
1 teaspoon vanilla extract
1 ¼ cups all-purpose flour
1 teaspoon baking soda
¾ teaspoon ground cinnamon
¼ teaspoon allspice
½ teaspoon salt
2 ¾ cups rolled or quick oats
1 cup raisins
1 cup chopped walnuts

Preheat oven to 375°F.

In large bowl, cream together the butter and sugars until smooth. Beat in the eggs and vanilla until fluffy. Stir together the flour, baking soda, cinnamon, allspice, and salt. Gradually beat into the butter mixture. Stir in oats, raisins, and walnuts. Drop by teaspoonfuls onto ungreased cookie sheets.

Bake 10–12 minutes or until golden brown. Cool slightly, and then remove from sheet to wire rack. Cool completely.

MAKES 4 DOZEN COOKIES.

Center Point Publishing
600 Brooks Road ● PO Box 1
Thorndike ME 04986-0001 USA

(207) 568-3717

US & Canada:
1 800 929-9108
www.centerpointlargeprint.com